ZUBAAN-PENGUIN BOOKS

LIKE A DIAMOND IN THE SKY

Shazia Omar is a social psychologist. She completed her bachelor's degree at Dartmouth, then worked for a year as an investment banker in New York. After three years of travelling, visiting ashrams and learning yoga, she completed a master's at the London School of Economics. Shazia is a member of Writers Block Bangladesh. She works at a development agency and teaches pilates. She lives with her beautiful family in Dhaka.

LIKE A DIAMOND IN THE SKY

SHAZIA OMAR

PENGUIN BOOKS

ZUBAAN
128 B, 1st Floor, Shahpur Jat, New Delhi 110 049, India

in collaboration with

PENGUIN BOOKS
Published by the Penguin Group
Penguin Books India Pvt. Ltd, 11 Community Centre, Panchsheel Park,
New Delhi 110 017, India
Penguin Group (USA), 375 Hudson Street, New York, New York 10014, USA
(a division of Penguin Group (USA) Inc.)
Penguin Group (Canada), 90 Eglinton Avenue East, Suite 700, Toronto, Ontario,
M4P 2Y3, Canada (a division of Pearson Penguin Canada Inc.)
Penguin Group (UK), 80 Strand, London WC2R 0RL, England
(a division of Penguin Books Ltd)
Penguin Group (Ireland), 25 St Stephen's Green, Dublin 2, Ireland
(a division of Penguin Books Ltd)
Penguin Group (Australia), 250 Camberwell Road, Camberwell,
Victoria 3124, Australia (a division of Pearson Australia Group Pty Ltd)
Penguin Group (NZ), 67 Apollo Drive, Rosedale, North Shore 0632,
New Zealand (a division of Pearson New Zealand Ltd)
Penguin Group (South Africa), 24 Sturdee Avenue, Rosebank, Johannesburg
2196, South Africa

Penguin Books Ltd, Registered Offices: 80 Strand, London WC2R 0RL, England

First published by Penguin Books India and Zubaan Books 2009
Copyright © Shazia Omar 2009

All rights reserved
10 9 8 7 6 5 4 3 2 1

ISBN 978-81-89884-14-7

This is a work of fiction. Names, characters, places and incidents are either the
product of the author's imagination or are used fictitiously and any resemblance to
any actual person, living or dead, events or locales is entirely coincidental.

Typeset at Tulika Print Communication Services, New Delhi
Printed at Pauls Press, New Delhi

To Shazly,
who had the patience to endure,
the perspective to guide,
and the love to keep me going.

✦ ONE ✦

Deen peered over the edge of his newspaper at the targets. First in line stood a lady in a flimsy sari, leather purse, preoccupied with her screaming child. Easy. Three teenage girls in sequinned kamizes stood together giggling, glittering purses on their shoulders. Easy. A thin man in a collared shirt, talking on his phone, expensive gold watch. Easy.

A gaunt guard in a green uniform paced the doorway of the ATM booth and patted the antiquated rifle slung over his shoulder. He gathered phlegm in his throat and walked to the roadside to spit. He noticed Deen watching him and explained, "The other booths are out of order. That's why its so busy."

Deen offered him a cigarette. The guard scratched his greasy hair then declined the offer, motioning to the line as if to say he couldn't smoke on duty. Deen passed the cigarette to AJ and lit one for himself.

AJ tapped his shoe impatiently. A lady with a scarf over her hair stepped into the booth. "She's hot," he said. "I'd do her."

"Too conservative," said Deen, fanning himself with the papers. AJ pulled off his baseball cap to fan himself too. They were both sweating profusely despite the pleasant late-winter breeze.

The lady stepped out of the booth and was besieged by beggars. She pulled her achol over her purse and called for her parked car. A banana vendor hurried to her side and lowered a basket off his head. She rummaged through to select a bunch of ripe bananas while he tried to shoo away the beggars.

"How much do you think she had?" asked Deen.

"Enough for groceries," guessed AJ.

An elderly man approached the booth. He stopped in a fit of coughs, then wiped his nose with the back of his palm. He mumbled something to himself and stepped into line.

"How about him?" asked Deen.

"Couple of thousand to pay for his lung operation," said AJ. "Hey, you think that thing works?" he nodded towards the rifle slung over the guard's shoulder.

"A guard shot a rickshaw walla last month. Fired it by accident."

"Did he die?"

"On the spot. I read it in the papers."

A black Mercedes Benz pulled up to the sidewalk and a tall, lanky man wearing a pin-striped suit stepped out, leather briefcase in hand.

The security guard tapped his rifle on the bonnet of the Benz and directed the chauffeur to move on.

The chauffeur rolled down his tinted window to argue. He was bald and bulky, much larger than the average Bangladeshi. A black scar snaked across his shiny head. The suited man dismissed him with a wave and fell back into line.

AJ lowered his shades to take a closer look. "This one has promise," he announced.

Deen nodded. He had complete faith in his friend's judgment. AJ's easy confidence was contagious. The two of them had been partners in crime for years, though they were as dissimilar as two friends could be. Deen was quiet and laidback, while AJ was sharp-tongued and fidgety. They both sported the classic half-shut eyes of guys who avoid eye contact, though on closer inspection, AJ's eyes were fierce while Deen's were compassionate. From a distance, they looked like brothers, similarly sinewy and skeletal; the only difference was their hair: Deen's was long and wavy, while AJ had a buzz cut.

The suited man stepped out of the booth and into the sun. Deen and AJ watched with interest, waiting for him to call for his Benz. Instead, he lit a cigarette and whistled for a rickshaw. He folded down the hood of the rickshaw and started down Kemal Ataturk Avenue.

The boys hurried onto another rickshaw. Midday traffic was thick but they had no trouble trailing their target, his tall frame was visible fifty feet away. They followed him down the road, past the travel agencies and shops, past the Banani bridge, past the RAB checkpoint and into a crowded side street in front of Gulshan Club.

"Create a diversion at the intersection," instructed AJ. "Then get out of here. Whatever you do, don't come back this way."

Deen jumped off the rickshaw. He jogged down the road to a construction site by the intersection and hoisted himself onto a broken wall, next to a couple of labourers in tattered lungis who were smoking bidis. A piece of brick broke off into his hand. He tossed it in the air and caught it again.

From where he was seated, he could see the suited man approaching with a smug look on his face, the briefcase on his knees. Deen scanned the intersection. Nordic Club, with guards at the gates a few metres to his right. Danish Embassy, with guards at the gates, a few metres to his left. American

Ambassador's house, a few more metres to his right, flanked by ferocious Alsatians. Diplomat neighbourhood, not the best place to hijack a man.

Deen wondered if AJ had made an error in judgment. He was exceptionally fast and fearless. That somehow gave him immunity from danger, but still, he wasn't invincible.

Deen lit a cigarette and noticed the black Benz parked in front of the Nordic club. It was a sweet car, a 1966. "*Oh Lord, won't you buy me a Mercedes Benz,*" Deen sang in his head.

A white jeep pulled in next to the Benz and a blond girl stepped out. Her perky boobs were visible despite the orna draped across her chest. Deen watched her walk into the club then returned his gaze to the intersection. The target was less than a minute away, but there was no sign of AJ.

"Bhaiya, I'm hungry, please bhaiya." A beggar boy grabbed Deen's arm. Torn red shorts and a threadbare grey t-shirt. Deen could see his rib cage.

"Here." Deen handed him the piece of brick. "I'll give you 50 taka if you throw this at that blue jeep."

The boy looked at Deen incredulously. Deen flashed him a 50 taka note.

"Why?" asked the boy.

"For fun." Deen shoved the cash into his hand. The boy sniggered at the mischievous request. He ran up the road to the oncoming traffic and hurled the brick at the jeep. The crashing sound of shattering glass resonated through the air as the windshield splintered into a million pieces. The jeep's chauffeur jumped out, waving his fists and cursing, but it was too late, the boy had disappeared.

A crowd materialized immediately. Rickshaw wallas,

beggars, vendors, loiterers, construction workers and guards gathered to assess the situation. The traffic behind the jeep honked and hollered fruitlessly. Deen watched the suited man dismount the rickshaw. He seemed unaffected by the commotion, casually weaving through the crowd towards Deen. Suddenly there was a scuffle and AJ, in the midst of the crowd, grabbed the briefcase and ran off.

In a moment, the suited man realized what had happened. To Deen's surprise, he did not shout out 'chore' or turn to chase AJ. Instead, he walked briskly towards the Nordic Club, passing the wall where Deen was seated. He reeked of cologne. He stepped into the Benz and barked orders at the chauffeur. The car revved out of parking. He rolled down his window and handed some cash to a guard at the intersection who stopped traffic so they could pass.

Deen ran towards Kemal Ataturk Avenue. He had to warn AJ. Blood rushed to his head, his feet pounded clumsily against the uneven road. Sandals weren't the right gear, dammit.

He slowed his pace at the RAB checkpoint and tried to not draw attention to himself. The Rapid Action Battalion, armed law enforcers with a license to kill, were the last people he wanted on his case. A shepherd with goats approached on the sidewalk, forcing Deen to step dangerously close to a RAB officer. The pungent smell of sweat assaulted Deen's nostrils. The officer eyed him suspiciously but said nothing. Deen passed the checkpoint and began running again, darting across Banani bridge.

A van screeched, braking hard to avoid hitting him! Behind it was the black Benz. The suited man shouted orders to his chauffeur, his hand tucked inside his suit. Deen craned his neck to see if he had a gun. The van honked and Deen bolted.

He jumped into a scooter parked at the side of the road and ordered the scooter walla to take him to North South University.

"I'm off duty." The scooter walla blew out a languid puff of smoke. His face was wrinkled and his eyes were yellow.

"I'm in a rush!" Deen explained.

"Slow down," he said, grinning. "Life is sweet. Enjoy it."

"It's an emergency!" Deen insisted.

"There are hundred other scooters on the street. Take your pick." His teeth were crooked and stained with tobacco. His front tooth was missing.

Deen peeked out and saw a crowd of rickshaws around him but, oddly enough, not one scooter. The three-wheeled green taxis were much faster than rickshaws and he had no time to waste. "My friend's life is in danger!" he said, frantically trying to shake the scooter walla out of his torpor.

"I'm waiting for my drink" the man replied, unbothered by Deen's dilemma. He motioned towards a skinny juice vendor he had parked next to. The man had a cart full of sugar cane stalks which he pushed under a red wheel to squeeze out sweet juice. He turned the wheel slowly, the heat of the day making him lethargic as well, much to Deen's dismay.

"You want one?" the scooter walla asked Deen politely.

"No! I'll pay you double," Deen pleaded. "You don't have to stub out your bidi. Please, let's go."

The man reluctantly abandoned the juice he had ordered and started up the engine of his scooter.

Deen scanned the road. He had long lost sight of the Mercedes Benz. Traffic had cleared up and the wind felt cool on his face. The cramps in his stomach returned in full force making him nauseous. He instructed the scooter walla to drop him off a few metres before the university gates. He had given the last of his money to the beggar boy at the intersection so he handed the scooter walla a half-empty pack of cigarettes instead. He accepted without a grumble.

Deen entered the university building through a side door. He rushed through a narrow hallway and as he turned into the main hall he collided with a girl. She fell back and glared at him. He reached his hand out to help her up.

He felt the warmth of her hand.

Their eyes met.

She looked like an angel.

She smelt like tangerines.

Deen felt like he was soaring, his soul lifted up into the sky in an out-of-body experience. He was suddenly looking down on himself and on her, and they were like Adam and Eve, they were meant to be. His unkempt hair and her tight ponytail, his ripped jeans and her chiffon kamiz, his lanky frame and her voluptuous body, his tortured soul and her air of innocence. They were yin and yang, anima and animus, Radha Krishna, Romeo Juliet, Layli Mojnu. He longed to crash into her soft body again. His heart raced like a freight train. He wanted to hold her and let time stay stuck for eternity at that very moment.

"Sorry!" she exclaimed. "Professor Harun's class, I'm late."

Deen shook himself out of his trance. "My fault," he stammered.

The girl smiled then resumed her walk to class.

"Hey," Deen called out. "I'm Deen."

"I'm Maria."

Deen watched her move into the crowd. She was hot, sexy and confident. Regal like a queen. Graceful like a ballerina. All heads in the hallway turned to watch her. Her trail electrified the air like a celebrity. He had never seen another woman like her.

At the end of the hall, Deen caught sight of a bald head with a snaking scar bobbing amongst the crowd. He lowered his chin and let his curls cover his face.

Baldy trudged by without noticing him. Deen followed him to the lobby. Panicked students were rushing in through the front entrance. Baldy plowed through them, panting. Deen followed him out.

Balanced on a road divider in front of the university, the suited man was waving a gun in the air and cursing. Less than 40 feet away, AJ ran, dodging traffic, unwittingly avoiding the line of fire. He jumped over the bonnet of a car and almost slipped out of range when a cart full of fried lentils and peanuts was thrust unannounced onto the road. AJ collided with the cart and fell to the ground. The nuts and lentils sprayed into the sky in a shower of earthy browns. The cart walla groaned and beggar children scrambled to collect the spillage.

The suited man lifted his gun once again, one hand under his other wrist to stabilize his aim. Deen had a moment to consider his options. Without hesitation, he lunged at the man. Though tall, the man was not heavy, and they both came crashing down. The man fell into a mesh of barbed wire surrounding the divider. Deen scrambled to his feet and rushed towards AJ. Baldy started after him, then doubled over labouring for breath, and returned instead to help the suited man out of the mesh.

AJ had bruised his leg. He leaned against Deen as they hurried into a side street. "We're loaded." AJ grinned, gripping the briefcase tight.

Deen tried to hail down a scooter, but it drove past without stopping. AJ massaged his bruise then pushed a passing man off his motorcycle and climbed on. Deen apologized to the man and climbed on behind AJ. They sped off towards Airport Road.

"*I keep blowin' down the road,*" Deen sang out. "*I ain't got me nobody, I don't carry me no load. Oooh Mr. Breeze.*"

The midday sun smiled and the world was a little brighter.

✦ TWO ✦

Today he would do it. He would seduce her. He had only known her for 24 hours, but she was the one. She was the most beautiful girl in the galaxy and with her in his arms, nothing else would matter. Joy would sing in his heart like a nightingale.

A blue truck packed with pineapples bullied its way past Deen's rickshaw but Deen didn't notice. He was a man on a mission. He was about to rope his beloved into his life and even Falani, sweetest of sweets, she didn't matter for the while.

A woman in a black borkha, face covered except for her eyes, held up her hand to stop traffic. Two beggar children hurried behind her. The rickshaw walla dabbed his gamcha across his brow and peddled clumsily around them while Deen dreamt of Maria. The collision the day before had been his awakening. In her chiffon kamiz, all sexy and curvy, her long neck and glittering eyes, she was everything he had ever dreamed of. Deen wished he were a better man. She'd never go for him if she knew the truth.

Deen arrived at the university gates and handed a few crumpled notes to the rickshaw walla. He finished his cigarette then peered inside the lobby. A crowd of students gathered by the elevators but there was no sign of Maria. He walked out to the mango tree in front, leaned against its trunk and inhaled a deep breath of semi-fresh air.

A scraggly boy with a wide grin approached him. Deen ruffled his hair and dropped a few coins in his hand in return for the morning papers. Deen glanced at the headlines, *Muslims Prepare for Izthema*. He tucked the papers under his arm and lit a cigarette. Did Maria read the papers? What sort of books did she like? Deen waited, watching his watch, smoking his smokes, wondering about Maria. She was a fourth-year student and in three minutes her class would end and she would pass by him.

Deen sparked a match and watched the flame dance in a moment of freedom before it found its purpose at the tip of a joint. Light love's light. Deen remembered a song he had heard a fakir sing, *light love's light, it's all right, it's all right*. Warm affection rushed through him. If only he had something to sustain the feeling. A little something to hold him up, until that moment, when she would expand into his life and spread over him like dawn, touch him with her dainty hands, French manicure and ruby ring, touch his face, his lips, his soul. A little fuel, that's all he needed while he waited, waited in vain, waited in pain, waited for three slow minutes to pass. He could feel his barometer rising. He needed to see Falani soon. AJ said he would go too.

AJ would be late if he had spent the night at Sundari's place across town. Lately that's what he had been doing. Deen had known AJ since he was a kid, and still he was the same, a lover through and through. He had smooched hundreds of women but when he dated a girl, he gave her his heart with nothing held back. Chicks dig that.

Deen wondered if Maria would dig him. He wanted her so badly. He would make her happy. He would devote his life to her worship. It would be his pleasure. He would give her his everything, gladly.

Fear of rejection. *Oldest cliché in the book*, thought Deen, but still the fear irked him. He was nothing but a lousy third-year scoundrel. What would she see in him? What if she never gave him the chance to give her the love that was destroying him as he held it within him, imprisoned explosive energy?

Deen felt like retching. The world around him was becoming too loud: buzzing students, buzzing rickshaws, buzzing mosquitoes. He wanted to scream to hear his own voice. He looked urgently at his teasing watch. Two minutes left.

He caught sight of a professor in a white sari approaching from the lobby. He ducked behind the mango tree and buried his face in his papers. The panic in his gesture caught the interest of a student walking by. She looked at Deen disapprovingly as if she knew what he was all about. *Sheltered first-year*, thought Deen. She didn't know yet that university was merely an instrument in a conspiracy to turn them into robots for powerful multi-nationals to exploit. The professors were in collusion. The students were being socialized to accept things without debate so they could later fit into the system neatly, mere cogs in a wheel. There were better ways to spend tuition fees. The only good thing at university was Maria.

Maria was different. She was a crazy diamond. He could tell from the confidence in her swagger and her defiant eyes. She wasn't weak like the other girls. Where was she? Deen began to feel irritated. Every second was infuriatingly long. Each person who passed by was intolerably dull. Irrelevant people crossing his path, each making him a little angrier. He wanted to throw a brick at the next smiling face. Why were they so happy? What was so great about their lives? He resented their joy. He still had one minute left.

He examined his wallet. Not enough. Maybe Falani would lend him some money. In one minute, he would declare his love to Maria, and then make his way to Falani's place. He could hold out that long. He should take a rickshaw, it would cost less, but a scooter would get him there in less than forty minutes, if the driver wasn't some lousy old man with wrinkles. Deen considered calling AJ. He'd get there fastest on AJ's motorbike. Where was Maria? He loved her so much it hurt.

Deen flipped his lighter through his fingers and schemed. He needed 300 taka for the weekend. Who could he borrow from? Maybe his mother would leave her purse on the table. He hated borrowing from her, but it was the easiest option until AJ could pull off another stunt. They had already blown through the stash in the briefcase, paying off debts. Money burnt so damn fast.

Shit, where was Maria? Had he missed her? Had she passed by? Passed him by? Like a toad on a road? Shit, why had he let his mind wander in that last crucial minute before his life changed forever? Shit. Or maybe she would have hated him. Or loved him then hurt him. Or crushed him with her indifference. Fuck her. Deen stuffed his meagre wallet into his back pocket and lit a cigarette. He must have missed her. Ah well, there was always tomorrow.

Deen dialed AJ's number and matched his puffs to the rhythm of the dial tone, kicking a rock on the ground to shake off the cramp in his leg.

"Hello," AJ answered, just as Maria emerged at the gates.

"AJ, let me call you back!" Deen mumbled, doing a double take to make sure he had seen right. In an unplanned act of desperation, he stepped directly into her path. She collided into him, her head into his shoulders, and dropped her books.

"Watch it!" she scowled. Then her angular face softened slightly but her eyes were still haughty. "You again."

"Uh huh," said Deen. "That's what they all say."

She blushed and picked up her orna from the floor. "You're full of yourself today." She placed the chiffon back on her shoulders.

"I'm having a good day." He couldn't help but notice the way her orna rested on her breasts, afloat on mounds of tranquility.

"Oh ya," she crossed her arms across her chest. "Why?"

"I could tell you," Deen leaned in to her ear and whispered, "but then I'd have to kill you."

Maria raised her eyebrow. "You might put me out of misery."

"You need a hand?" Deen bent down to collect the books on the pavement. She had quite a load. T. S. Eliot, Rumi, Tagore, Salinger. Of course. Of course that's what she would be reading. That's just who she was. His soulmate. Their crossing of paths was no lucky coincidence, it was Fate.

"First you knock me over and then you want to help me?" Her voice was coated in icicles.

"Sounds like someone woke up on the wrong side of bed?" teased Deen.

"Which side I woke up on is none of your business," she snapped.

"Touché."

Two boys circled in to help Deen collect Maria's scattered

items. Deen glared at them. They smiled shyly at Maria and returned to their lives.

"Very kind of you," said Maria sarcastically, once Deen had collected her belongings. She reached over for her books. Her finger brushed against his arm and he was immediately aroused.

"Let me carry them for you," he volunteered.

"No, thanks, I can manage."

Deen wasn't sure if she was playing hard to get or if she didn't want to be seen with scum like him. "Just trying to be nice, with you getting out of Professor Hell Raiser's class and all," he said with a shrug, not surrendering her books.

"Who?" She addressed her question to the air while adjusting her ponytail, indifferent to his answer. Deen noticed a birthmark on her neck.

"Professor Hell Raiser aka Harun Rahman. In the summer I recommend you sit away from the front row in case he raises his arms. It's a whiff of hell!"

"Ew." Maria scrunched her nose, then added, "The funny thing is, I had to learn that the hard way."

"You should bump into me more often, how else will you learn these valuable lessons?" Her birthmark was shaped like the Arabian Peninsula. Deen was consumed by an urge to kiss it.

"Yes, how else would one learn these lessons?" She offered him a wan smile. Her lips were thick and pouty. Her left lip was thicker than her right lip, making her smile lop-sided.

"A smile. I must have woken up on the right side of bed."

"Don't push your luck," said Maria, coolly.

"If I wanted to push my luck, I would have come up with a cheesy pick up line, but somehow I figured you wouldn't warm to the concept."

"You bump into me twice and now you have me all figured out?" she challenged.

"Well, why don't you prove me wrong?"

"How do you propose I do that?" she asked.

"How about over a cup of the best drink in the world?"

"The new Coffee Eleven?" she said, without hiding her distaste.

"No, your highness, right this way, step into my office." Deen pointed to a dingy wooden cart across the road.

"What, that? That tea stall?" asked Maria, taken aback.

Deen nodded.

"Hmmm, never judge a man by the size of his tea stall?" She eyed Deen quizzically.

"Never judge a man. Period."

"So what makes that the best drink in the world?" she asked.

"It's all about the company. You'll be having tea with me."

"Ah, every girl's dream come true?"

Deen smiled, "I don't like to brag!"

Deen led her across the street to the wooden cart. It had a tin roof that folded outwards, a shade for thirsty labourers and rickshaw wallas. A jute rope suspended by nails at both ends of the stall bore bags of chips and bunches of bananas, clipped on with clothespins. A glass cabinet at the front displayed Mr. Butter Cookies, buns and cigarettes. "Wow," Maria mouthed.

The rickshaw wallas on the bench shuffled to make room for Maria and eyed her with as much curiosity as she eyed them.

Deen ordered two cups of tea and watched with amusement as Maria tried to hide her discomfort when the small, stained cups arrived. "It's delicious," he encouraged her, and lit a cigarette.

"Is she Bengali?" they overheard one rickshaw walla whisper to another.

Maria examined the cup. Grease stains on its edges and chips in the rim. Small bits of solidified milk floated on top. She rubbed her ring absent-mindedly.

A passing moori walla shook a tin can, vigorously mixing spicy peanuts with puffed rice. He stopped for a minute to stare at Maria.

Deen was suddenly aware of the contrast between her chiffon kamiz and everyone else's ragged lungis. She was the only woman on the street. The smell of chillies drifted to his nose. The rhythm of the can shaking seemed to match the pounding of his heart. "Let's go," said Deen abruptly.

"Let's stay," she said defiantly, pulling her orna around her body. She lifted the cup to her lips and took a brave sip. "Wow," she exclaimed. "I would never have guessed that something so dirty could taste so exquisite."

Her excitement calmed him down. A fresh twinkle sparkled in her eye. Deen wanted to spend the rest of his life with her. "*Lord have mercy, you don't have to love me baby, please stick around me some time*," he sang to her softly.

A smile of recognition crossed her lips. "You like Buddy Guy?"

Deen couldn't believe it. He had never met a woman who listened to the blues. Maria kept surprising him. He gazed at her through the hazy smoke of his cigarette, mesmerized. Butterflies danced in his stomach.

Dooo dooo dooo dooo. Deen's cell phone rang out the Mission Impossible theme song: the increasingly urgent cymbals crescendoed before breaking into the bass beat, *dooo dooo dooo*

dooo. It was AJ. Deen hesitated, caught in a moment of indecision. He needed to tell AJ to take him to Falani, but then here was Maria Immaculate, sitting before him. He had to hold his ground for at least two more minutes to plant the seed of their friendship.

"The tea was jose," said Maria, before Deen could answer the phone. "I should get going."

"Sure," said Deen, thankful to get up from the bench. His stomach was cramping. The phone continued to ring. Deen paid the vendor and slipped his hand into Maria's. She gripped it tightly.

"I enjoyed your luxury office," said Maria, sticking close to his body for protection against the traffic and staring men. "I have my car, do you need a ride?"

Deen looked at her in awe. She had discarded her original reserve and opened up like a flower. The warmth of her body where she leaned against him seared through his shirt and pulsed in his arms. He had never met a woman who could drive. Women just didn't drive on the streets of Bangladesh. He wondered if he should ask her to drop him off at Falani's. "Are you trying to seduce me into the backseat of your car?" he said.

"Do you want me to?" Maria dragged her words out, coyly pushing a rogue ringlet behind her diamond-studded ear.

Deen wanted to take her in his arms and kiss her passionately so she would understand the depth of his feelings and vow to be his forever, then he could go off to Falani. "I can't stop thinking about you."

"You don't know me," she replied. "I shouldn't shatter your illusions."

"Give me a chance." The words stumbled out too quickly,

aggressive, almost like an order. Deen hoped she hadn't noticed.

She placed a tender hand on his arm, "Friday night? Dinner?"

"Ok!" Deen said. He watched her step into her car and drive away. Perfect hips, slender waist, delicious breasts. Amazing. The hottest girl at NSU had just asked him out. Friday would be the start of something brilliant. His stomach groaned. He lit a cigarette and called AJ.

✤ THREE ✤

"I need to get to Falani," Deen announced on the phone.

"I've got no cash," said AJ.

"Shit, I'm turqing." Deen felt miserable. He had already sold his guitar. He didn't own anything else to pawn.

"I sold three of Quader bhai's rocks to Ronnie," said AJ. "The fucker hasn't paid me yet. He owes a bunch of people money and he's disappeared. Gone off to Singapore or Malaysia or some place and I still owe Quader bhai. He's going to screw me." AJ paused to take a puff. Quader bhai was a small-time diamond smuggler for whom AJ often did odd jobs. "I have one rock left to sell. Know anyone who wants to buy a diamond?"

Deen frowned. "Dosto, if I ask my mom to buy jewellery from you, she'll kill us both." Deen adored his mother, but things had changed.

"This diamond, dost, it might be the Kali. My luck has fucking plunged," complained AJ.

Deen had heard of the dark diamond. According to legend, it was evil, the antithesis of the Kohinoor. Just as the Kohinoor could shape the destinies of its possessor, so could the Kali. While the diamond of light brought good luck, the Kali brought death and destruction. It too was worth a fortune, but no one kept it for too long. Its unwitting owners lost their health, their wealth and sometimes their sanity, until they got rid of the cursed stone. It had belonged to the Mughals before their downfall and it was believed to have wiped out entire clans in India. Now nobody knew where it was.

"Dost, you have to help me out," said Deen.

"Ok, dost, don't worry. I've got a plan. I'll sell the diamond to Javed Bhai. He's got a shop, give me some time," said AJ. "Khor2core."

"Khor2core," Deen replied, smiling.

They had come up with the term years ago, when they were just smoking pot. Ganja Khors. Khor was the raw Bangla word for addict. They had no idea back then what it felt like to be truly addicted to a substance without which your muscles ached and your blood dried up and every tendril of hair on your body screamed for another hit. A genuine khor to the core. Deen hoped AJ would hurry up and find some cash, then they'd be on their way to solace.

* * *

AJ parked his motorbike and eyed the Benzes parked in the garage among restored classics, rare editions, a 1924 Bentley, a 1936 Rolls Royce, billionaire collectors' items. AJ had heard Raj was generous with his friends, lent his cars around like CDs.

Raj Gopal was one of the richest men in Bangladesh, and he wasn't even Bangladeshi, he was from West Bengal. His family had moved to Dhaka from Calcutta in 1947. In the heart of congested Dhanmundi, Raj lived in a sprawling mansion. According to rumour, it was a gift from a Saudi businessman who had hired Bombay's most renowned architect to build it in resemblance of a Rajasthani palace, full with a marble courtyard for dancing girls.

The walls surrounding the mansion were covered with terracotta art depicting stories of Indian kings. Few noticed the art though. Their eyes were drawn to the AK-47s slung on the shoulders of the guards patrolling the outskirts of the palace. Beefy ex-military men, unlike the undernourished watchmen scattered around town. Not that anyone would ever entertain the idea of robbing Raj Gopal, the Don of the Dhaka Underworld.

Raj was not rich from drugs or prostitution, over which he had a monopoly, but rather, from the years of smuggling arms and diamonds. He was a jovial man who loved dancing, and one might never guess that he was a cut-throat villain and a killer. He was known for throwing the grandest parties in the country and he didn't spare any cost when it came to entertaining his guests, the cream of Dhaka's elite: politicians, industrialists, stars and the occasional foreign dignitary. He offered them fine wines from France, fine cigars from Cuba, and of course, dancing girls, the finest from Jaipur. Not only were these girls symbolic of India's pride in its traditions and culture, they were also legends for their agility and rhythm, both on and off the dance floor. Raj housed several such courtesans in private apartments along the back of his property, for the benefit of his guests.

Raj Gopal made AJ sick with jealousy. Raj was wealthy, powerful and feared. What more could a man want? AJ skulked along the manicured pathway next to the water fountain and knocked aggressively on the door of Sundari's apartment.

He stepped in and scowled at the maid massaging Sundari's shoulders. The maid scurried out of the apartment, pulling the door shut behind her. Sundari draped a sheer red robe around her body and smiled. "What brings you to the far side of Dhaka, darling? Does Raj have a diamond for you to pawn or have you come to see me?" The room smelt of lavender and Sundari's freshly oiled skin glowed under the lapels of her robe.

"I was in the neighbourhood," AJ lied. He dragged a finger up her exposed leg. She was soft as a baby.

Sundari placed his head in her lap and stroked his hair. "How have you been? You didn't come last night. I thought you had forgotten me."

"How does one forget such a face?" AJ stared at her naked breasts. Sundari had an elegance that made her regal. She had been Raj's lead dancer up until a fateful party the year before, where a scandal had abruptly ended her career. It had also been the night she had met AJ. Since then she hadn't danced, but Raj considered her his personal favourite and let her keep her apartment. She spent her days teaching the other girls how to improve their techniques and she spent her nights with AJ.

"Any stories for me?" she asked.

AJ kissed her neck. "Do you have ciggies?" He was starting to crave a chase and Deen was turquing already. The poor guy needed to score. He was the smartest guy in town, a musical genius, but he couldn't scheme to save his life.

Sundari walked over to her dressing table, lingering for a moment to expose her nudity, then retrieved a silver cigarette case and silver lighter. She held the flame for AJ. His features were sharp when he was smoothly shaven. She ran her lower lip along the jagged contour of a scar that crept from the corner of his eyebrow to his cheekbone.

AJ pulled away to smoke his cigarette moodily. Sometimes he enjoyed being pampered by her. At other times her affection annoyed him, but he tolerated it because of the benefits.

"Raj has a new bunch in. Have you spoken to him?" she asked.

"I don't want to talk about work." He knew where he was taking the conversation. He had only one goal, but he had to keep his cool. He didn't want it to get ugly. He reminded himself that Sundari was a whore and he didn't care what she thought of him.

"Have you got money for rent?" she pursued. "Do you want to borrow some?" She tried to hold his hand, but he jerked it away.

"I don't need your pity." *Control,* AJ reminded himself, *keep it cool.* His grip on his temper was slipping, like it often did when he tried to fleece her. He always thought he could pull it off without getting angry, but when he couldn't, his rage took him by surprise. He didn't want to acknowledge that Sundari had that sort of power over him. He felt like a bull under her cape of red.

"What are you talking about, AJ? We're friends. It's all right to let down your defenses. I won't bite." Sundari returned to her dressing table and pulled out a glittering wallet from the drawer.

"Are you giving me money?" AJ yelled. He didn't want to be in her obligation and she was sure to expect something from him. Women always had expectations. He wasn't prepared to be there for her the way she wanted him to be, he had made it clear. It was beyond his capacity. "What's the money for? What do you want from me? I can't do anything for you. Do you understand that?" AJ was suddenly furious, not with Sundari, but with his life. Why had he come to her to beg? What was wrong with him? "What do you want from me?"

"Nothing. Ok? I want absolutely nothing," Sundari shouted.

A stiff silence settled in the room. AJ lit a cigarette and paced for a while. He could smell the lavender drifting off her glistening body. "A man has his pride," he said quietly, getting up to leave. "I don't want you to see me like this."

"You're being stupid. I'm sorry, ok. I don't know why you're so upset. Think of it as a loan? I know Raj has new diamonds you can pawn. You can pay me back later."

AJ frowned. There she was again, saying sorry, grovelling at his feet. Didn't she see she was degrading herself? Classless. It was in her DNA or something. She was a whore through and through. What did she have to apologize for? She was the one giving him her hard-earned money. How could he respect her when she couldn't respect herself? How could he respect himself, when he needed to bring her down every time he was broke? Next time he'd go somewhere else. This was the last time he'd hit her up for cash, the last time he'd come by at all, for that matter. He was ruining her chances of saving up for the future. She was better off without him. "I have to go."

Sundari bit her lip to keep it from quivering. "Come again soon," she whispered. She stuffed a wad of cash into his front pocket.

AJ shrugged and walked off. With the money.

* * *

Hasan stepped out of his Benz and strolled towards the Don's mansion. He had lost the briefcase, but it wasn't his fault. He would have shot the thief if that crazy curly haired kid hadn't gotten in the way. Shit happens. Raj didn't need to know about it. Except for that glitch, he had managed everything well. He was in for a pat on the back, maybe a bonus. Hasan ran his fingers through his silky hair and felt a little sharper than usual.

Branches of the krishna chura trees at the edge of Raj's property swung over the wall, offering a glimpse of their blush. Crimson bougainvillea crept through the barbed wire lacing the wall tops. The scent of fresh gardenia tickled his humour.

Hasan heard a dog panting. A mangy street dog with fur falling off its neck trailed close behind him. Hasan smiled sadistically. A vicious thought crossed his mind. It wasn't that he was afraid of dogs, he had been bitten once, 32 injections in his stomach, but he wasn't scared. They were simply repulsive, scrounging through shit looking for a spot to piss. Dirty fuckers. Hasan picked up his pace.

The gates of the mansion were in sight. The guards called out salaams to Hasan. He nodded in acknowledgement then glanced over his shoulders to see if the dog had followed him. It had. "Ayc, aye, aye," he summoned. The dog wagged its tail and pranced towards him. Hasan thrust a kick straight into the dog's face. The dog howled, whimpered and limped away.

"Filthy bitch," said Hasan, then froze in his path. The guards were stiff and alert. The crows were silent. Raj Gopal stood at the gates with cold eyes.

"I saw what you did," he said. "Don't ever let me catch you oppressing powerless creatures again." He turned sharply and resumed his morning walk. His white shoes trod lightly on the pebbled path. His jogging pants were rolled up around his ankles. Birds of paradise and daisies lined the walkway.

Hasan scratched his head and wondered what Raj meant. Was he referring to the job last night? Raj had given him the signal, had he changed his mind? Was there a problem with the shipment? Sometimes Raj asked for too much. An unoppressing assassin, who'd ever heard of such a thing?

Hasan was debating over the meaning of Raj's words when a scruffy looking guy with a buzz cut approached the gates from one of the many walkways in the grove. He smiled at Hasan and mounted his motorbike.

Hasan scowled in reply. The boy looked familiar, but he couldn't quite place him.

✦ FOUR ✦

Deen finished a joint and sauntered into the canteen. A plate of phuchka spilt on the floor caught his attention. Tamarind sauce covered a pile of chickpeas like lava on a mound of volcanic rubble. Flies swarmed in delight. There was nothing to do but kill time till AJ found some money. Unless he stole from someone. There were a few rich kids scattered around the canteen, but Deen didn't love stealing. He'd give AJ an hour.

Deen noticed Parvez balancing on a railing behind the table tennis table with a group of first-years. "Hey kid," he called out.

"Hey bhaiya, what's up?" Parvez jumped down to greet Deen.

Deen threw his arm around his taller, bulkier friend. He had known Parvez since they were kids. They used to be neighbours, back when Deen lived in Gulshan.

"Wanna hit the ball?" asked Parvez.

Speedball? thought Deen, with a half-smile. Not that Parvez would ever mean speedball. He was a nice, clean kid. His father, Mintu chacha, was a brutal politician, but none of those genes were expressed in him. He had a heart of gold. Parvez handed Deen a paddle.

Ping. "What's on your mind, bhaiya?" Parvez served the ball.

Pong. "A sexy goddess." Deen volleyed the ball with a forehand. So many thoughts in the mind of a man at any given moment. Sixty thousand thoughts in a day. Six billion people in the world. Helluva lot of thoughts floating out there.

Ping. "Who's the lucky woman?" Cross table slam.

Pong. "Her name is Maria." *Mariasariataria, I love you!* Deen thought, saving the slam with a quick backhand that Parvez couldn't recover.

Parvez laughed, catching the ball. "One, love. She's a hotty. Voice like Macy Gray." *Ping*. He served a high ball.

Pong. "You know her?" Deen imagined her with her husky voice enticing him in the bedroom, wearing nothing but lacy underwear.

Ping. "I like her best friend, Nina," said Parvez enthusiastically.

Pong. "Aren't you a little young for seniors?" Deen teased.

Ping. "Me and Nina, it's written in the stars."

Pong. "Ya ok," mumbled Deen. He felt nauseous and the game was starting to drag. "You win, game over."

Parvez laughed. "Ok, I have class in ten minutes anyway. I'm throwing a Pohela Boishakh party at my dad's apartment in Uttara in a few weeks. It's empty, lots of space to dance."

"Jose! I'll set up the music system and DJ for a bit." Deen loved selecting tunes, setting the mood. Mintu chacha's pad was probably a plush penthouse. Maybe he could invite Maria. The Bangla New Year was a great excuse to celebrate.

"See you later, bhaiya," said Parvez.

"Bye, kid," mumbled Deen, happy to sit down. He watched Parvez bounce out of the canteen, stopping every few steps to shake hands or say hello to other students. Deen liked Parvez. The kid was zesty and refreshing. The only genuine guy in town. Unlike the slippery people Deen was surrounded by. Slippery snakes drag you down. Parvez was a ladder. He helped people climb out of ruts.

Deen's mood plummeted as the weed wore off. What, again? Again he was craving? Just as he had yesterday. And the day before that and the day before that. Dammit. Deen was tired of his zombie hours spent waiting, painful hours spent waiting, scheming steaming stealing dealing hours spent waiting for another hit. Tomorrow would be the same. Withdrawals in the morning. He'd need money again. Same old shit. He wondered if Maria was rich. Wealthy woman waiting to be his sugar mommy. His candygirl. *Sugar, sugar, oooh, honey honey.* Sick, he admonished himself. He didn't deserve her. He was becoming more of a snake than a ladder.

Deen wondered how Maria would kiss. It had only been twenty minutes since they had sipped tea together, but it felt like two lifetimes ago. Time warp. From the corner of his eye, Deen noticed Rahul stroll into the canteen. Rahul was a lousy conversationalist with no sense of humour, a self-consumed energy sucker. Deen lit a cigarette and pretended not to see him.

Rahul bounded up to his side and yelled "Hello!"

Maybe he'll have something mildly amusing to say. Deen warned himself not to be judgmental. Everyone deserved a chance.

"I just got back from Londonistan. I went to this club where the cover was 200 pounds! I met Wayne Rooney's girlfriend.

Guess how much we spent on drinks? I'll give you a clue, VIP room!"

There. He had done it. Reaffirmed all expectations. The first words he had uttered were mundane and worthless. Who the hell wants to talk about money wasted on drinks? "Want to buy us some phuchka?" Deen politely tried to gauge if Rahul had money on him.

"No. Hey, did you know Chinx is in a coma?" said Rahul in his second breath.

Deen choked. He felt like someone had punched him in the stomach. Chinx was a junky he had known since high school. The bad news was sinking in when AJ and Shagor arrived.

"I've got some peth." AJ flashed three vials from the pocket of his khaki pants.

Shagor was fidgeting with excitement, always ready to walk on the wild side. He was a big guy with a huge ego and everyone knew he was a kleptomaniac. They protected their cell phones when he was around. He was as likely to steal from his friends as from strangers. He had stolen 17 cell phones from Rahul alone; mostly when they were both smacked out in the basti. Rahul tried to recover his property, but Shagor sold off the phones almost instantly and had no way of returning them even if he wanted to. Shagor could sell anything. He sold his own shoes and told his father that he had been mugged. He stole Rahul's car and tried to sell it to AJ. Two weeks ago, he had picked up Deen and driven him to the basti in a public bus. He had clobbered the bus driver and thrown all the passengers out. He had driven around in the bus for two days until a group of angry passengers, waiting at the sidewalk, jumped on and clobbered him.

"AJ, dost," said Deen, "Forget the peth. Let's go to Falani's."

"What do you have?" asked Rahul, peering at AJ's vials.

"Nothing, man, don't you have class or something?" said AJ.

"What does he have?" Rahul asked Deen.

"Come on, come on. Let's go," Shagor urged.

"Hey, can I come?" Rahul asked Deen.

Deen shrugged. He wasn't in the mood to do pethidine, in fact he hated syringes, but he didn't have the strength to argue. His cramps were getting the best of him.

"I've got three shots, one for you, don't make me waste it," AJ stated, reading Deen's mind. "Dallas and then Falani's."

Shagor and AJ were keen for their fixes so they rushed ahead. Deen followed reluctantly, listening to Rahul complain.

Dallas was an empty plot of land not far from university, where the overgrown grass and guava trees provided shade for young couples. Deen remembered the first time he had ever smoked up. It was with AJ, several years ago. They had laughed for hours and named the place Dallas, after the soap opera they watched on BTV, back when Bangladesh had only one station. Dallas was their place to chill and smoke, though there was no convenient cover for needles. He didn't want to shoot up, anyway. Pethidine was not his thing. Maybe he would walk to Café Mango and order scrambled eggs with onions and tomatoes. The thought of food made him want to retch. He lit another cigarette.

Dallas was busy, with couples flirting under every tree and rickshaw wallas lining the peripheral sidewalks. The boys found a guava tree with only one couple under it and stared them into leaving. Deen lit a joint and hummed, *"Sweet Jane. Whoa. Sweet Jane. Oh-oh-a. Sweet Jane."*

Shagor tucked behind the tree to take a hit in his vein. "Ah, the feelings," he sighed. He passed the syringe to AJ.

AJ linked in a fresh vial and pressed the needle into his vein. He pulled the stopper back, drawing his own blood out to mix with the white morphine-based liquid in the vial. The red swirled with the white, turning dark and murky for a moment. AJ plunged the stopper and shot in his dose.

Deen refused to take a shot. Rahul volunteered to take it in his place. "I've never pushed a needle," he admitted. "Dosto, will you do it for me?" he asked Shagor.

"Look man, this place is too open. I can't shoot it for you, it'll be too obvious. Either shoot it yourself or wait till we go back to uni, I'll do it for you in the bathroom."

Rahul nodded and watched with disappointment as the others buzzed. AJ hummed the theme song from *Dallas*, "He's rich, he's rich, his wife is a bitch, she drives in a pink limousine. He lives in a palace in the centre of Dallas and he calls himself the Queen."

Ten minutes into the revelry Rahul caved, "Ya cool, let me do it myself." Shagor passed him a loaded syringe and tapped the spot on his arm where he had to aim. Rahul fiddled with the needle, unable to locate the vein. He stabbed it in finally and yelped "Jackpot!" as he pushed in the peth.

In less than five seconds, an egg-sized air bubble formed under his skin and his face turned red.

"Shit," AJ freaked out. "You missed the vein, man!"

Rahul stood up in panic. "Well, what the fuck should I do?" Everyone around could see the needle sticking out of his arm, next to the egg. Rahul's face was sweaty and swollen and a red rash erupted along his arm and neck as the poison spread.

"Pull it out!" AJ passed him a tissue to press against the incision.

Rahul was trembling, his body possessed by shakes. He forced himself to sit down. His jittery hands yanked out the needle. He screamed as he caught sight of the rash on his arm. "I feel hot, AJ. What the fuck is happening?"

The other students in the plot were craning their necks to watch the commotion. The rickshaw wallas stared openly. AJ cursed. Shagor had disappeared. "I think you missed your vein. The shit went into your muscle. That's all. Be cool."

"My muscle? What's going to happen?" Rahul gasped, trying to breathe. The memory of Rob's OD hung over him like an unheeded omen.

"I don't know. I've never seen this happen before." AJ shrugged, bored of the drama, irritated that his own high was being wasted because Rahul was a fool.

"Deen, should we go to a doctor?" Rahul whispered, in between waves of convulsions.

AJ pointed out that any doctor would know he had pushed peth and call the cops. It was better to go home and phone the clinic, anonymously. Deen grabbed a bottle of water from Café Mango and doused Rahul, while AJ hailed down a cab. Rahul rushed home. Deen and AJ lit cigarettes and walked to AJ's bike.

* * *

Zhoooooooooosh! On the back of AJ's speeding motorcycle, the world seemed to shrink. Wind slapped against Deen's face. Blue trucks blared the trumpets of judgment day as they raced forward like juggernauts. Nothing else mattered, just the

destination. Deen twitched anxiously as they made their way
up Airport Road, right at the gas station towards Tongi, sharp
left into the dirt road in front of the basti, braking to a bumpy
halt at the dilapidated brick wall that had been erected by the
Prime Minister to hide the ugliness of poverty. The road smelt
of piss and was deserted apart from a few skeletal children.

Deen and AJ stepped behind the wall, past the tea stall and
the mosque, and entered the basti. The stale air of the shanty
town enveloped them, heavy with the smell of fresh cow dung
and burning garbage. They made their way through the narrow
alleys cramped in between rows of tin shacks and ducked under
clothes lines draped with yellowed t-shirts with American idols
printed on them. Rejected export merchandise for rejected
local people.

AJ cursed as he stumbled on a wet bit of mud next to a
plastic bodna with which someone must have washed his ass.
They passed piles of plastic bottles and rusty cans, recyclable
treasures children had collected from dumpsters in town. At
the far end of the basti, a lane of shacks rested on stilts, secured
above a stinking river.

The boys arrived at the last shack on the embankment. A
krishna chura tree in full bloom canopied over the roof, with
flaming orange flowers. They dropped their sandals on the
bricks lining the doorway and entered their sanctuary.

The bamboo structure that held up the tin sheets of roof-
ing created an internal clothes rack from which hung two
blouses, one sari, plastic bags, a cotton blanket and an out-
dated Grameen Bank calendar. Precariously balanced on the
intersection of two bamboos, was a can of coconut oil with
the picture of a woman combing her silky hair while soaking
in a luxurious tub of bubbles. Underneath a bench in the cor-

ner of the room were a pile of pots and a kerosene lantern for the evenings.

Sitting on the hard mud floor, between Majid and Kala, was Falani. She had a bailey flower garland wrapped in her hair, scented and fresh. She was chewing paan. Her lips were wet and red from the betel nut.

She beamed deeply stained teeth at Deen and moved to make space for them to sit. "I've got some nice sweets for you today, you boys will be happy." She pulled out a plastic packet from her peacock-feather purse and handed it to Kala, who was slouching next to her.

"What's up?" said Deen to Kala.

The petite man smiled as he pulled off the foil wrapper of a chocolate bar. His pitch black hair was combed back neatly, no traces of white. He wore a fresh shirt and a soiled lungi. He sat cross-legged, with calloused feet caked in mud. Clean on top, dirty below, classic junky style, thought Deen.

"It's goddam Izthema next week," said Majid taking a swig from a bottle of cheap liquor. He was only four years older than Falani, but he looked more like her father than her brother. The combination of a lifetime of manual labour in the oppressive Bangladeshi sun and an intense addiction had left him a skeletal man with a confrontational attitude towards everyone, especially Falani. Deen hated the way Majid barked orders at her, but Falani did not seem to care, accustomed to the violence of frustrated men. Instead, she gushed an endless stream of affection over Majid.

"We can't keep stuff here during Izthema. There'll be too many people around," Falani warned gently.

"Fuck the mullahs." AJ shrugged. He had no respect for religion or religious men and the second largest Muslim pilgrimage in the world meant only one thing to him – an obstacle to his addiction.

"It's crazy. Millions of Muslims from all over Bangladesh pitch tents along this riverside. Stay for days! Why can't they pray in their own goddam space rather than crowding up mine?" Majid had not chased in a while and he was becoming belligerent.

"Crowding your space, are they?" Falani asked playfully. "It's our baba's land, isn't it?"

"It is my land!" Majid roared. "I'm the one that lives here and sleeps here and shits here."

"They're poor people. God is all they've got," said Deen, happy to stoke Majid's frenzy.

"That's not why they're here," Majid countered. "It's not devotion, it's fear. They're scared of Hell! Goddam God-fearing. They've come to beg for forgiveness. I see their ugly faces year after year, calling to God, before they go back home to sleep with whores and drink keru." Majid pulled his bottle to his lips. "Like me, only I'm not a hypocrite."

Kala glanced up. Majid was getting out of control. The foil was cut, the pipe was ready. Kala hurried to prepare the tillis.

"Nobody's scared," said AJ. "They're greedy bastards. Come to pray for fast cars and pretty wives. Come to pray for better lives. Simple minded folks. They don't know that God isn't listening."

"God-forsaken and GOB-forsaken." Deen sighed, referring to the Government of Bangladesh.

"God only loves the wealthy," continued AJ.

"Perhaps they pray to thank God for their blessings?" said Falani.

"Prayers are powerful. Can keep a man happy if he believes,"

Kala joined in. The smoke was ready. Kala was a tiny man, not a labourer, but like Majid, skeletal from years of addiction. He spent his days hanging around the basti waiting for Falani's clients to arrive. He prepared the smoke for them in return for a few drags to feed his own addiction. He could not afford a stash for himself so the boys were usually generous with him, unless their urges were too strong.

Kala gave AJ the first drag. Majid fumbled around to prepare a chase. Soon it was Deen's turn.

Deen admired the brown lump placed neatly at the edge of the foil and lit a cigarette. Kala balanced the foil between his fingers and led a flame beneath the smack. Deen followed the trail with his pipe, breathing in the snake of fumes. Immediately his muscles tensed and he stifled the impulse to vomit. He took a long drag from his cigarette then exhaled the smoke from his lungs. He felt his body release, let go, immediate relief, aaaaaaaah, the heroin feeding his thirsty, addicted cells, letting them swell with smack happiness, his sinus clearing up, the clogged veins in his body expanding so the rush of blood was once again smooth, his eyes heavy, his mind ascending out of darkness to a state of normalcy, losing gravity, the world spinning moving revolving around him as the stars realigned so that everything made sense as he drifted off into a calm, content space where even Maria did not exist.

"Dosto, I'm so high!" said Deen.

"High as a kite," AJ agreed.

"No, higher."

"High as a jet…" said AJ.

"No," Deen chuckled. "Higher."

"Dosto, how high are you?" asked AJ.

Deen pointed upwards and said solemnly. "High as diamonds in the sky."

"Aww, dost," said AJ. "That's cheesy."

✦ FIVE ✦

Deen wiped his muddy sandals on the welcome mat and rang the doorbell. He patted down the pockets of his jeans. There should have been three puriahs in the right pocket and two in the left pocket, but he could only feel two and two.

Deen's mother opened the door. He walked past her, careful to avoid eye contact, red eyes were a sure giveaway and he was in no mood for a confrontation.

"Deen, I need to talk to you," she said.

"Ya, ok," he said. "I just need a second, Ma." He had never brought sugar home before and he felt a bit paranoid. He needed to check if everything was ok. He stepped into his bathroom and locked the door. He pulled out the puriahs from his pocket. All five were intact. He flipped open the newspaper Falani had handed him. There were two pieces of foil and a pipe. She was really looking after him. Deen opened one of the puriahs and brought the sugar to his nose. It smelt bitter. She had packed in a good amount. An excited chill ran down his back. He calculated when he would smoke next. He could wait till the morning and smoke before uni. Or perhaps he'd smoke in a while, before going to bed.

A knock on the bathroom door jolted him out of his reverie.

"One sec!" he shouted. He folded the sugar back into the packets and placed them in his pockets. Two in the left pocket, three in the right. Split it up, just to be safe. He hid the newspaper with the foils and pipe underneath the toilet tank cover, careful to balance it so it wouldn't get wet. He noticed his reflection in the mirror. Dark circles outlined his bloodshot eyes. He splashed water on his face and brushed his teeth. He gelled his dishevelled hair to restore order to his face and lit a cigarette.

He opened the bathroom door. There stood his mother, with her hands on her hips. She hadn't entered his room in a while. Deen followed her gaze as she scanned his room. It was orderly and sparse, as if he did not live there. The numerous shelves around the room were empty. He had sold his books long ago. The only sign of his existence was a growing pile of cigarette stubs in the ashtray. His bed frame was broken, but he refused to repair it. It was this bed his father had died on. He shook his head to throw out the thought. Five years had passed and still uninvited flashbacks strolled in.

"How long can you go on like this?" asked his mother gently.

Deen didn't respond. He wasn't in the mood. Their face-offs broke his heart. He wished she would just let him live his life. They used to spend hours sitting together on the living room couch, watching movies, discussing philosophy, singing songs. He used to play his guitar for her, all her favourites by Bob Marley, and comb her hair before she went to bed. When he returned from school, her eyes would light up, and he would greet her with a bear hug. He was the light of her life. Now only sad emptiness existed between them.

"You're running out of time," she continued. "What would your Baba say?"

That pissed him off. Why did she have to pull his father into every conversation? What would he say? He would say, *it's dull down here, in my grave, wish the maggots would leave me alone*. What else could he say? Deen resented his mother. She could push him from sadness to anger in a split second.

"Are you still going to class?" she pursued.

How could he explain it to her? He didn't want to be part of that system. BBA, MBA, fast track to the grand life where you spend your precious hours like a greedy bastard salivating over balance sheets for some foreign firm that rips resources off your land and degrades your people to poverty. Corporate people were the worst snakes of all, no integrity.

She opened her mouth to speak, then decided against it. A look of distress clouded her eyes. Deen could see the bones in her face. She had lost weight. Wasn't she eating properly? That was the problem with his mother. She was always worrying about him and then she'd turn the tables so that he had to worry about her. Deen didn't want to worry about anything.

"You're so impassive!" she shouted suddenly. She began sobbing. Deen pulled out a chair for her to sit on. She stayed standing, but leaned against the chair with one hand. The other hand she held over her mouth to stifle her sobs. Deen wanted to hold her in his arms, comfort her. He wanted to stroke her hair and assure her that he was ok. He wanted to tell her that he loved her, but somehow he could not say it.

Deen noticed a photo on the table. She must have taken it out of a carton, it hadn't been dusted as yet. It was a photo of his father, his mother and himself, when he was sixteen, standing in front of a stage. He had performed with his band that day, a fundraiser, at the DOHS football field. They raised 12 lakhs for flood victims. He had played an electric bass and the crowd loved him.

After the concert, his parents wanted him to go home with them, but instead he went to the basti with his friends. At the time he'd thought it unfair that they expected him home after the biggest event of his life. He had his friends and his fans and his high to ride out. When he got home much later that night, wasted out of his mind, they were up waiting for him. His mother had cooked tehari, his favourite dish, and his father had blown balloons for the occasion. Balloons of all things, as if it were his fifth birthday or something. Still, it made him damn sorry that he hadn't gone home to celebrate with them.

But these regrets, what was the point of dwelling on them? He had enough regrets to steam a hot air balloon right up to the moon. They made him so blue he wanted to blow out his brains. It hadn't even been an hour since he had chased last, but his mother had totally massacred his buzz. Deen patted the packets in his pocket.

"Deen," she said finally looking up. She always said his name slowly, as if she may mispronounce it. "Deen," she said again. "Deen, you can't live here anymore. Your khalas say I'm too lenient and that's why you've turned out like this. They say if you realize how difficult the real world is then you might clean up your act. So I want you to leave. Not permanently, of course, just until you have sorted out your head."

Deen nodded, no longer listening. He needed to chase, but where could he do it? Back at the basti? Or perhaps at AJ's flat?

"You mustn't blame them, Deen," she said in defense of her sisters. "They love you. They're concerned. I love you too, you know I do. It's just that I haven't been able to raise you by myself. It's been really hard. I wish your Baba were around."

Deen nodded again. He could see how much the conversation hurt her and he wanted to get out of her way. He turned to leave.

"Deen," she called after him. "Do you want to stay for dinner?"

"No," he mumbled. He wanted to stay. Part of him wanted to stay. He wasn't hungry. In fact, he was sort of nauseous, but he knew she would end up eating alone again. Lonely people really messed up his head. Loneliness was the worst curse and his own mother was suffering from it. It broke his heart, but what could he do? She had spent the past five years blaming him for his father's death. He couldn't change the past and now all he wanted to do was run away.

"Deen," she called out again. "Where will you go?"

Deen shrugged. He didn't know the answer to that. It was a full moon night, at least he wouldn't get lost in the dark.

* * *

Deen settled on the edge of the nouka and lit a joint as the nouka walla began to row. The river shimmered in the moonlight. The wind was cool. This was life. What could be better? *Baby let's cruise, away from here,* Deen hummed.

The stench of rotten food and burnt plastic permeated the air. Toxic shit engulfed an emaciated man as he waded through the blackness in search of some unknown treasure. Deen remembered swimming in the river with his father. There were trees on both banks and the water was clean back then. Back before Dhaka became a concrete jungle and the river became a polluted poison pit. In one decade, the mighty Torag River had been reduced to a stinking sliver of sewer. It could have been a majestic Thames or Seine running through the city, but for greed.

Greed and fear, the two driving forces of humanity. Capitalist bastards, using both forces to motivate the masses. Crushing all opposition: burn the witches, beat the dogs, ban the drugs, demolish spirituality. Harness religion to define dreams, mind control. Burden language with ideologies that favour the rich. Money is might, right? Buy their precious time with false promises. Work hard, be good, pie in the sky when you die. Just a piece of pie. Not peace of mind. Sugar free pie. An eternity of blandness. Two bland eternities enveloping the fleeting moment called Life. No value for life. Especially not in Bangladesh, the sewer of India, the ass wipe of America, the sycophantic beggar child of Islamic fundamentalists. Swaying this way or that, however anyone wants. No hope, watch helplessly, a country without leadership, a story with no hero, nothing to do but pray.

Allahu akbar, Allahu akbar.
Allahu akbar, Allahu akbar.
Ashhadu al la ilaha illallah.
Ashhadu al la ilaha illallah.

The azaan floated through the air, interrupting Deen's contemplation. It came from a mosque on the receding banks of Tongi. The muezzin's melodious baritone invited the faithful to pray. Morning prayers to set the tone for the day. Deen wanted to join the congregation. He craved a connection with something higher than himself. Suddenly a second screechy voice blared from another loudspeaker, and then two others, scratchier still. Deen strained to isolate the first voice, but the noise increased as mullahs across town competed to be heard.

With the cacophony came carcinogenic doubts, creeping in through the cracks and crevices of Deen's parched skin, spreading through his blood into his soul. He felt ill. Conformity was an excuse lesser men relied on for a sense of belonging. Complete cop out. Organized religion was nothing more than an elite power structure. Power defined by institutions. Popes, scientists, investment bankers. Alternative ways of being were banned, eradicated, disempowered. Deen wanted to fight the power, smash G8, but struggles against the system resulted in a failure to fit in. Pariah! Reject! Outcast!

Deen felt lost. He needed to connect to God in a language he could understand. Questions cluttered his head. Ever since God split Adam and Eve, since the separation of nature from religion, since the day he was born, man's greatest need had been to transcend the loneliness that engulfed him, but how? Deen wished for a feeling of oneness to save him from the abyss of aloneness. Faith, love, giving, these were the paths he needed to take, but he was stuck in the swamp of his ego. He didn't know how to let it go. Surrender. Rise above it and ascend to Nirvana.

Deen noticed a kite soaring above him. It had a brown body and white head, like an eagle, only slimmer. Suddenly *Ave Maria* erupted in Deen's mind, an orchestra in full bloom, with Pavarotti singing. Violins, cellos, flutes, clarinets. He could hear each instrument in perfect clarity, each note calmed him, reassuring him of God's omnipresence, and above all that, Pavarotti boomed,

Ave Maria
Listen to our prayer
You can hear us in the wild
You can save amid despair
We slumber safely till tomorrow
Though we be men outcast, reviled
Maria hear our sorrow.

Peace and harmony descended upon Deen as dawn tore through the sky. The bird circled upwards, large loops, thirty feet, fifty feet, eighty feet, one hundred feet above the water. Deen felt light, as if he were rising up with the bird, above the world of turmoil, floating gently towards heaven.

Suddenly the kite swooped down in one straight, fast diagonal from the sky, disrupting the spell. It plunged its claws into the water and ripped out a fish. Silver scales sparkled in the sun. The fish wriggled, rising up from sweet life, up to death, in the clutches of the kite, up, up and away.

Deen squinted to follow it into the distance. Several kites were circling above him. How had he missed them before? He shaded his eyes with his hand and tried to count the birds. The sky was full of them, a flock perhaps. A family? Deen wondered what had happened to the gulls, herons and kingfishers that used to populate the river. Hundreds of them. Dead now? Extinct?

Deen's thoughts drifted to Maria. She was the only thing alive and vibrant in his life. She probably cared about endangered animals and the environment. She was probably a radiant citizen, a hero like his mother had been.

His mother was an activist. She fought for the downtrodden and protested against oppression. She embraced motherhood with the same fervour and nurtured her passion in Deen. He became the canvas of her dreams. As a boy, he was everything she wanted; confident, motivated and concerned. He organized fundraisers, led food drives and delivered supplies to flood devastated families in villages outside Dhaka. He won an award for a poem he wrote about peace. He wanted to be a doctor. He carried the weight of the world on his shoulders, as she had, until he finally decided it was too much for him. He went from being her greatest strength to her deepest disappointment.

Deen wondered what she was doing. Probably awake already, just finishing her fazr prayers. Sitting, perhaps, at the dining table to have breakfast, a cup of tea and a banana. She hardly went out anymore; afraid of what she might hear, unable to defend her son from gossip, weighed down by the stigma of being a junky's mother. Bereaved, disappointed and worried. Her husband was dead, her son was pathetic, her friendships had drifted away. She was alone. Dammit.

The nouka walla hummed a dirge to the river goddess as he struggled to manoeuvre the boat. The sweaty wrinkles on his neck glistened in the morning sun. He looked old enough to be Deen's nana. Deen offered to row. The nouka walla frowned and growled something about *no free rides*. Deen sat back down, heavy-hearted. No one wanted a helping hand, what they wanted, what they desperately needed, was money. The greatest human need had become money. Man-made money. Deen grumpily fingered his fleshless wallet.

They arrived at the banks of Tongi and Deen handed the old man a few coins. Humidity surrounded him like a sauna. His t-shirt clung to his body. Without the wind, the day was hot already. Spring was on its way, and with it, storm season.

It made him crave a chase. Deen stopped at a tea stall on the roadside and sat down next to the only other person there, a dark man with a moustache and a walking stick. Deen bought a pack of Bensons and a cup of tea.

"He doesn't ask much of us," remarked the man, pointing to God, shaking his head in dismay. "And yet we fail."

"Don't be too hard on yourself, chacha." Deen smiled respectfully, noticing the bright red lighter in the man's palm.

"In the evening of your life, you will realize, life is simple. All you have to do is stay positive."

The man's lips were the same shade as the lighter, a surreal comic book red. Deen wondered if anyone else had noticed the odd intensity of the colour.

"Positive people can give," continued the man. "Negative people become obsessed with their own problems. I've been a negative bastard my whole life, selfish and greedy."

The gamcha tied around the man's neck had become a dazzling red too, as well as the shop vendor's eyes. It was as if God had suddenly gotten bored with the dull reds in this patch of universe and had rectified it with an intense red airbrush. "How do you stay positive, chacha?" asked Deen.

"Pray. That's all it takes. I never prayed for myself. Never. Not once. I only prayed three times in my life. I prayed for my mother when she died. She was a good woman. I prayed for my daughter when she died. She was still beautiful when we buried her, though jaundice had stained her face. I prayed for Mr. Karim when he died. He opened a school, M. K. School for Boys, in my village in Bikrampur. It was a free school, now, you tell me, that's love, *no*? Because of him I learnt to read, but who cares, here I am pulling a rickshaw, can I even afford meals? I finished high school, but still no real jobs for me. I blame the government. They call themselves leaders, looting the country, while we toil penniless."

Deen zoned out. *M.K. School for Boys.* Deen knew the school well. M. Karim was, after all, his father. Mujabbir Karim had been a wealthy man, a business tycoon and owner of a prospering tea estate in Sylhet. He had a house with a pool in the posh neighbourhood of Gulshan. He took his family on extended vacations to Europe and Africa. He had a small school in Bikrampur which he cherished. He taught there occasionally when he could make the time.

Deen's father was a self-made millionaire, but like all honest men in corrupt countries, he had his balls unceremoniously ripped out by the first government with the guts and the gall to do it. In less than one decade, his entire wealth evaporated and he moved into a two-bedroom apartment in DOHS with his wife and son. When M. Karim passed away five years ago, there were no friends at his funeral, although 2000 people had attended his 25th anniversary the year before. Friends forget those whom fortune forgets. Nothing was left of the great wealth he had accumulated, except a small village school for boys.

Deen lit a cigarette and ordered another cup of tea. His father suffered for a year, the chemotherapy hardly helped. Deen had tried to stay off heroin then, but he couldn't. He hurt his father more than the cancer itself. Deen blinked to hold back his tears. He had wanted to be there for his family, to do the right thing, but he didn't have the strength. After his father died, his mother blamed him for the quick demise, a burden he now had to bear.

This is a divine message, Deen thought wistfully. He was

the legacy of a noble family and he was wasting his life. He sat on a seat of privilege from where he could make a difference, start schools like his father had done. *D.K. School for GOB-forsaken, God-forsaken Boys.* Instead he stole from his mother to buy drugs. A familiar self-loathing spread through his gut and made him nauseous.

Deen remembered the summer his father taught him to swim and the school of yellow fish they saw underwater, hundreds of yellow fish engulfed them like buttercups in bloom. *They are safe because they have each other*, his father had explained. He meant more than strength in numbers, he meant support systems, security networks, family. Deen wanted to be connected, but he didn't know how. He was a lousy son, a waste of time, a khor2core. He would die soon, unlamented. He felt lonely and consumed by a need to see Maria. He shook hands with the rickshaw walla and rushed off to university to find her.

* * *

Deen didn't believe in monogamy. It was too draining. Straining. Refrain from flirting. Restrain your instincts. Retrain your brain. Remain faithful. He'd been with many girls, but they didn't light his fire. They were dull, immature, easy. Maria was unusual. Her contemptuous indifference made him want her more. Was she too good for him? He wanted to know her better. He wanted her to know him. He craved a union, a settling down that would then give way to a deeper connection, an expansion of horizons for them both. He wanted to consummate their relationship.

Deen fingered the puriahs in his pocket. The intensity of his infatuation was shocking. "*I saw her face, now I'm a believer, without a trace, of doubt in my mind! I'm in love, I couldn't leave her even if I tried,*" he hummed in delight.

A street vendor with pineapples walked past and the tangy whiff of fruit lingered. It smelt like Maria. The future looked golden. Deen imagined Maria in a golden sari, breast feeding their baby, golden sunlight pouring in through the bedroom window. He imagined her by his side, on a golden beach, at sunset. He imagined her at night, glowing in his arms, tired and beautiful. He felt excited. He was tingling with electric love. He was singing in the rain. He was floating in the stars, in an orbit around her. She was the epicentre of his life.

Deen saw Maria approaching, with an armful of books. "Fancy meeting you here," he said, pulling a cigarette to his lips.

"What, you couldn't survive a day without me?" she replied, her expression unaltered by Deen's sudden appearance. Her hair was pulled back in a tidy braid that reached well past her breasts, almost to her lower back.

"I wanted to see you again." He tried to sound casual. He couldn't let her know he had waited by the university gates for over an hour. That might come across as obsessive stalker behaviour. She might misunderstand.

"I'm heading home," said Maria. "You want to come?"

"Sure!" He hadn't expected an invitation so early on, she barely knew him. He followed her through a crowd of students towards the parking lot.

"My chariot," she announced at the door of a run-down Corolla. Deen stepped into the passenger seat. The windshield was cracked. The car smelt of bailey flowers, a fresh garland hung from her rear view mirror. Maria revved the engine and reversed out of parking. It all felt surreal to Deen. Sitting in the car with Maria, life was suddenly magical.

Maria turned on the CD player. "*Mmmm, it's always better when we're together,*" rang through in guitar. Deen was stunned. She had picked a song straight off the soundtrack of love he had created in his head while he waited for her that morning. He began to sing along. Maria hesitated, then joined in, harmonizing with him, her voice deep and melodious. The song ended, leaving Deen breathless, in awe of the coincidence and his good fortune.

Maria smiled, then leaned across the gear shift and kissed him on the cheek. A beggar rapped violently at her window interrupting their moment. She blushed. The beggar continued to bang on the window, oblivious to their intruded privacy. Maria gripped her steering wheel, knuckles white. Keeping her eyes on the road, she launched into a monologue about her day.

Deen listened to her catharsis, amused. It didn't matter what she said, the way she curled her lips around her words was enough fuel to keep him going for the rest of his life. Or at least enough to keep him going until the evening. By evening he would be ready for another hit. He fingered the puriahs in his pocket. He'd go over to AJ's place to chase. He'd crash there, too. He'd be fine. Life was good and here was sweet Maria.

"Are your parents home?" he asked as they pulled into the parking lot of a fancy apartment in Gulshan.

"I live alone," said Maria. "My mom's moved in with my

nani. It's good, she needs to be babied. I can look after myself."

Deen followed Maria through her home. The place was a disorderly mess. Broken lamp shades, piles of newspapers, dust collecting on every surface. Deen wondered if he should ask if he could move in. It was an uncanny coincidence that she lived alone and he needed a place to stay. Then again, he couldn't really chase at her place. AJ's flat would be more convenient.

Maria stepped gingerly through the chaos into her colourful bedroom. The room smelt of vanilla candles. Deen walked around absorbing the details. There were photographs taped messily on her walls. Places she had been to, he guessed. The banks of the Ganges, a cascading waterfall, the New York skyline. A feeling of inadequacy gnawed at him. The room felt cold, the AC was turned up high. Sea shells lined the window sills. A laughing Buddha sat on her desk, next to a pack of cigarettes, Benson Lights. She smoked the same brand as he did.

"Do you want one?" asked Maria, passing him the pack.

He offered her one which she tucked behind her ear. He pulled one out for himself and examined her ashtray. It was made of clay, with Kama Sutra positions etched on its sides.

Yellow post-its with quotes and a to-do list framed Maria's computer and mirror. Deen noticed his reflection. He looked ghastly. Anyone could tell he had spent the night wandering around. He hoped she wouldn't notice. "Carpe diem?" he asked. He pulled a post-it off the mirror and approached her. She let him corner her against the desk.

"Seize the day, just do it, you know," she replied.

She also looked like she hadn't slept in days. Deen wondered what she had been up to. Was she sleeping around? "Do what?"

He pulled her into his arms and posted the post-it on her cleavage.

She pushed him back playfully and walked to her bed. "I have plans, I'll have you know. I'm not just another pretty face." She distorted her cheeks and opened her mouth as if bearing fangs.

"Tell me your plans, vampire lady," said Deen. She was like a little girl, spontaneous and uninhibited. He loved the way she bounced. It pulled him out of his gloom.

He noticed the a calendar on her desk. Each month was a different Dylan record cover, heavily scribbled in with birthdays and reminders. Of course she loved Dylan too. Deen was a sucker for such coincidences. Her periods would start in a week, he noticed. She had marked it in with red ink.

Maria dug under her bed and pulled out two wine glasses. She ran out of her room and returned with a half bottle of red wine. "It's from Amma's booze cabinet. I know where she hides the keys." Maria handed Deen a glass.

Deen lit their cigarettes. Maria held hers in between straight fingers, like a V, military style. The wine tasted dense.

"When I graduate in May," Maria stretched out languidly on her hyacinth couch, "I'll open a shop."

Deen settled on the carpet in front of her, resting his chin on her legs. He noticed a guitar tucked under her couch. "What will you sell?"

"Lingerie," she replied softly, forcing Deen to lean in closer to hear her. She smelt like fresh fruit.

"I'll run odd errands," he offered. "Serve you tea and kisses."

"The shop is only for women. No men allowed." She pulled her orna around her head demurely.

"What's the name of the shop?" Deen asked. "Maria's Secrets?"

"No, my secrets are not for sale. They're much too dark." Maria's eyes were bright and inviting. Deen wanted to escape his turbulent world and become a part of her charming reality. He placed his hand on her stomach. She smiled and brushed it away.

"Sometimes I feel like I'm not doing enough for the country," she said, suddenly serious. "Then again, what difference can I make? I don't have power. I don't want power. Power corrupts. I wish I could be happy living a small life, making small contributions to the women around me, bringing a spark to their bedrooms. Someone has to sell lingerie in Bangladesh, why not me? But it creeps up on me, this feeling that I need to do more, be more, you know?" A frown settled on her otherwise peaceful face.

Her abrupt outburst surprised him. "You don't have to do anything," he replied, stroking her flimsy shalwar. He could feel her creamy thighs beneath. He loved the way she swung from one topic to another, opening her heart up to him. "You can just *be* and that's ok. *Be* and enjoy *being*."

"That's comforting," said Maria, unconvinced. She pushed her fingers into his hand, French manicure, ruby ring. "What're your plans after graduation?"

"I want to make a million dollars," said Deen. He caressed her baby smooth arms. He could see she enjoyed his touch.

"Nice self-centered goal." Maria ran her fingers through his hair.

Desire rippled through his body. He pinched her thigh, gently but firmly. "Then I'll start hundreds of schools and change the education system in Bangladesh."

"That's very noble," Maria teased, prying open his grip, pushing his fingers away. "I wish you weren't all talk and no action."

"You think I'm all talk?" Deen pinned her down on her couch.

"Ya." Maria pushed against his weight. "I'd like to see you do the things you dream of."

"You want me to do the things I dream of?" said Deen.

Maria nodded with a naughty smile.

"As you wish." Deen slowly undid the hooks of her shalwar. He could feel her breath quicken.

Maria pulled Deen's roaming hand up into hers, blushing. "Wait... *how* will you do *it*?"

"I'll lead a revolution for you," whispered Deen. He pulled her deeper into him. She arched her back and pushed her breasts against his chest. A moan escaped her lips. "I'll overthrow the government and the madrassahs. I'll destroy every man who stands in my way. I'll do it with my bare hands." Deen stroked the birthmark on her neck. The world around them melted. Breathing in Maria, the tenderness of her skin, the citrus in her hair, the lust in her eyes, Deen felt overwhelmed. The butterflies in his stomach were going wild.

"My brave Deen," said Maria. "You could get hurt."

Deen noticed a bead of sweat on her forehead. "For you, I could sacrifice my life in an instant." He wasn't pretending, the words flowing out of his mouth were true. He was completely in love and suddenly the feeling was selfless, all that mattered was Maria's happiness. He wanted to do everything for her. He pushed his groin in between her legs.

She nuzzled into his face. "What do you like *most* about me?"

"Your mermaid hair," he replied. He was ravenously hungry

for her. He wanted to rip off her clothes and lick her body.

Maria twirled her braid in her fingers, then seductively brushed its end over Deen's face.

Goosebumps erupted on his arms. He kissed her neck. "But that's not it," he continued. "I like your naughty eyes."

Maria batted her lashes dramatically.

"But that's not my favourite either." Deen kissed her nose. "It's your delicious lips that have me trapped."

Maria lifted her mouth to his and gave him a soft kiss that progressed into a passionate frenzy of lips desperate to surrender, tongues anxious to escape loneliness, souls frantic to connect.

* * *

On his rooftop was a glass room with a state-of-the-art treadmill and a rack of weights. Raj Gopal lay on his massage bed. Five men in suits fidgeted nervously, waiting to deliver the week's update.

An obsequious man in a yellow tie stuttered, "Sir, the dividends have gone up since Sunday."

Raj motioned to the masseuse to move further down his back.

The men stiffened, their reports heavy in their briefcases. No one dared displease Raj. The consequences were dire. The yellow tie reflected the bright day into their eyes. An air of awe hung over them.

"Your sweater sales in Germany have doubled," the man continued hesitantly. "Sweden is close behind." His voice faltered as Hasan stepped onto the roof, smoking an irreverent cigarette. The others parted to let Hasan through. Raj sat up, tying a towel around his waist.

"Sales have gone up," squeaked Hasan. "They want more." His high-pitched voice didn't quite match his tall frame. The others watched cautiously from the corners of their eyes. Hasan was notorious for his volatile temper and violent rage.

Raj lit a thick cigar and nodded.

"We'll be sending one hundred kilos monthly, under the cover of frozen pineapples. The next load leaves in the evening," he whispered. The others strained to listen.

"Any problems?" asked Raj.

"The port. We can't have them checking us at the ports."

Raj nodded. Hasan laughed and left the roof with a 'Khodafez.'

Raj returned to his massage table.

The suited men shuffled. Each knew at least a dozen legends about Raj – the friends he had in all the important places, the brutalities he had committed, his business deals, his unbelievable wealth, and his ladies, actresses, models and princesses. Though these gentlemen were young, they had each experienced at least one personal moment of terror as well as endless moments of sheer wonder in Raj's presence. Once you were working with Raj, you were hooked up, taken care of, paths were cleared for you, but you were also on the dark side, trapped suddenly in a world where law and order took on a new definition, where Raj was judge, jury and executioner.

The yellow-tied man recalled the last incident at the port, it had happened a few months earlier. The port labourers were on strike. A union leader had been arrested and they were demanding his release. Raj Gopal's cotton, imported from Uzbekistan, had just arrived. Raj happened to be in Chittagong so he called Mr. Khan, the interim leader of the labour union, to his house.

Mr Khan was a diminutive man with a red henna beard. He arrived at Raj's house in nervous dread, with none of his usual self-assurance. His local power was nothing compared to Raj's. He walked in fawning over Mr Gopal, sir, and asked what he could do for him.

Raj said his cargo needed to be released immediately as it was stalling the work at his factory. Mr. Khan begged Raj's forgiveness, but said there was nothing he could do. It was a nation-wide labour strike and if he tried to help Raj, he'd lose his power over the union. Raj didn't argue.

The next day, Mr Khan's son strolled out of school and found a black Mercedes Benz waiting for him. Mr Khan's wife was frantic by the time he reached home, little Tanvir was missing. Mr Khan rushed over to Raj's home, a man desperate and afraid.

"Mr Gopal, sir, my son is missing. He didn't come home from school today. Do you, um, do you know where he may be?"

Raj chuckled. "Don't worry, Mr. Khan, we've shifted him to a special school. He'll have chutti as soon as my cargo is released."

Mr Khan wrung his hands behind his back, beads of sweat collected in his beard. The previous trade union leader had been arrested on charges of corruption. He was known to be Raj Gopal's right hand man. With him in jail, Mr Khan was next in the line of power, but what Raj asked of him was impossible. It would jeopardize his career and his life. He'd be thrown into prison. "Mr Gopal sir, please understand sir, I cannot help you though I want to." Mr Khan shuddered at the thought of Chittagong district jail and its alleged torture techniques. The images blended in with images of Tanvir terrified within the confines of a deranged special school.

"My cargo will be released, Mr Khan, whether it's you who helps me or not," said Raj.

Mr Khan left Raj's house in a daze. He nearly drove into an oncoming truck and when he got to his office, there was a package waiting for him. Something wrapped in the morning's newspaper. He opened it and discovered a severed finger. Tanvir's baby finger staining the headlines with its blood.

Mr Khan recoiled at the sight and found himself remembering the last time he had seen blood. It was last Eid. He spent his savings on a bokri, but in the days leading up to Eid, Tanvir had adopted the goat as his friend, even gave it a name. Khushi. Mr Khan remembered his son's face when the knife hacked into Khushi's neck. The bokri didn't stop bleating. It bleated as blood spurted in all directions and its eyeballs popped out.

Mr Khan had only seen that much blood once before, six short years earlier, when his darling wife pushed out their bundle of joy. He remembered holding her hands and praying, please God, let the baby have all ten fingers, all ten toes. He remembered Tanvir's soft hands, so tiny and perfect.

Mr Khan called Raj in desperation and was told he had to not only release the cargo but also put it on a truck and ensure its safe arrival in Dhaka. The entire process took two days after which Mr Khan returned home and found little Tanvir playing with a new remote control toy. All ten fingers on his hands.

✦ SIX ✦

Deen tried to disengage from Maria's embrace. Even in her sleep, she responded to his body, moving to mould into every new position he took. Deen had discovered, much to his wonder, that it was possible to spend the entire night intertwined with Maria, they were like two strands of a braid. He also came to know that she always tied her hair up, in the daytime in a ponytail, and at night, in a braid. Her nails were meticulously manicured and she wore only freshly laundered clothes. She presented herself as flawlessly pulled together, but in many ways she was as lost as him. It was an idiosyncrasy he had come to adore.

The week had flown by. He had spent almost every waking moment by her side, every blissful night in her embrace. In her bedroom, he explored the curves of her body by candlelight. On her rooftop, they drank wine, smooched under the stars and talked until glorious dawn. In her car, they drove around the city, strolling through snapshots of their past; the football field where he played as team captain, the dilapidated theatre where she took voice lessons as a child. They had a common love for music. She had a guitar that Deen strummed as she sang along, her voice deep and emotional. He gave her a book that made her cry and look at him differently. She taught him how to braid her hair.

She bunked class for the first time, liberated from her obligations under Deen's influence. They jumped on an overnight bus to the beaches of Cox's Bazaar, where they had sex. Mind-blowing sex. She stole him away from his mundane life and gave him a taste of what it would be like to be happy. With her around, he felt normal, like a normal ordinary guy in love. She made life perfect. Perfectly perfect. Except for one thing. He had finished the last of his puriahs and he was itching for another fix.

Deen pulled away again. This time Maria let go of her grip. Her legs untangled from his, reluctantly. The room smelt musky. She reached over to grab him, but he eluded her touch. "I have to go," he whispered.

"Where?" She peeked out of sleepy eyes.

"Football game," he explained. "I'll pick you up after."

"Football? At this hour?" she asked in disbelief. "That's some spirit." She planted a tantalizing kiss on his mouth.

Deen felt sexed up again, but he had to go. It was a qualifying game. Parvez really wanted his team to make it to the DOHS football tournament so Deen had promised to play. Besides, he hadn't been in his neighbourhood in a while and he felt homesick.

* * *

Deen received a pass and raced forward three metres, then sent the ball sailing smoothly to Parvez. Parvez weaved the ball up field, in between three bulky players, and passed it on to a friend who kicked it into the goal. Deen jogged back out to the defense.

Parvez ran by to slap him on the back. The slap nearly knocked him over. Parvez was much taller than him now, and stronger too, though as kids, it was Deen whom their parents had predicted would be taller.

Their parents had been friends throughout Deen's childhood. He had memories of a family trip to the Sunderbans, when he was as young as ten and Parvez was seven. They had trekked through the mangrove jungle with a long haired guide who told them about Gangetic dolphins that inhabited the area. They were looking out for snakes when they spotted a Royal Bengal tiger swimming across a narrow canal in the distance, a burning moment of glory and hope, grander than life, bobbing in the murky waters.

Parvez and Deen had shared many such incredible experiences over the years. Before he became a smackie, Deen spent most of his evenings in Parvez's mansion, listening to music, watching Spanish flicks, talking about comic book villains, jamming. Parvez played lead and Deen played bass. They spent endless hours on his rooftop too. Parvez was Spiderman. He could balance on ledges and jump from rooftop to rooftop without the slightest of stumbles. His mother tried to prevent his climbing, but no amount of scolding could keep him grounded.

Parvez's father, Mintu chacha, was a minister of GOB. He was a particularly powerful minister because he was as shrewd as he was intimidating. He was the kind of man who could get you out of jail, but throw you back in just as easily. He was rarely home, but the few times Deen had run into him, the man had interrogated him about his studies.

Parvez's mom was the opposite, always home, annoying them with her dedicated molly-coddling. Parvez was her only child. Deen felt thankful that his mother was not as irritating. He really should appreciate her more. She was probably sitting at the dining table by herself, praying that he was ok.

Deen ran to intercept the ball from an opponent and manipulated it away with a stylish feint and turn. Dexterity out of habit. Or passion? He sent the ball flying across the field to Parvez. Parvez, the playmaker. He could receive the ball from out of nowhere, run it up field through the other team's legs, and pass it at just the right moment to set someone up for a goal. Smiling all the while. Like Ronaldinho.

Deen wondered if he should call his mother, tell her he was ok. She'd ask where he had spent the week and he'd have to lie. He couldn't tell her about Maria. Deen didn't feel like lying so he didn't call. He knew she was worrying about him. That's how mothers were. They'd kick you out of the house then worry about where you were staying.

Deen felt a stab in his heart. Disappointments churned in his stomach like rotten eggs and bad music. He wasn't the son he wanted to be. He knew she needed him, but what could he do? He couldn't give up smack, not for her, not for anyone. It was the only thing that kept him going. If she stopped interfering, she wouldn't have to know how badly he was addicted.

His father would know though. Watching from the sky. Deen launched into negativity as he jogged through memories of his father's lectures on addiction. He had hated his father for that, but now he'd do anything to have him back. Even if it meant more lectures. At least his mother wouldn't be so damn alone.

Deen missed a direct pass and felt angry at himself for opening the floodgates of his emotions. He should be master of his thoughts, not slave to their catastrophic pull, but his negativity was stronger than his willpower, so he continued remembering, and each time the episodes were worse and regrets rushed in.

"Bhaiya," Parvez interrupted, "don't push yourself. It's a hot day! There's a bottle of water with my stuff."

"Thanks," Deen mumbled. Parvez was a good kid. Always helpful. Deen had seen him take the clothes off his back once, to give to a mad beggar who was freezing to death on the roadside. Deen remembered the beggar's eyes. Desperation. What had driven him to madness, was it an addiction? Deen's stash of smack had completely run out. He needed to make a trip to Falani's. His arms were starting to itch.

Deen panted, lagging far behind the rest of his team, nostalgic for the strength of his once-powerful thighs. His body was decaying, atrophied muscles clinging to brittle bones, black lungs, poisoned blood. His stomach, arms and cheeks had caved in. Still he continued with dogged determination. They had only been playing for seven minutes and he was unwilling to accept that those kids were better players than him. He remembered the games he had played three years ago (or was it in a different lifetime?) at that very field. He was the star player, back-heel goals and the works, a regular Maradona.

He realized suddenly how weak he had become. His stamina was shit. His kicks had no power. He could barely walk. Or talk. Or rock. He could barely do anything anymore. Deen craved his youth. He craved the high he used to get from football. None of that existed anymore. Only smack mattered and he needed a hit badly. Afraid of facing reality, Deen played on for three more minutes, then collapsed on a bench with Parvez's bottle of water.

Dooo dooo dooo dooo. The cell phone wailed in his pocket.

"Where are you?" AJ asked on the other end. "I'm at your house."

"Playing football with Parvez," said Deen. "Ma kicked me out. I'm staying with Maria."

"Maria from NSU? Score, dosto! Listen man, I'm turquing hardcore," AJ announced. "Let's go to Falani's."

"No money."

"Shit. Borrow from someone?"

"Like who?" Deen asked.

"Try Parvez, he's loaded."

"Ya right, I'm not asking a kid for money."

"Let's take Parvez with us," said AJ. "Smoke him up and get him to pay after."

"That's really fucked up!" Deen exploded.

"I'm not asking you to steal from him," AJ pursued. "He'll like it. Everybody does."

"I'm only going to say this once," said Deen with cool, collected rage. "Leave Parvez alone."

"Ok, ok, ok. Chill out. Where the hell can we get some cash?"

"I don't know. I've got to pick up Maria." Deen hung up abruptly. He felt like punching AJ.

* * *

The chot-putti stand at the edge of the DOHS football field was usually busy, a favourite among food lovers in the neighbourhood. Since it was Friday, the stand was bursting at the seams. Behind the counter, two skinny men struggled to meet the orders of hungry customers. The field buzzed with life. A family of three, short and stocky, a snotty-nosed child clambering around, followed closely by his cautious mother and her uxorious husband. A group of high school boys discussing nude scenes in movies, over a game of catch. A group of old men discussing politics, enjoying the festive air. A couple of cats, one grey, one black. Laughing beggar children flying a red kite. Perched on the periphery of the field were rickshaw wallas and cotton candy vendors with neon pink cotton candy.

"I'm in a good mood," cooed Maria, toying with the phuchka on her plate.

"Me too," lied Deen, planting a salty kiss on her cheek.

"There's an art exhibition coming up." Maria sipped her masala chai and readjusted her ponytail. "It's called *Alive in Wonderland*. Do you like plants?"

"Yes." Deen scratched his arm. He had seen something similar. A junky in the basti had carved sculptures out of plants. Real heartfelt art. He tried selling them to passers-by on Airport Road until he got arrested… or something.

"Do you know where the biggest banyan tree in Asia is?" asked Maria enthusiastically.

"Shantiniketan?" guessed Deen.

"No, it's in Bangladesh! In Kaligonj, a half hour from Tongi!" Maria told Deen about the banyan tree that reached out beyond twenty acres and was over one hundred years old. A man had tried to cut off its branches to make fuel. After a severe illness and prolonged suffering, he died. "It's an enchanted tree. You have to be suicidal to attack it. We should go see it!"

Deen adored Maria's attitude. She was curious about the world, thirsty for knowledge, eager to explore. He liked how her mind meandered. She could totally mess up punch lines. She was unconventional, without even knowing it. He admired the dreams she had of how things could be different. Her beliefs were aligned with his, same wavelength. He loved her, it was no longer lust. And best of all, the feeling was mutual. He could tell by the way she looked at him.

"There's going to be a concert." Maria continued. "Bangla, the band, have you heard of them? They'll be singing baul songs."

"Sure," replied Deen. Baul songs were more than Bengali folk music, they were a form of worship, mystic devotion. Deen knew Bangla, the band. They were famous, fusing baul songs with a range of instruments: electric guitar, bass, drums alongside dhols, bashis and ektaras. Anusheh, their vocalist, was a legend. Her lung capacity, her stamina, her control over her classically trained voice, had thrown her into stardom. She was a musical genius who used her voice to revive the baul spirit among Bangladeshi youths.

"We've simply got to go," said Maria, clasping her hands together. "The concert's on a boat! Only 50 tickets. A tribute to Lalon. Do you like Lalon?"

"He's a Messiah," said Deen. Fakir Lalon Shah. A boy in rags who rose up from the depths of famines and floods, with songs of spiritual transcendence. A guru to dervishes. Music set him free.

"I saw a documentary about him," piped Maria.

Deen had seen it too, with AJ and Shagor, in the Dhaka

University Auditorium. The film-makers had depicted Lalon as a clean, conservative kid though he was really a king khor, a red eyed ganja smoking fakir, a hippie and an anarchist. They didn't watch the entire film. They left during the interval, sat under a banyan tree in the centre of campus and smoked four fat joints in honour of Lalon.

"Have you been to the Lalon mela?" Deen asked. Maria shook her head. A strand of her wild curls came loose. Deen stretched it out like a spring, pulling it to his nose. "It's a festival," he continued. "A gathering of musicians, pot-heads and spiritualists from all over."

"A local Woodstock!" said Maria, in delight.

Deen was crazy about the way her eyes lit up when she was excited. Her tangential thoughts were perfectly in sync with her unbalanced personality and quirky mood swings. Deen loved it all, but something about her was a little *off*. Deen wondered what it was. Was she flaky? Or fake? There was something wrong with the *way* in which she was unpredictable, something unsettling. Or was he looking for faults, excuses to hold back, afraid of his feelings? The week with Maria had been magical, and yet, he wanted to get away from her now. For a bit.

The beggar children gathered in a sad huddle and tried to untangle their prized possession. The red kite was lodged high in the branches of a guava tree. Though they jumped with all their might, they could not reach the first branch of leverage.

Maria poured tamarind sauce into a phuchka shell and brought the watery bite to her mouth carefully. "Are you and AJ tight?"

"He's like an older brother," replied Deen. Annoyance rushed through his blood as he recalled his earlier conversation with AJ. But he did need to smoke and how would they pay?

Deen's eyes strayed towards Maria's purse lying on the seat next to her.

"Is he a nice guy?" Maria pursued.

"He's a rebel," said Deen. "He led me to my first ciggie and my first dance with Mary Jane." *And my first chase,* he thought. Maria always had cash. He had seen her wallet lying around in her room, but it hadn't crossed his mind before. Now it seemed like a gift from God.

"I don't have any true friends," Maria stated quietly.

Deen laughed. "Ms. Popular has no friends?" He wouldn't need to borrow much, just 500 taka for smack and maybe a bit more to take her out for dinner.

"I am not popular," Maria insisted, "And I have no *true* friends. I know a lot of people, but none of them really know me. Do you think I'm a closed person?"

"It takes effort to open oneself up, and trust," said Deen. He needed to create a diversion. He eyed the chot-putti stand. It was thirty feet away. He couldn't ask her to buy him anything, she'd have to take her purse.

"Deen, it's funny, I feel I can tell you everything."

"It's not funny, Maria. I feel that way too." Deen felt lousy. Maria had admitted to telling him *everything* before. Deen could honestly say she was very special, but there was a world he could never share with her. Then he spotted it, the perfect opportunity, the box of napkins behind the counter of the stand. Deen leaned in to kiss Maria and knocked over the plate of phuchka. It fell upon her lap in a messy heap of tamarind sauce and chickpeas. "Oh shit!" said Deen.

"Ew!" squealed Maria, jumping up. The soggy mess dropped from her lap to the floor. Tamarind sauce covered the chickpeas like lava on a mound of volcanic rubble.

"Napkins are over there!" Deen pointed to the stand. Maria rushed off to get some. Deen grabbed her purse. It was stuffed with receipts, lipsticks, rubber bands and junk. He scrambled to find her wallet, glancing up to see if she was looking. She had just reached the stand and was asking for napkins. Deen found the wallet. It was thick with cash. Maria was cleaning herself off at the stand. Deen counted, 7000 taka. He grabbed five thousand and closed the wallet, pushing it back into her purse and onto the chair, just in time.

Maria returned to their table. She marched past her seat and straight to her purse. Deen started to sweat. She lifted her purse from the chair. Deen wondered if she had seen him. She sat down, putting the purse on the ground.

"I'm sorry," said Deen. "I'm really sorry."

"It's ok," said Maria, her eyes still sparkling with love.

Deen felt lucky, she adored him. She was amazing, she was his Kohinoor. He would take her out to a fancy restaurant, some place with candles. *Dooo dooo dooo dooo*. Mission Impossible wailed on Deen's ringer.

"It's me. I've got some money. I'm picking you up," said AJ.

"Ok, bye." Deen mumbled into the phone. "I've got to go," he said abruptly to Maria.

"You're leaving me?" she asked with a pout.

"Ya." Deen could feel her displeasure. She couldn't stand being away from him. Women, ever-demanding, but oh so sweet.

"Where are you going?" she asked.

"I need to meet AJ," Deen explained vaguely. "How about we go out for dinner? I'll call you." He wanted to spend time with her too, but his thoughts were racing to his next hit. He would meet up with her later, do something romantic. Flowers maybe. Girls love flowers.

SEVEN

Deen stared into the glossy eyes of a massive, black bull yoked to a bamboo cart next to their car. They were barely moving, locked in place by the surrounding cars, scooters, rickshaws, gas-guzzling jeeps, ducks, trucks, schmucks, motorcycles, ox-carts, pedestrians, beggars, street vendors and buses exploding with passengers. People, people, people. Deen tried to ignore his itchy skin.

"Let's park here and walk," suggested AJ. They were still a good fifteen minutes away from the basti but Shagor and Deen agreed immediately.

As they walked, Deen realized he was not surrounded by people, people, people, but men, men, men. Men everywhere. The street was clogged with men. Men chanting *Allah*. Men dressed in thobes inching forward with Qurans and religious zeal. White robes billowed in the wind like spectres. Even for Bangladesh, with 150 million people squeezed into 150 square miles of land, this congregation was an especially cramped mess.

"What's going on?" asked Shagor.

"Izthema," said Deen. Three million believers crowded on the banks of the Turag River in the tiny town of Tongi.

By the time they reached their shack, the boys were sweating. The indifferent sun, the unsubdueable urges, the suffocating nearness of hundreds of religious enthusiasts was becoming too much. Falani let them in and offered them cold water.

"Give us some smack," Shagor demanded.

"I don't have any, bhaiya," Falani replied.

"What do you mean? Find some." Shagor ordered.

"Can't you see it's Izthema," said Majid, sitting on the ground smoking a cigarette, his tattered lungi covered with ashes.

"I don't care," warned Shagor.

"Falani, we're in bad shape," explained AJ.

Falani looked at Deen beseechingly. "I don't have any. What can I do? It's not safe today, even for you all, but Kala said there's smack in Musa's shack. You know Musa? The dealer in the basti across the street?"

"We'll never find him alone," said Shagor. "Take us to him."

"I can't leave my girls alone here, too many people around," said Falani firmly. "Kala is at the tea stall, he'll take you."

Deen thanked Falani as they headed out.

Kala was smoking a cigarette and sipping tea with some friends. "You see all kinds of men," he said to the boys. "They spend their yearly savings to come this far. I met a man yesterday who traveled three days by bus and ferry!"

"Hey, take us to Musa," barked Shagor.

Kala frowned, visibly disturbed by the mention of Musa. He pulled the boys aside and told them to keep their voices down, warning them that the place was crawling with cops. The boys refused to leave, forcing Kala to comply.

Together they waded through the sea of chanting men. An old man with one leg and a crutch, *Allah,* three blind men,

Allah, a boy with skin disease, *Allah,* a man in strange sunglasses, *Allah,* a man with a pockmarked face, *Allah,* a man with a mattress in his arms, *Allah,* a man with a henna red beard, *Allah,* a man with a beard that reached his groin, *Allah,* a man with his father in a wheelchair, *Allah,* a young man in an ex-export Guns N' Roses t-shirt, *Allah,* a man with a large sack balanced on his head and skinny neck, *Allah,* a dark man in a white kurta, *Allah.*

Inside Musa's shack, four men were playing carom. One of them looked just like Musa, his brother probably, a taller more skeletal version with beadier eyes. Deen thought he resembled a giant praying-mantis hovering over the game. The men glanced up with blank faces when Kala introduced the boys and asked for smack. They knew Kala, but the boys were strangers and they were not about to be busted by undercover cops. They did not trust Kala, or anyone else for that matter. In the sewers of society, anyone could be a rat. They continued to pretend innocence till Shagor lost his temper and waved a wad of cash in Musa's face. Musa called him into the inner room, gave him a pouch of smack, took his money and asked them to leave. Shagor had no pockets so he threw the pouch to Deen.

The throngs of men on the main road had grown and a mullah with a loud-speaker preached to them as they inched forward. The sudden appearance of the boys disrupted his sermon, but after a long stare he continued with increased urgency. The crowd shuffled in agitation. Deen felt the weight of their disapproving gaze as they passed moral judgments on his character. *They don't know me!* Deen thought. They didn't know his life, his circumstances, the history behind his actions. They didn't know what dips and desperations had led him there. Besides, why was his addiction such a crime? He never hurt anyone. Except his mother. And himself.

They leered at him, careful not to brush against his body, erecting symbolic boundaries between him and themselves. The distance they created, almost palpable, made Deen feel like a leper. He wanted to grab the next passing mullah and kiss him. A wet sloppy kiss full of junky germs. He wanted to exhale a puff of smoke into their faces and shout, *now what would you like to do to me?* They would stone him to death, for sure, then leave his dead body unburied at the side of the road. They pummelled him with their looks. Conform! Conform! They seemed to be saying. Conform or lose yourself to the DEVIL!

Angry religions for angry men.

Do they know why I'm here? Deen wondered if his eyes were red, surprised to find he wanted to hide, suddenly ashamed. The smack in his pocket scorched a hole through his pants, through the flesh of his legs, into his blood stream, poisoning him. His sweaty shirt clung to his back, he felt dizzy. He looked at Shagor and AJ, but they seemed unbothered. Deen quickened his pace. "Hurry up! Let's get out of here." He began running as best he could through the maddening crowd. He saw the face of the Devil among the worshippers, smiling at him diabolically, as he ran against the grain, against the flow of people heading towards God.

AJ laughed, quickening his step to keep up. "Are you turquing?"

"Shut up!" Deen shouted. "Shut up and hurry up."

"Are you scared?" jeered Shagor, "Bheethoo! Bheethoo!"

Deen could hear his heart pounding faster and faster with every breath, *dhoog-dhug, dhoog-dhug, dhoog-dhug.* He caught a glimpse of the Devil again, following him at a measured distance. The crowd blended into an abstract collection of colours. He heard Kala call him from behind, but he didn't stop. He saw people part to make space for him, but he ran, avoiding the spaces, plunging instead into the thick of the crowd, creating mild havoc in his path. *Watch out,* cried the masses. *Watch where you're going. Jerk! Hindu!* they cursed. Khor, khor, khor, Deen heard them chant, as he rammed his way through.

Deen reached Falani's shack in a state of frenzy. He banged on the door and she let him in. Kala and the boys piled in shortly after. Kala saw the look of terror on Deen's face and quickly prepared a chase for him. He led the flame under the lump of sugar, back and forth, back and forth, singing a shaky line across the foil as Deen inhaled.

Whoooooooooosh.
Whoooooooooosh.
Whoooooooooosh.

Deen took a puff of his cigarette and collapsed on the floor.

"You guys shouldn't have come here," said Majid. "There are people everywhere."

"So?" shrugged Shagor.

"Well nothing's gonna happen to you rich boys," said Majid vehemently. "No one's gonna fuck your pretty ass. But you're leading a trail right up to Falani. Think about it."

"Stop it, Majid," Falani admonished. She bit into a paan. Her lips turned red and wet. "Where were they supposed to go? You can come here whenever you want," she said to Deen.

Deen blushed. His ears were hot. He didn't want to put Falani in danger, but then Falani was their dealer. A dealer takes certain risks. If the boys took their business to another shack, Falani would be left with no income. They were Falani's lifeline just as she was theirs. And Majid, who depended on his sister for smack, food and shelter, needed them too.

"Where'd you get cash?" asked Deen, after they had all smoked.

"From Parvez," said AJ coolly.

"Ya," laughed Deen, recalling his earlier rage. "No, seriously?"

"Parvez," said AJ.

"What?"

"After I spoke to you, I went to the field to pick you up. You had already left but Parvez and his buddies were still there. I told him I needed some cash."

"You just told him outright? 'Hi, Parvez, I need cash?'"

"No. I did the small talk. He said you weren't being yourself so I said you were probably turquing."

"What the hell?! Thanks AJ, you don't need to broadcast that."

"Relax dost. He knows you're a khor. Everyone in university knows. It's a small circle, people love to talk. Anyway, he asked if he could help, so I told him you were broke and turquing. He offered the money himself."

"What the hell?" shouted Deen.

"Hey, I didn't lie or anything," said AJ defensively.

"Chill, man," interrupted Shagor. "Parvez's a big boy."

"I can't believe you did that," said Deen.

"It's Ronnie's fault," said AJ. "He still owes me money. I'm going to kill that cheat when I get my hands on him."

Deen was seething. He had already smoked so he couldn't say much. He felt used and betrayed. AJ had manipulated his friend. Deen's confidence plunged like an anchor. He resented Parvez's sympathy. His life was a result of deliberate choices, he did not need anyone's sympathy. *Let it go,* Deen told himself, trying to concentrate on his smoke. He stared at the coconut oil can balanced on the bamboo. Falani oiled her hair occasionally, on holidays like Eid or Pohela Boishakh, when she strung little bailey flowers in her braid.

Deen could hear her daughters playing in the back room. Falani's shack was split into two rooms by a sheet of woven cane. She lived with her daughters in the back room and served the boys in the front. Her husband used to sell smack before she threw him out for breaking her jaw. After he left, she kept the room clean for a few months, but desperation drove her back to the only trade she had ever known. Deen remembered the first time he had come to Falani's shack. AJ had picked him up on a brand new motorcycle, gripping a wad of cash in his hand. He was jittery with joy over a 2.6 karat diamond he had stolen and sold to some punk. Shagor told him about a basti in Tongi, beside a mosque by Airport Road, which had recently received a fresh load of smack. AJ drove like a madman and Deen hung on for dear life, singing at the top of his lungs, "*C'mon brown sugar, how come you taste so good?*"

Falani was skeletal then, even now she was skinny, but back then she was emaciated. After the boys started buying from her, Falani's life improved. She fixed the roof of her shack with corrugated tin. She put her daughters in school. She purchased two saris, some pots and pans and an audio cassette. Deen had given her a tape player so they could listen to music while they chased. The melodies lifted her spirit, though she did not understand a word of English. When she had saved

up a bit, she splurged on a Bangla casette and taught her
daughters all the songs.

She did her best to keep the boys happy, not only because
they were her livelihood, but also because she had grown fond
of them over the years. The arrangement worked out nicely,
except when the monsoons hit and the smack did not arrive.
Then everyone suffered. The boys scraped by, scavenging off
whatever they could find. Falani was left to fend for herself,
no money for doctors, school, food, clean water.

"Why doesn't the government do anything to improve their
state?" asked Deen, suddenly bothered by the poverty around
him. He usually ignored it but sometimes it pierced through
his shield, reared its mammoth head and knocked the air out
of his lungs. As a child he never came so close to the harsh
reality, now he faced it every day in the basti. *Where the people
are many and their hands are all empty, where hunger is ugly,
where souls are forgotten.*

"Who cares?" said Shagor.

"Exploit the poor so the rich can get richer," said AJ.

Deen knew AJ's cynicism was not entirely groundless. All
the rich businessmen in Bangladesh were, coincidentally,
corrupt politicians who were happily letting their people down
in order to bolster their own bank accounts. "Fuck GOB," he
said, though he knew it was not only the Government of
Bangladesh at fault. It was something more fundamental, in
the very DNA of mankind, something that made men brutally
hungry for power.

"Fuck GOB," repeated AJ in solemn agreement.

And God, Deen thought in dismay. What hope was there
for his country?

"Hey," said Falani, softly interrupting their conversation.

"Whatever's happening on all those levels, GOB, tob, at the end of the day, *we* poor people *are* happy. Allah has given us that strength. It's no small blessing, let me tell you. I am thankful."

Deen frowned. He could not figure out if Falani was really happy, or if it was a false consciousness she had been conditioned into during childhood. Be content with what God's given you. System justifying bullshit. Opium for the masses. And if that were the case, was her happiness fake? Was it less real? Once in her reality, who cares how it got there? Maybe that's what she needed, promises of bliss hereafter. What was bliss, anyhow? The ecstasy of salvation? Complete fulfilment? At peace, released from worldly needs? Deen felt blissed out and wanted another smoke to sink into the pleasant, sedated stupor his body adored. "Falani, can you honestly tell me you are happy?"

"There are different ways to be happy," she said, doe eyes gazing at him. "If you're born in a basti, you learn to be content with what you've got. It's the only way to save yourself from despair."

* * *

From the moment he had come to know of her, Sergeant Allauddin Akbar had been on her case. Filthy Falani. He hated her more than the other peddlers on his list. It was despicable enough that men might dabble in drugs and other such dung, but how could women, sacred carriers of the future, wombs holding innocent Life itself, ordained by Allah to be pure and submissive, how could they stoop so low? He secretly fantasized about her lips, but it made him feel un-Islamic.

Torn between his desire to be pious and the instinctive temptations of the flesh, he hated her. Such sirens should not be allowed to roam free, damning souls.

The sergeant waited like a patient tiger. The boys that Falani served were rich and well connected, so he had to wait for proof so compelling, so juicy and ugly, that no one would dare lift a finger to save the goddess of gloom. He knew if he waited long enough, he would unearth something buried deep down.

He stroked his beard, devising a strategy. His greasy hair was parted to the side to cover a patch of baldness. He caught his reflection in the window and thought he looked young, despite his growing belly, which anyway, was hidden by the pleats of his pants. His forehead had a dark patch of skin at the centre, from years of prostrating in prayer. He was a true devotee.

Sergeant Akbar paced the room. Certain things are wrong, wrong, wrong, no matter how you put it. *Haraam*! Addiction is *haraam*! It says so in the Quran. There's no confusion about it. Drugs, alcohol, pre- and extra-marital sex. No, no and no-no! Drugaddicts were not only criminals, they were sinners.

Sergeant Akbar's desk was piled high with reports filed by harassed people. Only the papers at the top, generously funded by bribes, made it to the sergeant's inspection. He was too busy chasing drugaddicts, there were so many of them. The sergeant glanced at the photograph tucked under the glass surface of his desk. Pretty little Daisy. Good name: Fatima Binta Akbar. She was growing up so quickly. Already five years old. Next year, kindergarten! She wrinkled her nose when she smiled. She told her friends that her father was a Police Man.

She took great pride in him and he took great pride in her.

He shuddered at the thought of the villains roaming the streets. Not that Daisy would ever be allowed on the streets alone. NEVER! And she would be in *purdah* once she was seven. Allah, the most merciful, had offered women the veil to protect them from the eyes of lecherous men. A simple yet effective precaution. The sergeant wanted to lobby for a law that would make the purdah compulsory, but Chief Detective Khan rejected his suggestion. He resented the detective. Such liberal mindsets were an affront to Allah, the most merciful.

Sergeant Akbar's room was adjacent to several smaller offices. He poked his head into the doorways to see if his inefficient officers were lazing over a cup of tea. Yes, they were underpaid, but rightfully so, they didn't deserve anything more. The sergeant returned to his office feeling disappointed. He sat heavily into his cushy swivel chair, a token of friendship from the Home Minister. It was a friendship the sergeant valued deeply though it meant turning a blind eye to certain matters. No matter, with so many criminals out there, there was no time to bother with the minister's minor offences. The criminals to fear were the ones who roamed free of reign: anarchists, Hindus and drugaddicts.

"Samad! SAMAD!" called the sergeant.

A boy in an oversized uniform appeared at the doorway, wiping sleep out of his eyes. "Sir? Yes Sir? You called Sir?"

"Yes Samad, bring me some tea and samosas. Beef samosas. None of that aloo vegetable stuff, ok?" said Sergeant Akbar. A worn out prayer rug, carefully folded, hung over the back of his chair. The walls of his office were green and lumpy, peeling with the dampness of many humid summers. The tube-light over his desk gave off a garish light, creating the atmosphere of an old operating theatre. No money to touch up the office, but no matter, he consoled himself, his work was out there, on the streets and in the slums, where the pagan fungus of society carried out its sinful debaucheries.

❖ EIGHT ❖

Sundari lifted the cascades of her sari and stepped onto the marble courtyard where she would soon begin the Dance of Sita. Her ankle bells jingled as she stepped, one slow foot beckoning the next. Her toe tips were red. A trail of henna paisleys snaked its way from her toes, up her ankles, up her slender calves. The gentlemen wondered how far underneath the sari the red stain meandered on… did it make its way up to her hot core?

The younger dancers looked upon Sundari with an admiration that she graciously accepted with a twinkling eye. It had been one year since she had last performed and though it was known that she was the indirect cause of Raghav Mehta's death, the scars of the scandal had healed somewhat and no one seemed to think of it here. Here all reputations were bloodstained, the sullied past blended with the bleak future in a haze, money was everything and no love was lost. Here Sundari's radiance made her a symbol of hope for lonely men and they were eager to watch her dance again.

Raj Gopal's property was adorned with fairy lights and streamers of colourful silk. Three dozen waiters served martinis and hors d'oeuvres in the courtyard. Politicians and businessmen milled around the bar. The Australian Ambassador was already plastered. Scattered along the periphery of the garden were groups of people lounging on silk cushions, smoking hookahs. Beyond the fountain was a grill with an assortment of barbequed meats and sausages, including pork chops, which were rare to come by in Bangladesh. An elaborate buffet laid out on silver dishes suspended above permanent flames offered everything from tandoori lobster to mint mutton biriani.

A shiny Range Rover arrived at the gates, flanked by two cars full of guards. A minister in a black suit stepped out, with a champagne bottle in his hands. Raj walked to the gates to greet him. They shook hands heartily and Raj accepted the bottle.

"I've heard the government will be tendering out the construction of three new bridges," said the minister, as they walked towards the bar. Deal-making had become a sure jackpot with the current government running the game.

"I know a steel trader in Dubai," suggested Raj. "An old friend of mine. He'll give you good rates."

The minister nodded in appreciation.

Raj offered the minister a drink. "Demand for my pineapples has gone up," he said. "I hope my cargo won't be subject to the usual inspections at the port. The process is too slow, the fruit spoils."

"Of course," said the minister empathetically, taking a sip of his cocktail. "I completely understand. And what about the problem I spoke to you about last time, the young man from Old Town?"

"I've taken care of him," said Raj. "Settled your score." Raj led his friend to the courtyard to enjoy the dancing, then returned to the gates to greet his guests.

The evening's performance had drawn in some particularly notorious gentlemen richly dipped in new money. They sipped their gin and measured Sundari with coolly confident eyes, but tonight their longing stares were wasted, because she was looking for just one man in that crowd.

AJ skulked by the terrace, hidden in the shadows with his drink. He hated the idea of Sundari performing for other men. They'd probably fantasize about her in their grimy bedrooms. AJ had tried to talk her out of dancing, but Raj had personally asked her to perform. It was his birthday and she felt she could not deny his request. *No one dared deny Raj anything*, thought AJ bitterly. Men of power. Money and power. Money is power.

The tabalchi began with a slow rhythm, *dha, dhin, dhin, dha.* Sundari circled the courtyard, moving her foot with every third beat, eyes downcast. The audience swelled with hushed anticipation. To AJ, it felt like chloroform. He swallowed his twelfth glass of whiskey and ordered a waiter to bring him a refill. The tabalchi increased the pace and Sundari lifted her head up to heaven, submitting herself to the music like a true devotee.

Red eyed and enraged, AJ followed Sundari's movements, the sway of her hips, the wave of her arms, the arch of her neck, as the beat gained momentum.

Dha. *How dare they stare?*
Dhin. *Lascivious fucks.*
Dhin. *She's my girl.*
Dha. *Why should anyone see her like this?*

Dha. *Fuck Raj.*
Dhin. *Fuck them all.*

Dhin. *I don't care who they are.*
Dha. *I'll kill them.*

Na. *Bash their skulls.*
Tin. *Against the marble floor.*
Tin. *Rip out their eyeballs.*
Na. *Teach them to stare.*

Tete. *Bludgeon them with that damn sitar.*
Dhin. *Hack their bodies to pieces.*
Dhin. *Throw their remains into the river.*
Dha. *Wipe out their families.*

Rage. Jealousy. Hatred. AJ froze when the crowd cheered as Sundari smiled.

When Bablu Haq whistled at Sundari, he had no idea what was coming. He was sitting in the back row on a throw cushion, leaning against the terrace, belly hanging out, enjoying his martini, sharing lewd jokes with his friends, when Sundari lifted her veil and smiled at the audience. He thought the smile was directed at him so he let out a loud whistle of appreciation. A moment later, he felt the grip of ice cold hands on his neck.

The hands lifted him right off his cushion. He gasped to breathe.

"What the hell did you mean by that?" AJ whispered into his ear ferociously.

Bablu struggled to pull the vice-like grip off his neck.

AJ released one hand and revved his fist back to throw a punch. A guard caught him from behind, intercepting the blow. Another guard plucked him off the floor like a rag doll. As the guards carried him away, AJ muttered under his breath,

Bulls, quick as lightning. Goddam trained, ex-navy pricks. Fucking Raj Gopal's fucking impenetrable wall. Even in his state of belligerence, AJ did not dare say it out loud.

Sundari returned to her apartment late that night to find AJ passed out on her bed. She sighed with relief, happy to see him there. She pressed her body against his. Whiskey emanated from his pores. There'd be a torrential fight in the morning, because he loved her, though he would never admit it.

* * *

Tonight would be the night of unmasking. Deen lit a joint and headed to meet Maria with three bottles of red wine in his bag. His heart warmed as he thought of her delicious breasts and pouty lips. He was high off their romance, it reached beyond his wildest dreams.

She needed him. Ensnared in lofty ideals, she demanded too much of herself. Stooped under her own ambition, she had become a masochistic perfectionist, militant about her studies and overly self-critical. She needed him to pull her out of her destructive obsessions. He was her distraction, her respite. Just as she was his.

Deen thought of their impulsive trip to Cox's Bazaar, a requiem from the busy streets of Dhaka and the dead end avenues of unexpressed feelings. The six-hour bus ride, their x-rated behaviour, frantic fingers, new lovers exploring each others' bodies, minds, souls. How did it happen so fast?

The posh beach avenue lined with hotels and their dingy room a few streets away, she had named it *no.ac@holidayhotel.com.* They made love in the sticky heat till dawn. That night was special. They both knew it. It was their plunge into eternity together. It was a promise in both their hearts.

Deen loved the feeling of Maria in his arms, soft tender warm, all woman. In discovering her, he was discovering himself, stirring emotions he had never known before. He thought of the breezy rickshaw ride the morning after and how he felt fine and mellow yellow, hello: just inexpressibly happy. Feeling groovy, without any smack. She did that to him. Just Maria. She was a trip.

They splashed in the water, lounged on the sand, drank spiked coconut juice and ate spicy rupchanda. And then they made love. Again and again and again. The bonfire by the beach set their spirits ablaze. The bottle of tequila and the romancing stars. The teasing, pleasing rhythm of the waves whispering songs of sunken sailors who had once loved so deeply. There they were, dancing under the ancient moon with all its memories of passions gone by and brought back again by the twists of Fate, reincarnated to bathe in each other's affection.

Then it was morning already and time to return, not to his home in DOHS, but to her apartment in Gulshan, to spend the rest of his life in her arms. His feelings were growing with every moment, now he wanted something more. He wanted a connection that was stronger, deeper than that of flesh and blood. He longed for her to melt into him so that they could be one, but their union was blocked by the prickly old LIE growing fat in between them.

He had to tell her the truth. Tonight, in the candlelight, he would unburden his soul. He would declare his love and then he would confess his addiction. He would tell her so that she could know him completely and love him for who he was. He lit a cigarette and tried to string together the words to say it.

* * *

Sitting alone in the candlelight, Maria began to wonder if her hopes were pinned on the wrong guy. He was unquestionably the handsomest guy in university, but he was also unreliable, unmotivated and broke. *Oasis,* the fanciest restaurant in Dhaka, seemed bland to Maria as she waited. The garden outside was a cluster of palm trees and fountains.

Maria wondered if Deen was an oasis in her parched world, or a mirage. She couldn't help but think, *she* should be the one waited upon, not the one waiting. The restaurant resembled a Bedouin tent with camel saddles and sketches of masked falcons hanging from the walls. Rustic lamps carved out of coconut shell cast eerie shadows that danced with the flicker of the candles on the tables.

In Deen's presence, she could forget the hatred that curdled in her blood. Though they had spent only a week together, she felt like she had known him forever. She was happier than she had been in months, maybe years. Deen had become the masculine energy she lacked in her universe.

Maria toyed with the candle, pouring wax patterns onto the menu. Ever since her father abandoned her mother for the neighbour's uncouth maid, six months ago, things had gone terribly wrong. Her mother collapsed on the kitchen floor, destroyed by the double blow of bigamy and betrayal. She was rushed to the hospital and then never quite recovered. She moved out of their apartment and in with Maria's grandmother, leaving Maria on her own.

Maria tried to resume her life, but suddenly it had grown ugly. She saw her mediocrity, her failures, one after the other, like unfinished stories hanging on a clothesline. With nothing else going right, she threw her energy into her relationship with Deen, and now he had disappeared. It was her father's fault. If he could cheat, lie and abandon them, how could any man be trusted? She needed to rely on herself alone.

Eudemonia? thought Maria, feeling miserable. Wasn't that the ultimate goal? What would make her happy? Love? Some grand achievement? Maria pulled out a flask of whiskey from her purse and took a sip. Were her dreams too big for her? Like ill-fitted stilettoes, you couldn't walk in them without stumbling, all you could do was stand still, feeling lofty and unbalanced. The last time she felt confident was in high school, when the future teemed with endless possibilities and her life was a sky sparkling with dreams, distant and beautiful. Only recently it had dawned on her, not all your wishes come true.

She was used to the good life. Her father was a businessman and her mother was the daughter of an industrialist, but now, with her father out of the picture and her mother burning through her dwindling inheritance, Maria was only moments away from bankruptcy. Financially and emotionally. Penniless pointless life. What good was life without money?

Nothing in the world scared Maria more, not even death. Death was kinder than poverty. She didn't fear roadside beggar poverty. She could never fall that low. Could she? Relative poverty was a monster much more real, too close for comfort. Middle class mediocrity poverty. Curtailed freedom of choice poverty. Can't pay your bills poverty. Where no one dares dream big dreams. Where imagination is a luxury. Where desperation makes people selfish.

She couldn't let herself slip through the cracks of society. She needed to get a job. At some bank. Some boring bank where she could do boring things so that some boring guy's check reached some other boring guy's account, or something equally boring. Though she would never make any lasting contribution to humanity or be excited at work, at least she would be able to afford the basics. It was the most *practical* choice.

Maria reached for her flask and took another swig. She grimaced as the bitter taste spread through her. Mmmm. . . Sure, it'd be easy. She would just numb her brain. She would work like a dog till she saved enough money to take off and explore some unbeaten path, down which lay greater happiness and purpose. And perhaps fame.

Deen was broke, with no ambitious plan to propel him into success, and yet, he wasn't stressed. He made her calm too, pulled her away from her gnawing worries. He helped her enjoy life. She had never been happy just *being* before. Still, their relationship wasn't going anywhere. Where could it go?

She could never marry a man who had even less money than her. They'd starve, for starters. She wasn't ready for marriage, but it did loom ahead. Before her mother was abandoned, she'd been on the hunt for Maria, gathering bio-datas of eligible bachelors from her charity club friends. Men in the in-crowd. Probably boring. And dorky. But rich. She needed to survive. Or maybe it didn't matter. Who needs money when you have love?

Maria remembered Deen's lips and the smoky-ashy flavour of his kiss. Dense and intoxicating, it took her breath away. Even after it had long ended, the tantalizing flavour lurked in her mouth. And his touch, gentle yet demanding. He was a real number.

What would she do if he left her? Left her for another woman? She wouldn't let Deen get away with it. She wouldn't fall apart like her mom. She would kill him in his sleep. Kill the bitch first, in some brutal way, and then kill him. Maria chewed her lips as she fell into the abyss of her imagination.

* * *

Deen stubbed out his cigarette and approached the restaurant. He could see Maria in the window. Her raven locks held up by a jewelled clip, her smooth neck exposed. A slinky sari hugged her curvy body. Silver bangles on her arms. But she was crying, wasn't she? Something was wrong.

"Where were you?" Maria demanded. "Where the fuck were you?"

"Izthema." Deen motioned her to lower her voice, she was drawing everyone's attention.

"Izthema?" Maria whispered furiously, throwing punches at his chest. "I thought you had met another girl. I could see you touching her, in my mind."

"Maria, calm down," Deen said gently.

"Calm down? No, Deen. It gets worse. When I was fuming with jealousy and you still didn't show up, then I thought you had died!" The anxiety in her voice crescendoed into a scream. "Do you know what it's like to sit in a restaurant alone, thinking you've just lost your best friend? It's unbearable! Why do you drag me through these emotions?" She collapsed into sobs.

Deen, shocked and shaken, took her in his arms and stole a glance at the time. Shit, he was two hours late.

"Deen, I hate you! I needed you! You left me!" she screamed.

"Just kill me, I can't bear to be this unhappy! I want to die."
Maria's livid sobs grew louder until she was howling
hysterically.

"It's ok, baby," Deen soothed. "I'm here now. I'm here."
He pulled her into his body. He had never seen her like this.
He didn't know how to help her. She needed medication or
counseling. All he could offer her was love. And lies. He felt
afraid, what if she did try to hurt herself?

"Don't ever do that again, Deen," said Maria, finally calming
down a bit. "Don't abandon me."

"I won't," he promised, looking into her eyes. He couldn't
remember when he had last done so. Her eyes were bewitching
even when brimming with confusion. His shirt was moist
with her tears. It made his heart ache. Girls could be so
vulnerable sometimes. He wanted to save her. He felt lonely.
His secret felt heavy inside him. He could not tell her who he
really was. Not today. Maybe not ever.

"I didn't know you were religious," said Maria, teardrops
glistening on her eyelashes.

"Everyone needs a prayer now and then," said Deen.

"Why go all the way to Tongi?" she asked. "Why couldn't
you come *here* and whisper a prayer? God is omnipresent."

"Group energy," said Deen, stroking Maria's arm. "That's
what they say about congregations. God's more likely to hear
our prayers if we pray together."

"You stole from me," Maria interrupted.

"What? No I didn't," Deen avoided her eyes. Her accusation
caught him by surprise.

"You stole 5000 taka. Did you think I wouldn't notice?"

"I'll pay you back," said Deen.

"Ya right," Maria shouted. "How?"

A waiter shuffled away nervously. Deen rubbed his sweaty palms together and said nothing.

"You're a liar, Deen. Besides, you're going nowhere with your life. I need to get over you. Don't call me." Maria grabbed her purse and stormed out.

Deen was stunned. Tonight was supposed to be their night of connection. He was going to reach out to her so she could help him become a better man. Instead the suicidal psycho had dumped him? Deen poured himself a glass of wine. Maria was just a girl. He didn't need her or anybody else.

✦ NINE ✦

Deen woke up to a jolt of pain in his stomach. He rubbed his forehead. A hangover pounded in his skull. He looked around his bedroom and vaguely remembered the night before. Maria had dumped him. He stayed on at *Oasis* and finished the wine himself. He didn't recall climbing the trellis up to his window, but he must have. How else would he have broken into his room?

There was a loud knock at his door. *Knock, knock, who's there.* "Who's there?" Deen shouted.

"Let me in, it's Parvez," mumbled a sickly voice at his door.

Deen crawled out of bed to open the door and Parvez fell in.

"I have to puke," he yelled. Deen lunged for the bin and placed it under Parvez's mouth. Yellow bile poured out of Parvez's gut. "I'm sorry bhaiya." He murmured something about smack and AJ and moori, then collapsed on the floor. Deen brought him a glass of water, but he had already passed out.

Deen's head hurt. What just happened? Parvez sprawled out on the floor reminded Deen of his wasted youth. He was infuriated with AJ for destroying the only friendship he had that was clean.

There was a time when Deen had been keen on recruiting others, but that was mostly before he chased smack. Before he was hardcore, much earlier in the *progression*. He started young. Cigarettes at the age of eleven. Then alcohol stolen from friends' parents. Then ganja. Then phencydil, amphetamines and coke. Then coke and smack. Sometimes horse tranquilizers and yabba. Then just smack. Smack, smack, smack.

Smack had its own progression. Someone introduces you to sugar, usually because he wants your money. Sugar daddy. Someone has to feed it to you. Virgins don't know how to chase. If there's one thing a smackie is OCD about, it's the *procedure*. Kala was the hand that fed them. Good old Kala. The next step: chase the smack yourself. Prepare your own pipe, drag your own flame, still smoking in the basti with the crew, but chasing your own line. Then you start buying puriahs and taking the H home to chase by yourself. On your own. All alone. Hoarding your stash. Selfish. Greedy. Desperate. Hoorah! In your lonely corner of the world. At the doorway of a black hole.

While Deen had not completely isolated himself yet, he was past the point of pulling others in. He didn't want to share the stash, except maybe with AJ for the convenience of his bike. Sometimes Shagor too. He came with perks. He was a khor anyway, but to pull in Parvez was purely malicious.

Deen had done it once, pulled someone into heroin intentionally. One dimwit named Naved who had hooked up with his ex-girlfriend. He knew even then, that it was a horrible thing to do, to push Naved into the black sea of negativity from which no one ever emerges. He did it anyway. That was three years ago. Naved was still a junky. They hung out with different crowds, but Deen ran into him at parties. His cheeks were sunken, his body skeletal, madness in his eyes. But Naved was a slippery snake, unlike Parvez.

Deen and AJ had been friends for years. Partners in crime, thought Deen. If addiction was a crime. Was addiction a crime? Or a sin? Or a slow suicide? You can't quit though it's killing you, poisoning your blood, conquering your mind, destroying your relationships, and maybe condemning your soul. Deen wondered if all smackies were damned to hell. Or perhaps there was no hereafter. No hell, just death, and maggots to devour your decaying flesh, in the damp graveyard, if somebody buried your bones.

The weight of Parvez's collapse hung heavily around Deen's neck. He was the reason behind AJ's treachery. AJ resented Deen's affection for Parvez and he could not let it go. He would not leave Parvez unsullied. Welcome to the club. All junkies club. Club Khor.

Deen called AJ. "Hey man, Parvez is passed out on my floor. Do you know anything about it?"

AJ laughed. "Why? What did he say?"

"Nothing, he's passed out. What the hell is going on?"

"Don't worry, it was his first chase, that's all," said AJ coolly.

"Chase? Where the hell did he get smack? Why the hell was he smoking? Were you with him?" Deen demanded.

"I don't like this superior Mother Hen thing you've got going on. The boy wanted to try it, so I let him."

"You sick bastard. Why do you need to pull everybody into your black sea? Did you take pleasure in watching Parvez smoke?"

"I don't see you doing anything to help us get our next fix."

"What do you want me to do? Pull money out of my ass?"

Teeeeeeeeeeeeeeeeeeeeeeeeeeeeeeeeeeeeeeeeeeeeeeeeeeeeeeeeeeeeeeee.

Deen stared at the phone in disbelief. *He hung up on me? He had the nerve to hang up on me?* "Go to hell, AJ!" Deen shouted into the dead phone.

"What's the matter? Deen is that you?" Deen's mother called from outside his door.

"Hi Ma," Deen called out.

"How did you get in? Are you ok?"

Deen heard her voice quiver. He realized suddenly he hadn't spoken to her in over a week. His heart clamped up at the sound of her concern. "I'm fine, Ma," he called back.

"Tell me if you want something to eat," she said. She sounded apologetic.

Deen grabbed a towel from his bathroom and wiped Parvez's face and shirt. He hauled him off the floor and laid him on the bed. The pain in Deen's stomach returned. He lay down next to Parvez to give his head a moment of rest before he went out to kill AJ.

* * *

AJ felt betrayed. Ever since his brothers had abandoned him, Deen had become more than a friend, he was family. Now suddenly Deen was turning on him. For what? AJ was no bastard. He did not take *pleasure* in smoking Parvez up. It did not give him an orgasm. Parvez chose to chase. Simple. What the hell was the black sea? *Deen's a hypocrite,* thought AJ bitterly. *As bad as my brothers.*

His brothers were back-stabbing bastards. They owed him

everything. Though they were older, in some ways they were like his kids. He practically raised them. AJ flipped through the stations on his television, bored and resentful. When their father left them, with a debt of 38 lakhs, AJ was seventeen years old. He dropped out of school to look after their mother, to service their debts and to pay for the education of both his brothers. What did he know about making money? He put his innocence up for sale. Sacrificed precious youth. While other teens were partying and necking girls, he was busy saving his ass.

Fourteen passports, money can buy anything, fumed AJ. He parked on the sports channel to watch an Arsenal vs. Liverpool game. Dubai did not issue overnight visas, so to expedite his mission, he travelled with backdated tickets and multiple passports. Dubai had no restriction on the transport of gold so he could take it straight through the boarding gate. The leather briefcase stowed under his feet during take off, no worries, but it was illegal to bring gold into Bangladesh so when the airhostess announced the ground temperature just before landing at Zia International Airport, Dhaka City, AJ made his way to the bathroom with his gold.

AJ flinched as he remembered his briefcase, his anxiety and the vaseline. Stuff them up there. 18 biscuits of gold. 2" by 1". 11.665 grams. One tola. Purity of 999.999. Didn't matter how painful or bloody it got, he had no choice, the gold was someone else's. If he tried to get off the plane with the gold in his hands, he'd be thrown in jail. If he walked out empty handed, left the gold in the plane, he'd be a dead man. And so, with the airhostess banging at his door, *Excuse me, you can't be in the toilet now sir, the plane is landing, you must be seated,* and the turbulence of the downward flight swinging him off balance, and his ears popping and his head hurting and his ass bleeding, young AJ shoved with all his might. Shoved the gold up his ass. Then opened the bathroom door and hobbled back to his seat.

AJ poured himself a double jack on the rocks and flipped through the channels again till he settled on *Tom and Jerry*. Nice and gory. Great soundtrack. Little guy screwing the big guy. In those days they paid him 5000 taka per biscuit. Peanuts compared to how much they made. He knew they were screwing him, but he had no choice. His ass had become his most lucrative asset. Anal Canal Gold Mine.

By the age of twenty-two, he had paid off his debts and gotten to know the players in the field, so he moved up the ladder. The customs officers who intercepted smuggled gold at the airport reported only half of what they found. The other half, they distributed among themselves. Perks of the job, but gold was a dangerous commodity. They had no way of trading it in for cash. They called on AJ who drove his motorcycle out to their suburban homes and picked up their biscuits to pawn for them. His profit margins increased significantly. Eventually, the mafia got to know of him and called on him to run their errands. By twenty-six, AJ was trading diamonds.

After the rise of global terrorism, the Interpol started monitoring all large transactions in international prime banks, creating problems for the drug industry. Unable to make prime bank payments, drug traffickers switched to diamonds. The rocks were purchased from registered diamond companies in the Far East. The merchants were not aware of what the buyers were doing with their diamonds, so their transactions were authentic, truthful in a way. They conveniently chose to ignore that their diamonds were selling at a huge premium, for cash on the spot. They were happy. Their buyers were happy. It was all official.

Ten million dollars in any other form, cash or gold, would need two duffle bags to transport. 250 grams of diamonds fit in a small packet, 3" by 1". The packets were marked with a red '10'. Ten million dollars, in your back pocket. Dazzling diamonds in barter for dirty drugs. Why not?

Traders paid for drugs with these packets which then circulated in the underworld, transferring from hand to hand, lightweight currency. Finally it reached an end user who disposed of it, sold it to another registered diamond company, somewhere else in the world. He didn't get ten million dollars, eight maybe, but it didn't matter because he was already fat off the profit. On paper, it was just one big transaction, from one diamond company to another. All official and shit.

No one ever checked the diamonds, no gangsters with kooky gadgets in their eye sockets. Industry trust. Who would dare mess around? The thought had crossed AJ's mind though. A '10' in his back pocket, that'd be nice, but where would he hide? They'd find him anywhere, Dubai, India, Singapore, London. AJ knew how it worked. If they valued your life, you lived, if you were a risk to their investments, you died. Strictly business.

It almost cost him his life once. He failed to make a payment, because he was too smacked out, and then rather than apologize, he let his ego get in the way. His arrogance and his grandiosity always got him into trouble. He was picked up from his home at 3 am, beaten to a pulp, blindfolded and pushed into a car, driven to the airport and boarded onto a private jet. He arrived in Singapore without a passport. They kept him in the airport for eight hours while a passport was created and then they took him out to meet Chotta Gulab, India's most powerful mafia lord. Chotta mistakenly thought AJ had stolen from him. AJ explained that it was Alim who had conned them both and run off with Chotta's money. Chotta sent his men to take care of Alim. That was the last mistake Alim ever made. Chotta appreciated AJ's honesty and flew him back to Dhaka, first class. Barely alive.

AJ poured himself another double. He had been so selective, hoarding his affection. He rarely let anyone get close to him, and even then, everyone he loved betrayed him. He felt like chasing and cursed himself for being broke. He'd kill Ronnie when he found him.

* * *

Deen awoke from a nightmare and saw that Parvez had left. Only the pungent smell of bile assured him that it had all really happened. 4:20 pm. The red numbers on his alarm clock stared at him like the eyes of a demon.

Deen lit a cigarette and recalled his dream. He was with Maria at a swanky party. Well-dressed people, lots of booze. Maria asked him to get her some water. She looked stunning, in a slinky sari, bangles on her arms. He went to the kitchen to get her a glass and ran into Parvez, only Parvez was a junky, haggard and tired, cheeks caved in, mad eyes. Deen returned to the party to find Maria, drunk as a madman, smooching a first-year, one of Parvez's friends. Pain gripped Deen's heart and he felt a jealousy he had not yet experienced in real life. At that cracking moment, he woke up.

Nothing but a dream, he told himself. Parvez would not become a junky, he would never let that happen, and Maria could kiss all the first-years in the world, it didn't matter. She had dumped him. And for good reason. He didn't deserve her. Bad guys don't get good girls.

He tried to focus on blowing smoke rings to distract himself from the image of Maria in another man's arms. Her breakdown the night before had scared him, he had never seen anything like it before. She needed help, but he wasn't going to be the one to help her. She didn't want his help. He wasn't going places with his life. She wanted nothing to do with him. She had dumped his sorry ass, and it was for the better. He didn't need her either.

Deen lit a joint and watched the end glow as he inhaled. His thoughts drifted to Parvez. Innocent Parvez, oblivious to the danger he was in. He didn't know that smack creeps into your veins when you're not looking and lodges itself in the centre of your jugular, threatening your life blood. More dangerous than moralistic bullshit or capitalist propaganda or false promises. Physically destructive poison. Imprisons you in the aching, vomiting, blinding, boa constrictor around your intestines crushing the living loving laughing life out of you, broken bone smithereens lodged in all your important organs, punctured lungs, bleeding heart, rotten liver, money vaporizing, obsessing, paranoid, lonely world of despair. Nothing else matters. Low, low, low. Glass fucking empty. Never satisfied. Always craving. Say goodbye to the world you know. Welcome to the black sea of negative thoughts, where no light can enter, where happiness does not exist.

He wouldn't let that happen to Parvez. The kid had only chased once, he might not be hooked as yet. Unless he was predestined to doom. Was luck on his side? Had the Fates conspired against him? A heavy feeling of responsibility grew within Deen, flashing in neon green lights in his head, SAVE PARVEZ, SAVE PARVEZ. He'd talk some sense into that stupid kid. Then he would warn Falani not to sell to Parvez. Then he'd beat the shit out of AJ. Deen crawled out his bedroom window and headed off to rescue his friend.

✦ TEN ✦

The scooter walla shooed the beggars who gathered around the vehicle when it stopped at the railway crossing. Blind beggar boy, armless man, stub man with no limbs, mother with crying infant in arms, toothless woman on crutches, little girl in pigtails trying to sell candy. Candy to flavour your rich palate and feed her hungry family. Deen felt claustrophobic as they hovered around him. "I have nothing!" he told them, but they remained unconvinced. A city dweller, gelled hair, cruising in a scooter, he could not be as broke as they were.

"One taka, two taka, anything, bhaiya," the girl insisted, shoving three sweets into Deen's shirt pocket. "Please bhaiya, please."

Deen reached for his wallet just as the lights turned green. He fumbled through its contents, old concert tickets, photo of Maria, receipts, extra foil, folded tissue, a photocopied prayer his mother had given him, driving license, expired gym card, university ID. The girl ran along with the moving scooter, dodging dangerous traffic to keep up with Deen.

"Like I said, it's empty," said Deen. Her smile fell and she slowed down her pace, trailing off, pink shorts and pigtails bobbing in the sea of traffic.

"My sweets!" she cried suddenly. She put forth a burst of energy to catch up with the scooter, but it was too late. They had already hurtled out of reach and she was lost in the on-coming bustle.

Deen's heart felt heavy. He put a sugar lozenge in his mouth. Strawberries and cream. Pink shorts, pigtails, dismay in her eyes. He could not help her. All she wanted was two taka. He didn't even have money to pay the scooter walla, but it didn't matter. Fuck her. Fuck them all. None of that mattered. The only thing that mattered was to stop Parvez from chasing again.

Dooo dooo dooo dooo. The ringer wailed in Deen's pocket. Deen let the whole thing play out. The drum and bass version of Mission Impossible by Mullen and Clayton took his mind off the beggars. They were too fucking hopeless. The phone rang again. The caller was persistent.

"Your phone," shouted the scooter walla, turning to face Deen.

"Thanks, keep your eyes on the road, chacha." Deen pulled the phone out of his pocket. It was Maria. "Hello."

"Hi Deen. Where are you?" She was crying hysterically.

"What's wrong?" Deen's body tensed.

"Can you come here? It's an emergency."

"What happened?"

"I'll tell you when you get here." She hung up.

Deen redirected the scooter walla who launched into a lecture about the price of natural gas in an attempt to renegotiate his fees, but Deen was not listening. Maria's mom had moved out, leaving Maria alone with the maid. Deen usually thanked his stars for the set up, but now it seemed terribly unsafe. He shouldn't have left her on her own. She was unstable, depressed and maybe crazy enough to do something stupid. She needed his help.

He was still mad at her though. She had dumped him and then, in his dream, smooched a kid. Though it had no physical reality, the dream had irrevocably altered something in Deen's mind. It made him realize how deeply he cared for Maria. Parvez would have to wait. It was time to tell Maria that he truly loved her (he would marry her!), but he was just a junky. She was emotionally dependent on him and suicidal. He hoped the news wouldn't destroy her. If she hated him after his confession, he would cut off the relationship before screwing her happiness further. She had dumped him and maybe that was best for her. He couldn't be the man she needed. He had let his father die. He sure as hell didn't want another death on his shoulders.

* * *

Majid fidgeted uncomfortably. The garish light behind the desk offended his eyes, making him squint as he faced the sergeant.

"In the end, the truth shall be revealed," said the sergeant pompously. "So Allah, the most merciful, has ordained."

Sergeant Akbar's garlic breath pummelled Majid. He nodded to create air between himself and the sergeant.

"And be not mistaken, khor," Sergeant Akbar continued onerously, "there is only ONE truth and that is the truth of the Quran. In the Quran, the One Truth given to us in kindness by Allah, the most merciful, he has said, so clearly he has said, YOU MUST NOT BE ADDICTED. Do you under-

stand, khor? But of course you do, you drugaddicts all understand all too well, understanding everything always, always.
You think you are so sma-art, out-sma-arting the police always, always, but HOLD! Yes, Hold. Do you KNOW who
you are really out-sma-arting, khor? Yourself! Yes, YOUR-
SELF!! Because Allah, the most merciful, is not fooled by
you fools."

Majid stared directly at the sergeant's bald spot.

Sergeant Akbar cleared his throat with a noisy cough, then
spat phlegm out the window. "Khor, you are in trouble. Yes,
big trouble. We caught you with half a kilogram of heroin.
So what should we do now?"

Majid continued staring. *Bad luck,* he thought. They arrested him at the railway station. The cops must have been
tipped off by some jerk. Maybe Javed, he had been acting
funny lately. There was no other reason for the random search.
It was a routine transaction, he had done it a million times
before. Banani station 6 am, Roger, the Chakma boy. Roger
received a steady supply of smack from across the border and
he was desperate. His tribe had it bad, practically extinct now,
massacred by the government. Majid was doing them a favour
by buying from them. He had bought half a kilo to sell to
Falani.

"Tell me where you were going to sell this?" The sergeant
waved the bag in front of Majid's face then tucked it into his
drawer. "Then I'll let you off the hook."

"I'm not a rat," said Majid indignantly.

"I have reason to believe," Sergeant Akbar cleared his throat
again. "You were going to give that load to a certain dealer
known as Falani." His eyes narrowed with greed.

Majid cringed. So the sergeant knew about Falani. What else did he know? Did he know they were siblings? Did he know where they lived? "If I tell you, you'll let me go?" he asked cautiously. Could he give the sergeant Musa's address and get away with it? Musa was a dealer too. The sergeant would get what he wanted, and they would be ok.

Sergeant Akbar continued slyly, "Let's just say, I need you to tell me where Falani lives and testify on record that you were trafficking heroin for her. Let me warn you, khor, if you try anything funny, you will be in trouble. Not only will Allah, the most merciful, throw his wrath upon you, but also you will taste the fury of the Bangladesh Police Force!"

Majid ran his fingers through his oily hair. He was not a filthy snitch, but what were his options? The cops had caught him with enough heroin to put him behind bars for life. Majid hated the cops, corrupt crooks; he hated the laws, only enforced upon those who could not afford lawyers; he hated the squealing rats; but most of all, he hated Sergeant Akbar, with his fat condescension and his religious bullshit. Majid suddenly felt protective about Falani and vowed to get her out of this mess. He would kill the sergeant. "I won't cooperate," he said defiantly.

Sergeant Akbar grinned. He picked up the telephone on his desk, an old analogue model, and dialled a number. He mumbled something into the receiver. Four police officers stepped into the room. One grabbed Majid by the shirt and threw him to the floor.

Majid felt the ground crash against him. Pain ripped through his body. Through the tears in his eyes, he could make out a shiny black boot coming towards his face. He tried to move, but the boot whammed into his nose. The bones in his face crunched. He was covered in blood and fighting to stay conscious. He could hear a squeaky voice warning the others not to kill him.

"Let me do it!" Sergeant Akbar growled. The men moved aside. The sergeant aimed a kick at Majid's lower back, targeting the smackie's weakest spot.

Whack. Majid screamed.

Whack. Majid whimpered.

Whack. Majid pleaded for mercy. Blood covered his *lungi*.

Whack. Majid begged them to stop and promised to confess.

Sergeant Akbar motioned to one of his men. A scrawny cop grabbed Majid by the hair and lifted his smashed face off the ground. Another cop held a tape recorder to Majid's mouth, careful not to dip his sleeve in the pool of blood.

"Now," said Sergeant Akbar. "Tell me what I want to hear."

Majid struggled to breathe. "Her shack is in the basti off Airport Road on the way to Tongi," he mumbled. "It's the last shack in the settlement, by the krishna chura tree."

The sergeant grinned.

* * *

Sundari was in her bathtub when she heard the familiar banging on her door. Only AJ would knock so loudly, as if impatient to see her. She opened the door, wrapped in a towel, water droplets glowing on her skin, and greeted AJ with a kiss. He lit a cigarette and followed her into the bathroom. He seated himself on the closed lid of the toilet, as she settled back into her bubble bath. Bubbles collected around her breasts. Sundari lifted her legs out of the tub and ran one toe against the smooth skin of her slender calf. The scent of lavender drifted in the steamy air.

AJ pushed his hand through the bubbles to squeeze Sundari's thigh, but she moved. His hand landed on her cluster of dark curls. He stubbed out his cigarette and let her pull him, clothes and all, into the bubble bath. No words were spoken. He sucked on her breasts as she deftly undid the buttons of his shirt and the zipper of his pants. She stroked his chest and kissed his neck. He trembled with excitement. Sundari smiled. She knew she had mastered the art of seduction.

Sundari had learnt her art early. Her earliest memories were of growing up in the Sacred Heart Orphanage in the centre of Bombay, along with other children whose parents had either died, been arrested or abandoned them in various locations around the city. Even as a six-year-old, she realized she could get her way with the others simply by lowering her kohl-laden eyes coquettishly and then raising them beseechingly. Boys were mesmerized, girls fascinated. By twelve, she knew where a woman's real forte lay. Her eyes danced with sexual promise.

At fifteen, tired of the children's games and the officials' rules, Sundari ran away. The chief administrator of the orphanage, whom everybody called amma, took off her glasses, rubbed her weary eyes and stared out the window when told of Sundari's latest indiscretion. She sighed and turned her attention back to the new batch of children awaiting refuge.

Sundari had been on the streets for less than four hours when she was picked up by Chotta Gulab, South Bombay's most notorious pimp. She thought her future was made when she accepted a ride in his black Ambassador with tinted windows and glided up the driveway of one of Malabar Hill's swankiest apartment buildings. Once inside his richly-decorated duplex, she turned on her charms and began to massage his neck. But he had no time for such games. His interest, once he had had his customary fuck, lay solely in calculating how much income this latest addition to his repertoire would bring. This one was a winning lottery ticket.

Within a week, Sundari was living in a luxurious bungalow in the suburb of Bandra, along with six other 'high-quality' girls and a Madam named Swati. The girls were indulged with expensive saris and perfumes and tutored in Kathak by the top dancers in the country. Sundari had been there for nine years when Raj Gopal, a leading diamond sourcer, met her and decided he would much rather avail of her services from within the comforts of his own home in Bangladesh, and purchased her from Chotta for an undisclosed sum.

Sundari's love affair with diamonds began at Raj's house. They beckoned her from every corner of the mansion. They studded the cups Raj drank his chai from and gleamed from the hairbrush his wife used three times a day. Despite the abundance of gems around her, she still could not believe her eyes when Forhad Haque, a steel tycoon from Old Town, came over for dinner one night with the most lustrous diamonds she had ever seen.

As he ambled from the dining table to his guest room at the end of the night, she sashayed across his path and lowered her eyes suggestively. Moving with surprising speed for a man of his size, he whirled her around and pinned her against the wall. His rum-stained breath washed over her in waves and she felt his hardness against her stomach. "You've been looking at my stars all night, haven't you?" he said, with a thick Bangla accent. "Bet you've never seen diamonds like these before!"

Sundari moved her henna-adorned hand between their bodies and cupped his crotch expertly. "Surely you must be mistaken, sir. My interest lies solely in the jewels in my hand!"

His eyes wide in surprise, he allowed himself to be led into the guest room for a night of unadulterated pleasure. Sundari got her first diamond.

More than a dozen years had passed since then and Sundari had come to realize that diamonds could not buy happiness. But neither could love. Love was forbidden among courtesans and it was no mystery why. She had seen the devastation love left in its wake. It was a doomed fantasy that inevitably led to the downfall of dancers. She herself had been entangled in another man's dreams and watched him kill himself, in the name of love. Unrequited love, the worst love of all. She had never loved anyone before she met AJ and then she learnt that love dug trenches into the heart. Still, there was something about it that felt good.

She could not figure out what she adored about AJ, other than his dependency on her. He was a rude, crude, arrogant smackie, who wouldn't admit that he loved her, but Sundari knew how much he needed her, and in that, she experienced something new. It was the closest she had ever come to being loved.

Since she had been with AJ, Sundari had stopped taking customers to bed. It was understood that she was 'spoken for' though the other girls knew that AJ hadn't bought her time at all, but rather, lived off of her savings. The girls didn't mind him though. He had a good sense of humour and he was sort of handsome. Occasionally, he flirted with them, but they ignored his passes because they knew Sundari was so fond of him.

After the bubble bath, Sundari and AJ relaxed into a lovers' embrace. When Sundari awoke later that night, AJ was gone. She buried her nose into his pillow. She could smell AJ, the real AJ that existed beneath the tough exterior, the caring AJ whom only she knew, the AJ whom she loved.

She caressed her belly, in search of a bulge, though she knew it was too early. She wanted to tell him her secret, their secret, their secret growing inside of her, but she hesitated, unsure of how he would react. Would it fill him with hope, as it had filled her, or make him more frustrated with his life? She was afraid if she told him too soon, he would make her get rid of the baby. She was determined to have this child, determined to tie a knot between her and AJ, a living, breathing knot, to secure him into her life, once and for all. Then he would marry her and they could relax into a simple life with a lovely family, she wanted nothing more. She waited for the perfect moment to reveal the secret heavy in her womb.

* * *

Slit wrists, sleeping pills, diving off a roof? Deen rushed into Maria's bedroom in a panic. *Guantanamera* was playing on her speakers. Sketches were scattered all over the floor, pastel images of lovers entwined.

"*I'm in the mood, I'm in the mood for your love,*" Maria sang, draping her body on his. Her hair was a messy bird's nest.

"What happened?" Deen demanded.

"Deeeeeeeeeen!" she cooed. "I'm a ravenous sexaholic addicted to you. I tried to resist the urge, but I couldn't hold out any longer. I needed to taste you!" She ruffled his hair and licked his face. The smell of whiskey on her breath was distracting. "Can I get you a drink?" she asked, finishing off her glass.

"Sure." He was relieved to see her ok and not dead in the bathtub. She seemed almost ecstatic, but only ten minutes back she was in hysterics. Her mood swings were becoming more intense and less predictable. She looked hot though, sexy as hell. He had never seen her in a t-shirt before. It was snug around her body, her jeans low on her hips.

"Deen, darling!" she exclaimed. "I love the way you're always calm no matter what, I love the way you keep me sane, I love the way you sing, I love the way you love me strong and slow, mmmmmm, and then fierce and frantic, oooof! I love the way you smell at the end of the day, I love the way you feel under my body, or on top of my body, I love waking up next to you, naked and warm." Maria pressed her body against Deen and danced in rhythm with the song.

Deen pulled off her shirt and ran his fingers over her taut stomach. Her eyes were twinkling. He felt confused. She had dumped him. Was she ready to forgive him already? Could she accept other dirty truths about him?

"Why didn't you ask me for the cash? I would have lent it to you." She ran her fingers down his chest.

"I'm sorry," Deen murmured. He pushed his face against hers, avoiding her eyes. He needed to tell her that he was a junky, she needed to know.

"It's ok. I know you won't do it again." Maria jumped onto her bed. She stumbled, fell, giggled and then jumped back up. "You, with your charms and your disarming smile. I'm drawn to you, a nympho slave at your mercy. I want to be with you ALL the time! Come here, come to bed. I can't get enough. You put me in the moooooood."

Deen poured himself another drink, rushing to finish the bottle so that Maria would not have any more. She was too damn drunk. Like she had been in his nightmare. The vision flashed before him and he fumed again. She was capable of it. She was a smouldering seductress who flirted with everyone in sight. He loved her, he really loved her, but this time it was different. Something had slipped out of his dream and into his reality. He knew now, he could not live without her, and it made him miserably insecure.

"I hate everything in Bangladesh," said Maria suddenly. "There's no right and wrong. Did you read the papers today? The cops found a maid's body in a FREEZER! Some madam got pissed off and hacked her to pieces. She'll get away with it because she's rich. The story got coverage only because it happened in your neighbourhood, in DOHS! It got a small column on the fifth page, that's all it was worth."

"Shit happens everywhere," said Deen. She wanted him to placate her, tell her it'd be ok, but today he didn't feel like it. He felt damn depressed and he wanted her to feel that way, too. "Americans threw slaves into the ocean," he said. "Beautiful black people, alive, tied up in ropes, threw them overboard."

"How?" Maria protested. "What is wrong with the human psyche? How can we be so indifferent to the suffering of fellow human beings?"

"We are predators." As soon as he said it, he regretted it. He shouldn't have agitated her.

"We can't just sit around and do nothing, Deen," she screamed. "What's our role in the big picture?"

Maria seemed fragile, a distressed Atlas. Her breakdown at *Oasis* had come like a storm. He dreaded the next outburst. He didn't know how to help her.

"Say something!" she charged. "Why do I remorsefully confess my sins, my inaction. You're not even listening! You're busy thinking, *it ain't me babe, I'm not the one you're looking for.*"

"I wasn't thinking that," Deen replied.

Maria narrowed her eyes. "I've applied to a Masters programme in America," she said. "Journalism. We need to do something about the atrocities in Bangladesh. The future of our country depends on OUR generation. As a journalist, I will raise awareness and make a difference."

Her words sounded rehearsed. Deen felt like he had been hit by a truck. Maria wanted to leave him. "What?" He stuttered. His head reeled. What about their golden future? "You'll never come back."

"It's a one year programme. Of course I'll come back." She placed a flirtatious hand on his thigh. "Won't it be lovely?"

No! No, it would not be lovely! "I don't know," Deen said. The croak in his voice betrayed his hurt. "What'll happen to us?"

"We'll be long-distance lovers for a while. It's no big deal."

What will you do there? Screw American boys, intellectual fucking journalists, fuck their brains out? That's a fine plan Maria. Deen slipped into cognitive distortion. Visions of his dream returned with mad new dimensions, expanding and conquering his mind. Synapses in his brain fired off crazy sequences of thoughts he couldn't stop. His imagination was a rabid stallion, galloping through his head without concern for the tender emotions it was trampling underfoot, racing towards the cliff edges of his sanity. "I don't know if I can live without you," he murmured.

"If you think we can't survive a few months apart then you aren't thinking about us long-term, are you?" She was genuinely upset.

Deen pulled her into his arms. "I didn't mean it like that. It's just that… I need to think about it a little." He didn't want to think about it all. He wanted to run to Falani. He tried to focus on the feel of Maria's body in his arms, the physical reality of the moment. He tried to focus on his breathing, to calm himself. Why shouldn't she go? What could he offer her? He wasn't going places. He was a worthless smackie. He had no future. He deserved to lose her. Deen ran his fingers down her cheeks.

Maria let out a sigh. She pulled off her bra and placed his hand on top of her heart. She slowed her breathing to match his and stared into his sunken eyes. "What's the matter Deen? What's wrong?" she asked.

Where to begin? Nothing's wrong except my life. The life of a junky. Bad things happen to bad people. Deen wanted to tell Maria everything, the whole truth. "I had a dream. You were necking this kid. It made me mad. Now you say you're going away and it seems like maybe the dream's coming true."

"I'm not leaving you for another man. Would you care if I did?" she added coyly. "You don't really *love* me, do you?"

"I *love* you Maria. I do love you, but the dream made me so mad. I'll kill anybody who lays a finger on you. I don't care if he's in USA. I'll get on a plane and kill him and then come back to my sad life in Bangladesh."

"It was a dream." Maria laughed. "Am I to be responsible for my actions in your dreams?"

"No," Deen sulked. He could see she enjoyed his burst of insecurity. He searched her face for reassurance, but she kept it expressionless intentionally. "It's not going to be like that, is it? Do you want to fuck other men?"

Maria pulled him to her and whispered dirty words in his ears.

He pushed her away, on the verge of tears. "Do you want to fuck other men?" he asked with a forced calm. "I'll under-stand, but then we need to break up now. You deserve a better man anyway. I won't hold you back."

"Deen!" Maria smiled. "I need nothing else in life! Just you!"

Deen knew she was teasing him to lighten the moment and she was drunk, very drunk, but he wanted to believe her words. Was he all she needed? Could he make her happy? He pushed her gently onto the floor and unzipped her jeans, bury-ing his head in her breasts, planting kisses on her neck, press-ing the hardness of his body against the softness of hers.

⊁ ELEVEN ⊀

The sky was cloudy. Persistent rain drizzled down. Winter was departing. In a month or two, kal boishakhi storms would wash through the country and announce the arrival of the Bangla New Year.

The scooter walla inched forward carefully avoiding the toes of the destitute beggars crowding the road. Blind boy, armless man, stub man with no limbs, mother with crying infant in arms, toothless woman on crutches, girl in pink shorts selling sweets. All the same faces. Every day, every night, day in, day out, day in, day out. Deen had consumed a bottle of cat earlier that evening and it was making him drowsy. The rhythm of the traffic was tranquil, like raindrops, lulling Deen into a cough syrupy sense of harmony with the world. He did not do phencydil often anymore, but he enjoyed it on days such as these.

Rain sprinkled on his arm. The beggars were going to get wet. Deen thought about the jhors that would soon destroy their sad homes, the tents of blue plastic tied to trees on the roadside, wash them away. *It's a hard rain's a-gonna fall.* Dylan was twenty-one years old when he wrote that song. The lyrics were perfect. Each line was a poem on its own. Deen was twenty-one too. He longed to create a perfect song.

It was hard to say what made a song perfect, but there were many such songs out there. Some simple songs were perfect. A song with a catchy melody, for instance. *One love, one heart, let's get together and feel all right.* A song that made you smile. Or remember. Or get up and dance. A song that offered hope. Or love. A song that captured the strangeness of life. *What a wonderful world.* It was a combination of elements; the tune, the lyrics and the emotions the song could evoke.

Deen was trying to hum a tune that would capture it all, when he accidentally made eye contact with a beggar boy at the railway crossing. He hoped the scooter would not have to stop. Bad luck, blinking red light on the pole, train approaching. Red eyes staring at red lights. Deen lit a cigarette in anticipation of the oncoming attack.

"Bhaiya, give me some money, I'm poor, I'm hungry, bhaiya please give me some money. Bhaiya, give me some money, I'm poor, I'm hungry, bhaiya please give me some money. Bhaiya, give me some money, I'm poor, I'm hungry, bhaiya please give me some money. Bhaiya, give me some money, I'm poor, I'm hungry, bhaiya please give me some money. Bhaiya, give me some money, I'm poor, I'm hungry, bhaiya please give me some money. Bhaiya, give me some money, I'm poor, I'm hungry, bhaiya please give me some money. Bhaiya, give me some money, I'm poor, I'm hungry, bhaiya please give me some money. Bhaiya, give me some money, I'm poor, I'm hungry, bhaiya please give me some money. Bhaiya, give me some money, I'm poor, I'm hungry, bhaiya please give me some money. Bhaiya, give me some money,

I'm poor, I'm hungry, bhaiya please give me some money. Bhaiya, give me some money, I'm poor, I'm hungry, bhaiya please give me some money. Bhaiya, give me some money, I'm poor, I'm hungry, bhaiya please give me some money. Bhaiya, give me some money, I'm poor, I'm hungry, bhaiya please give me some money. Bhaiya, give me some money, I'm poor, I'm hungry, bhaiya please give me some money. Bhaiya, give me some money, I'm poor, I'm hungry, bhaiya please give me some money. Bhaiya, give me some money, I'm poor, I'm hungry, bhaiya please give me some money. Bhaiya, give me some money, I'm poor, I'm hungry, bhaiya please give me some money. Bhaiya, give me some money, I'm poor, I'm hungry, bhaiya please give me some money. Bhaiya, give me some money, I'm poor, I'm hungry, bhaiya please give me some money. Bhaiya, give me some money, I'm poor, I'm hungry, bhaiya please give me some money."

The beggar boy's voice faded though he continued to mouth the words.

Twenty-one times, Deen counted. The beggar boy at his window had repeated the same phrase twenty-one times, while they waited for the train to pass. Deen tried to convince the boy that he had no money. He never had any money. The boy continued chanting his mantra. Deen pushed against the claustrophobic green canvas of the scooter waving in his face and mulled over what it was like to be inside the head of someone who repeats the same line all day long, year after year, with no change in his life. Complete stagnation. How often did anyone drop change into his sweaty palm? How did he survive, eking out an existence on the loose change of irritated passers-by?

Parvez was not street smart. He was a Mama's Boy, a clean cut college kid. He wouldn't survive a day on the streets. Deen didn't live on the streets, but he knew a thing or two about survival. A smackie's survival depends on only one thing, and a smackie in need was desperate and ugly. He would not let Parvez go that way.

The armless man jostled with the repetitive beggar boy and took his spot next to Deen's scooter. "Bhaiya, I have no arms, bhaiya, I'm hungry, bhaiya, please one taka, two taka, bhaiya, Allah will reward you, bhaiya…" The armless man was worse off than the repetitive beggar boy, but better off than the stub man who had no arms *or* legs and spent his days in a push-cart on the corner of the sidewalk. At least the armless man wouldn't set adrift in the floodwaters later that year. Hierarchy of despondency among the Unfortunates of DOHS.

Laws of the streets. Gnarled deformed beggars populated the busy intersections, run by gangs, syndicates that ruled over the road. Notorious gangs who kidnapped children from villages and mutilated them, chopping off their arms so they could earn more sympathy money when they begged. Strategies of survival. Brutal, and yet, not so different from civilized laws.

Laws of GOB. Strategies of the rich. About two hundred families controlled the entire wealth of Bangladesh and about one hundred and fifty of them were corrupt. This was public knowledge, not secret intelligence, everyone could see what was going on. GOB lacked the subtlety that had been mastered by the thieves in the western world. Government officials, businessmen and cops, were in collusion to keep a tight grip on the nation's wealth. They too were notorious for chopping off hands. They upheld a social order that left the masses with no money and then chopped off their hands if they tried to steal.

Had the armless man been mutilated as a child by gangs or punished by cops because he was a cunning thief? Deen thought he looked a little sly. What had he stolen? A briefcase full of cash? Deen imagined the staff table, back there behind the gallows, meting out justice. The executioner, the hand-chopper and the nurse. Was she beautiful and kind? Nursing the blunt ends of his arms where hands had been. Who fed the armless man? Who cleaned him after he shat? Who trimmed his beard? Poor old bastard. God-forsaken. GOB-forsaken.

A blue truck drove by, piled high with pineapples, juicy fresh fruit for the rich. Painted on the truck was a thatched hut in a green field, two cows grazing, and behind, a river with ducks. Some artist's vision of happiness. Deen wondered about the truck driver. Was he smacked up? Most of them were. How else could they drive six hours to the Chittagong port and then turn around and drive back again? Stamina drugs for the poor.

Rich kids got their energy from yabba. Deen remembered when he used to do *y*. It kept him wired for days. He once went three weeks with no food or sleep, just *y*. It fucked with his sanity, rewired his brain. Thaar cheera. Hitler invented yabba to fuel his soldiers. Fucking yabba khor Gestapo.

The truck driver honked unnecessarily at the passing train. Deen wondered if the man had a wife. Did he visit brothels? Did he know about HIV? Did he have children? Did he beat them? Was he illiterate? Dropped out of school after grade two? Working like a dog to eat. Thrown into the throes of poverty like the other 150 million Bangladeshis. Staggering to survive. Grovelling at the feet of the rich. *Don't get bogged down by the poverty*, Deen told himself. Learn to accept. God give me the strength to accept the things I cannot change.

And God give me the courage to change the things I can. *God help me save Parvez*, Deen thought as he sniffled. His arms were itchy despite the cat and he felt irritable. The lights turned green and the scooter screeched forward finally. Deen played out a conversation in his head. It'd be a quick chat, he'd tell Parvez about desperation and explain to him that he wasn't cunning enough to handle it, and besides, he had a bright future which he should not jeopardize.

* * *

Parvez lived with his parents in a white mansion tucked away in the posh neighbourhood of Gulshan. The mansion was fenced in by a brick wall and a black iron gate. A guard slid the gate open to let Deen in. The driveway was cobblestone and there were three shiny Range Rovers parked in the garage. The garden between the driveway and the house was a multitude of colours. Flowers from all over the world, petunias, marigolds and daisies, lined proud guava trees. The house itself was an ostentatious structure with pillars, reminding Deen of the White House. *Probably on the CIA payroll*, he thought as he rang the doorbell.

"Deen!" cried Parvez's mother with a shrill voice. "I am so glad you're here! Parvez has been sick since yesterday. Oh, you know? You've come to cheer him up? You're such a good boy. Stomach upset, must have eaten something bad. I keep telling him not to eat out, the sanitation conditions of the restaurants are terrible, you know how it is. The food and health inspector visited ten restaurants and NONE of them met his standards. He found rotten fish and cockroaches in all of them. It's a travesty! Did you read the papers today?" Parvez's mother was wearing a sleeveless kamiz and the rolls of flab on her arms swung like tidal waves during the monsoons.

Deen tried to fake a smile. He had in fact read the papers that morning, skimmed through an article that suspected the government was issuing trade licenses to a consortium of businessmen who were exporting heroin to England in cartons marked as food items. Brave journalist, thought Deen, daring to spill such a story.

"Come, come, what shall I get for you? Some samosas? Babu!" she called out, "Babu! Fry some samosas quickly! Deen, you have lost weight, no? Tell me your secret! I walk in Gulshan Park every morning, but nothing is going off my tummy. What to do? At my age, it isn't easy. You are too skinny, no?"

I'm a smackie, I don't eat, thought Deen. "No aunty, I'm ok, I just ate." Deen hurried towards Parvez's room.

"Parvez! Look who's here!" she called in a sing-song voice, as if addressing a five-year-old.

Parvez's father was in the living room, in a grey lungi, reading the papers. "Salam'alaikum, Deen," he said sternly.

"Walaikum'asalam," Deen mumbled, avoiding eye contact, red eye to suspicious eye – bad combination. Mintu chacha was a busy man. Deen was surprised to see him at home.

"Are your classes going well?" he continued.

"Oh stop it!" interrupted Parvez's mom. "Always interrogating the boys about grades tades," she turned to Deen. "Your uncle is always fighting with Parvez because all he can talk about is grades. Communication blockage, I tell you. I've been telling your uncle to go to a counselor but he thinks he's ok. He's not hard-hearted, you know, no, no, no, but he doesn't know how to talk to his boy.'

Mintu chacha grumbled under his breath and returned to his papers.

Deen nodded politely and entered Parvez's room, closing the door behind him.

"Tell me when you are hungry!" Parvez's mom shouted from behind the closed door.

"Hey bhaiya! What's up?" said Parvez, brightly. He was on a couch flipping through a Sandman comic. *Rattle and Hum* blared on his speakers. Posters covered the walls: Floyd album covers painted on the backs of naked women, Grateful Dead jamming with Dylan, Bob Marley taking a drag. The walls were blue with white sponge strokes like clouds in the sky.

"Hi kid," said Deen, still lulled by the cat. "How's it going?"

"Good, good. Feel like shit though," Parvez laughed. "Red Bull?" He handed Deen a can.

Deen took a sip. The energy drink mixed poorly with the cough syrup and made him feel dizzy.

"AJ came by the football field yesterday, we were practising for the tournament," said Parvez. "He was turquing so I gave him some money."

Deen winced. He would beat the shit out of AJ when he was through with Parvez.

"AJ was reluctant, but I convinced him to take me with him." Parvez closed the comic book and launched into a monologue. They made it to Tongi in 20 minutes on AJ's bike. AJ took him straight to Falani's shack. 'It's funny, Deen, I've lived in Bangladesh my whole life, driven by a million bastis, but I've never been inside one," Parvez said.

Deen nodded. He wondered why Parvez was so animated, relating the tragedy without regrets, something about him was *off*.

Kala had cut small strips of paper he called tillis, Parvez continued. He placed a brown lump of smack on a piece of foil he called a panni, made from the wrapper of a Mimi chocolate, then lit a tilli and dragged it under the smack. AJ chased the smoke it released with a rolled up ten taka note. "And what a stench!" exclaimed Parvez. "I lit a joint and had a few drags trying to mind my own business, but I could barely breathe, so then I asked if I could try a hit."

Parvez's enthusiasm made Deen uncomfortable. He eyed Parvez's drink. Was it spiked, with vodka perhaps? He scanned the room. There were no traces of bottles anywhere, just several empty cans of Red Bull by his side. Deen wondered how many Parvez had consumed in the past hour. *Signs of addictive behaviour.*

Kala showed him how to stick a coin in the roof of his mouth, Parvez explained. Then he taught him the procedure: use the pipe to chase the trail of smoke, keep the pipe pressed against the coin so the resin collects on it, then, holding the smoke in, spit out the coin and take a drag of a cigarette, then release all the smoke at one go. "As soon as I chased, I started to puke. It felt terrible, I puked my guts out." Parvez looked at Deen. "Have another one." Parvez passed him a can. "My dad brought these from America. Too bad they aren't available here."

Deen scratched his arm and accepted the can without a word.

"Some guy sold 'energy drinks' here a few months ago," Parvez continued. Only he was really selling beer marked as energy drinks. 5% alcohol and all! He had a brewery in Dhaka. Can you believe the gall? Sold like hot cakes. Poor old

Bangladeshis starved for alcohol and denied it in the name of God. He didn't market too smartly though. Got greedy I guess. His cans were green like Heinekens. He minted money. He could have been a bit more discreet about it, you know, come up with his own design and label. He got busted by the government within a month. He claimed it was for the export market, but they closed him down. Too bad. We're a secular nation, why is religious dogma forced on us? Hey, bhaiya, do you have a cold?"

Deen shook his head. *No, just mild withdrawals.* He wondered if Parvez was already deeper into the black sea than he had realized. He was jabbering non-stop like a yabba khor.

Parvez opened another can and began again. He went to the tea stall with AJ and ordered a cold Fanta. His head was spinning, he could barely sit up, he felt like he might fall off the world, and then he puked out a whole load of orange puke. Then he spotted a moori walla across the street. He thought the moori might absorb the nausea and by then he really felt like shit. AJ helped him cross the road and they ordered moori, but as soon as he ate it he puked again. He told AJ it was all too much, but he was in no state to get on a bike, so they hailed down a cab. "I couldn't come home and face my mom, so I went to your place." Parvez laughed. "I hope you didn't have to clean up my mess?"

Deen's heart was heavy. He wanted to sob. He wanted to punch AJ. And Parvez. He wanted to beat the shit out of them both. "I'm not proud of what I do," he said. "And I don't want you doing it." His tone sounded foreign and chilly.

Parvez looked at Deen quizzically. "It's no big deal, bhaiya," he said. "I'm not as preppy as you think. It's not like I've never done drugs. I'm not a kid anymore, besides, I was curious."

"Don't fuck with smack!" Deen shouted. "You get HOOKED!" An awkward silence trailed his words and Deen thought about his own hypocrisy. He reached for a cigarette. Last one in his pack. He had no lighter so he fidgeted with his cigarette unlit.

Parvez's shock dissipated and was replaced by a broad grin. "Thanks for looking out for me, bhaiya. I appreciate it but seriously, don't worry." He handed Deen a lighter.

Deen looked him in the eye. "Tell me, khodar kossum, give me your word that you won't chase again."

Parvez kept smiling. "Ok bhaiya. Khodar kossum."

Deen wasn't sure if Parvez was telling the truth or ya-ing. Ya funda. Ya, ya, ya. Whatever you say. Ya. Sure. Ya. Agree to anything the other person wants just to shut him up. Ya. Zone out. Ya. Just nod. Ya. Deen used the ya funda often, with his mother, ya, with his professors, ya, sometimes with Maria, ya. It was odd to have the same trick played back on him, but once Parvez had said ya, there was nothing more to do.

Deen tried to relax and make small talk, but the conversation stayed aloof. In the midst of the banter, forced as it was, they formed a truce, an unspoken agreement to never broach the subject again, as if the entire incident had never happened. Deen left Parvez's place feeling unsettled. He wasn't sure if he had saved Parvez or pushed him further away.

* * *

Detective Khan pushed through the crowd of cops that had gathered at the doorway of Sergeant Akbar's office to witness a spectacle. Three men were kicking an emaciated man in a blood-soaked lungi. "What is going on?" demanded the detective.

"Sir, you have arrived just in time!" replied Sergeant Akbar. "We are interrogating a khor."

Detective Khan knelt down beside the man. He was barely breathing. "Take him to Dhaka Medical immediately," the detective commanded.

The cops looked imploringly at the sergeant, but he was unable to override the detective's order. The men arranged themselves reluctantly, disgusted with the pulpy body before them, lifting it up with as little contact as possible. The khor offered no resistance, he had already passed out.

Detective Khan turned to the spectators with a glare that pierced through their thick skin and pricked their conscience. The crowd disbursed meekly. He turned to the sergeant, "Mr. Akbar, how can I endorse your activities when you commit heinous acts of violence, violating basic human rights?"

Sergeant Akbar chuckled. "Sir, without such tactics, we would not be able to extract the information we need. Don't worry, this khor has no lawyer tawyer. Besides, he needed the beating to teach him a lesson."

The detective sat down with a sigh. His shoulders slouched as he loosened the buttons of his trench coat. Winter was over, but he insisted on wearing the coat. It was a gift from his ex-wife. It had brought him good luck in dangerous situations and it created a layer of psychic armor between himself and the outside world. The rest of his plain clothed battalion respected him, feared him even, and accepted this eccentricity without remark.

Detective Mandela Khan of the Criminal Investigation

Department was known among his colleagues to be a man of integrity and knowledge. He studied law before joining the CID and he never accepted bribes. He was born the day Nelson Mandela was sentenced to life in prison. His mother, who was bedridden throughout her pregnancy, had followed the build up on the news and named her son after the great man, in the hope that he too would someday fight for his people and uphold justice.

"Drug abusers are not criminals, Mr. Akbar," said Detective Khan. "They are ill. An addiction is like depression. It's a disease and they can't *afford* the cure. Shall we punish them for their illness when we can offer them no alternatives?"

The detective lowered his head into his hands. How could he enlighten the sergeant? Junkies were the saddest of all people. They needed years of counseling to break out of their destructive patterns. Detective Khan's own uncle was a heroin addict. He had destroyed his life and dragged his family through hell. They sent him to a rehab that was more like a penitentiary than a healing centre, run by people who believed addicts were criminals. No junky would recover in such a place.

But junkies were not the crux of the problem. They were victims of the drug trading empire. The businessmen who treated heroin like a commodity to be sold at market value, disregarding the value of human life, they were the masterminds who needed to be arrested. Of course, the sergeant probably *knew* the masterminds personally. He was probably on their payroll too. The detective didn't blame the sergeant. He was an underpaid, uneducated man. His was a corruption of need, not greed. Still, it was corruption all the same, infiltrating all levels, a cobweb of deception.

"I have a daughter!" Sergeant Akbar bellowed suddenly,

glaring with beady yellow eyes. "Would you have me leave these dangerous monsters on the streets to rape and murder her one of these days? I cannot! I cannot, sir, even if you can."

"Tell your men to respond to these cries for help." The detective waved his hand above the files piled on Sergeant Akbar's desk. "Leave the heroin situation to me."

"Sir, we've tracked down the biggest dealer in Tongi. We must make the bust soon, we can't delay!"

Detective Khan frowned. Thick-headed Sergeant Akbar and his misconceived notions of right and wrong. "Don't you SEE? The Golden Triangle, from Burma out to sea. The Golden Crescent, from poppies harvested in Afghanistan, Iran and Pakistan. What about India? Bangladesh is a geographical cherry on the cake of brown sugar!" The detective was enraged. Poor Bangladesh had become the unfortunate conduit for drug trade and the burgeoning business was symptomatic of wider problems on every level. The only way to make a difference, given the scale of the problem, was to focus on a critical point. "Who benefits from these addictions? We need to find the source."

"Maybe I do not see the CHERRY, sir, you don't see the khors! Sir, sitting in your AC office, you don't see the greed in their eyes. They are thieves of the worst order, stealing from other *poor* people to feed their habit. Damned to hell, it says so in the Quran, or perhaps Allah doesn't SEE either?" Abruptly the sergeant remembered he was addressing his senior and checked himself. "Excuse me, sir, it's zohr time, I must say my prayers." He took the prayer rug off his chair and stomped out of the room.

Detective Khan knew this was tricky. How could he explain the chemistry of addiction to a man who spoke the language of religion? Science and religion were always at odds, and strict religious morality, under the guise of law, was a dangerous weapon. Bangladesh was a secular nation so it was imperative to separate the law from the Book. Just as it was imperative to separate the judiciary from the government, though that hadn't been done either. The government had too much interest vested in its 'loyal' judges. The detective looked into his palms for an answer. The entire system needed reform, but where to begin?

Bangladesh was a young country, an independent nation since 1971, born of the hopes and dreams of idealistic people who wanted freedom and democracy. The detective remembered the celebration that broke out after the war, though he was just a child then. The streets were filled with music and dancing as people rejoiced their hard-earned victory. A victory that soon gave way to unbridled corruption.

Economic chaos, thought the detective. The history of Bangladesh was one of chaos, instability and unrest. Supporting a population of 150 million, the gap between rich and poor was immense and growing daily. The country lacked a critical, reformist consciousness and nationalist sympathies because the people with power were uneducated. Their Prime Minister had only completed grade six. Her party was a farce.

Educated upper-class citizens kept their heads below the parapet, sending their kids to colleges abroad. Inevitably, those children never returned to the hellhole they had just escaped from, settling for comfortable jobs on Wall Street instead. Those who stayed in Bangladesh were the ones whose fathers ran illegal operations on the home front, which they inherited and ran with the same iron fists (and bullets!) because there was no other way to survive in the political climate of

Bangladesh. With liberal, left-of-centre youths gone, and violent youths steeled in the corrupt milieus of their fathers remaining, Bangladesh was trapped in an ideologically vicious circle.

Conventions of democracy were a sham and freedom of speech didn't exist. Utter one word against the government and you could be wiped out. Goons, thugs and hit men, all crippled under the weight of poverty, could be hired for a mere 5,000 taka. Simple economics devaluing life. The Rapid Action Battalion, paramilitary forces set up by the government to stop the rampant crime in the country, were armed with guns and the license to kill, making them a menace, powerful and politically partial, with no accountability. They could blow a bullet through your brain and then have their lunch without batting an eyelid.

A revolution, thought the detective, *is the only way to achieve social change.* Bangladesh needed a leader, an educated man to motivate the masses, a Che. A benevolent visionary with courage and charisma, indifferent to power. They needed leaders with spiritual strength. Then again, not fanatics. The fundamentalists recently multiplying in the fertile misery of Bangladesh offered a dangerous illusion of hope to the masses, though they were themselves entrenched in violence and power struggles in the name of Allah.

Perhaps the people were not ready for democracy. Bangladesh was a child, confused in its mid-30s, reeling from the divorce of its parents, India and Pakistan, whose cultural and religious struggles still ran deep in its bones. Bangladesh had to grow up into its own. The imported ideals of democracy had to become institutionalized and culturally acceptable. A sense of identity needed to develop. Yes, the government needed to do much more, but progress took time. Globalization made information readily available, but it came with its own set of problems. *Not so simple,* thought the detective, *but there is still hope.*

✦ TWELVE ✦

There is still hope, thought AJ, as he waited on the burgundy couch in Raj Gopal's ornate living room. If the Don had heard about the drunken brawl at his party, AJ was finished. Raj wouldn't take such matters lightly, especially not if the guest AJ had tried to strangle was someone important. There was a slight chance though that Raj didn't know about the brawl and had summoned him for some unrelated reason, some diamond errand for instance, and not to wipe him out. The chandelier lit the room dimly. The Persian rug felt soft under his toes.

"It's been a while, hasn't it champ?" said Raj jovially. He entered the room alone, no weapons in his hands.

"Hello," said AJ, extending his hand. Raj shook it firmly.

AJ pulled a cigar out of his pocket. "I brought this for you."

"For me? How thoughtful." Raj laughed heartily, grabbed his clippers and lit the cigar. He passed it back to AJ. AJ tried to protest, but the jolly man insisted.

"So tell me, son, how have you been? Can I offer you a drink?"

"I'll have what you have," said AJ, in between puffs.

"Gin and tonic, clean and clear?" he asked.

"Yes please," said AJ.

Raj poured AJ and himself a drink. He sat down on the armchair next to AJ and laughed again. He had a deep, whole-hearted laugh that made his entire body shake. Each time he laughed, he threw his head back, like he was enjoying himself thoroughly. He wore a simple lungi, a Bengal Tigers t-shirt and a diamond on his ring finger, a 10 karat rock, no less. He was good looking despite his eccentric moustache that was oiled out to curls at the ends. The soft creases around his eyes made him more dashing than he had been in his youth. He was sophisticated, posh and articulate. His energy infused the room and AJ felt jittery.

"Here's the key to the locker." The Don tossed AJ a silver key.

AJ put the key in his pocket. He knew the ins and outs of locker business. Standard procedure was to make a duplicate key and leave the original in the locker itself. The original had a serial number that could be traced back to the locker, but the duplicate left no trail. Not worried about robbers. Even if they were daft enough to mess with Raj's stuff, they wouldn't make it past the ID check points at the banks. The keys were a simple precaution to avoid the bigger gangsters, the GOB. If they got hold of the key and traced it back to your stash, you were screwed. Officially screwed. Without the key, they had no proof, and banks, concerned about client confidenti-ality, wouldn't disclose anything to anyone: cops, detectives, politicians. Only under orders from the PM herself were they obliged to break client trust. If she was on your case, you had to skip town, anyway.

Not that men like Raj Gopal had to worry about GOB. If they showed up at his door, he'd call his lawyer, speed dial 1,

and his doctor, speed dial 2. The lawyer would say, this man is
innocent until proven guilty. The doctor would say, this man
is a heart patient, if you manhandle him he could have a heart
attack and his blood will officially be on your hands. That
would end the game right there. Raj Gopal was Unfuckable.
It was people like AJ who needed to worry.

"You resemble the man whom the locker is listed under,
carbon copy, it's a fortunate coincidence," Raj said with a
laugh. "That unfortunate fellow is no longer with us." His
voice trailed.

AJ nodded. Raj had a reputation for being brutal with of-
fenders. He had killed a man with his bare hands, for insult-
ing his wife.

"Have you ever been picked up by cops?" asked Raj.

"No," replied AJ honestly. *Clean record so far.*

"They can be nasty. No respect for human life." Raj laughed,
as if he were sharing a joke. "Not that we should expect anything more from them." He tugged on the edge of his majestic moustache. "They picked me up once, back in the '80s, in
the prime of my days, so to say. Things were different then.
Now I am but an old man, enjoying the sunset of my life."

AJ tried to protest. He wanted a sunset like Raj's. Sunset
Boulevard. Playboy mansion in Bangladesh. Benzes in his garage. Beautiful women at his beck and call. More power than
the PM.

"I am a content man, I don't resist the coming of old age,"
he chuckled again. "They arrested me without a warrant. Pulled
me out of bed, in my lungi!" Raj's smiling face suddenly became fierce. "Didn't allow me a single phone call. Took me to
the police station and gave me a thrashing. Now how do you
think they would dare do that?"

AJ had no clue how they would dare. He could not imagine anyone with the balls to cross Raj Gopal.

Raj's eyes glistened with rage. "The bastards rolled me inside a rug. A Persian rug from my own living room floor. Then they fisted me and kicked me to their hearts' content, like I was a dog off the road. Most painful night of my life. When they were done, I was unconscious. They returned me to my home. Tucked me in bed. Put my rug back in the living room. Thought it was funny. They were smart though, I had no bruises, no visible signs of assault. Whom could I turn to for justice?"

AJ trembled at the sight of the Don in rage.

"Do you know what it was all about?" asked Raj.

AJ shook his head.

"A woman." Raj chuckled. His face brightened and he grinned again. "Son, in the absence of a robust justice system, do you know what innocent civilians like you and I must do?"

Innocent? thought AJ, shaking his head.

"We must look after ourselves, protect our own." Raj refilled AJ's glass.

"Thanks," AJ mumbled.

"Enough chatting. There's business to attend to." Raj dialed a number on his cell phone and a tall man in a pin-stripe suit arrived with a briefcase. AJ recognized him instantly, they had mugged him a week ago. He clearly did not recognize AJ, because he shook his hand and sat down.

"Hasan here will tell you the details," the Don explained. "I hope we meet again soon. You take care of yourself, ok?" Raj shook AJ's hand and patted him on the back before he left the room.

AJ thought Hasan looked comical, like a gangster from a smoky bar in New York. He smelt like he had emptied an entire bottle of cologne on himself. AJ downed two shots of whiskey then mixed himself a fifth drink. "So Hasan, what's the scoop? What do you want me to do with this key?" he asked casually. "Am I putting something in the locker or getting something out?"

Hasan opened his briefcase and pulled out a 9 mm Beretta. AJ bolted upright. Was Hasan going to blow his head off? Punishment for the scene he had created at the party? Revenge, best served cold.

"Here," said Hasan, in a surprisingly feminine voice. "It's loaded. Eight bullets. For protection against thieves. You never know, the streets are not safe anymore." He handed AJ the gun.

The shiny black metal reflected the chandelier light. The handle was wooden, glazed and smooth, with a golden bow and arrow engraved on it. AJ had gone duck hunting with his father years ago, but they had used rifles. He had never held a pistol before. The weight of the weapon in his hand gave him a sense of power. He held it up and pointed it at Hasan's head.

"Hey!" shouted Hasan. "It's loaded, man!" He grabbed the gun and put it back in the briefcase. "Do you know how to use it or do I need to show you?"

"I can figure it out," replied AJ, cocky arrogance returning.

"The diamonds," Hasan instructed, "are a rare collection from South Africa. Protect them with your life, if you know what's good for you. The pouch is in locker 31A of the AB Bank in Mirpur. Your name is Javed Ali. Bring the pouch straight to me. Locker 31A. Can you remember that?"

"Sure," said AJ. Did Hasan think he was an idiot?

"Bring me the pouch, the key and the gun by tomorrow. Can you manage that?"

"Sure," said AJ. Why was Hasan treating him like an amateur?

"You get paid when the job is done. 75,000 taka. Cash."

"How much are these diamonds worth?" asked AJ.

Hasan grinned. "Worth a helluva lot more than your ass."

Suddenly AJ lost his temper. "Fuck you."

"What?" said Hasan in disbelief. "What did you say?"

"Fuck you."

"Listen, you little prick," said Hasan sternly. "I know your type. Because Raj Gopal's given you a job, suddenly you think you're invincible? You're just a small fish in a big sea. Ok?"

"Fuck you, you mother fucker." said AJ with a straight face. He could feel his barometer rising. He knew he would regret cursing Hasan's mother, but he could not stop himself. Mr Hyde had emerged. "You think you are some sort of hot shot? I know Quader *bhai*. I know all the ministers. I know each and every cop in Dhaka City. I'm not scared of you, you fucking queer."

"You know who MY boss is, so respect!" shouted Hasan.

"I fuck your boss' whore every night," shouted AJ.

"Ok," said Hasan with a tight lip. "Let's keep it cool. Just get the diamonds to me by tonight. Don't try any cheap tricks."

AJ fumed. Did Hasan take him for a fool? Who would dare cross Raj Gopal? You don't fuck with the King. Raj could erase him in a second if he so chose, but Hasan was a nonentity. "I'm going to make a duplicate."

"You won't get away with it," Hasan warned. "I'll personally see to it that your extra key is thrown into the grave with you."

"Ya, fuck you." AJ stormed off with the gun and the key to the locker with the pouch worth more than his life.

* * *

For all it was worth, life was good. Starry sky, cool sea breeze, good music. What more could a man want? Deen grabbed a beer from the cooler and stretched himself out on the roof deck of the cruise ship. Maria had gotten hold of five tickets for the Bangla performance and she, AJ, Shagor, Nina and Deen had packed into Shagor's car and made their way to Meghna ghaat where the ship was anchored.

Meghna ghaat was only an hour outside Dhaka, but it was a different world altogether. No congested traffic, no throngs of people, no buildings, no noise, no lights, no pollution. Just the incredible energy of the Meghna, and a few fishing boats docked on the side. During the day, the ghaat was a bustle of fishermen and traders, but at night, it was silent and mystical.

The ship was lit with candles. Clusters of music junkies were scattered on blankets on the deck. Deen spotted Parvez sitting on the lower deck with a group of younger kids, and waved. Parvez came running over to say hello. They chatted about the band and about the boishakhi party Parvez was throwing at his dad's pad. Deen promised to set up the music system and select some tunes for the night. Parvez invited Maria and Nina to the party then returned to the lower deck.

Deen sniffled, his head cold was creeping in. Shagor rolled a joint and passed it around. Deen watched, amused, as Maria took a shallow puff and burst into a fit of coughs. He took a drag, then laid his head on Maria's lap. He stared up at the diamond sky and mused over the nature of the expanding universe. What lay beyond? How can we comprehend the realm of God, while stuck in thoughts delineated by languages created by men. Stuck eternally to our paradigms of conception. Stuck in our antiquated notion of time and space. Stuck in the 10 percent grey matter we've learnt to use. All the wonders of the universe reduced to fit our frameworks. Why make sense of it? Why systemize the chaos? Moloch, the man who invented the clock and cast humanity into a rush. *Ticking away, the moments that make up a dull day. Fritter and waste the hours in an off-hand way. The sun is the same, in a relative way, but you're older. Shorter of breath, and one day closer to death.* Deen scratched his arm.

Maria ruffled his hair and played with his ear lobe, whispering visions of their life together as it would be in America. Deen could move there while she studied journalism. They'd go out dancing every Thursday and drink cappuccinos in park cafes. Deen listened as Maria fantasized, mapping out the future. Cartography of dreams. Ah, the best laid plans.

The musicians tuned their instruments at the front of the boat. The band was accompanied by a group of bauls from the Lalon mazaar, wrinkled old men in dhotis and saffron robes, with tangled beards, matted hair and tulsi beads around their necks. They passed along a bamboo kolki full of ganja. A red eyed fakir took a long drag then let out a heartfelt cry to God before returning to the tuning at hand.

Devoted bauls, wrapped in musical worship, true to the gypsy lifestyle and the Sufi spirit. Deen admired their dedication. Could music save his mortal soul?

Anusheh emerged and the crowd cheered as she made her way to the front of the boat. She was beautiful, with long wavy hair and lashes that reached out to the stars. The bauls sat upright with their bashis, ektaras and dhols, ready to accompany her powerful voice. Her voice was enchanting, like a flying carpet. Every time Deen heard it, it grabbed him and held on to him and took him on a spiritual trip.

AJ walked by and looked Deen in the eye. No words were exchanged. "Honeybaby," said Deen to Maria, "I'm going down to get us some wine."

"Hurry back," Maria pleaded. "They're going to start soon."

Deen climbed down the roof ladder, down the spiral stairwell and into the hallway of rooms two decks below. AJ was in the first cabin. Deen stepped in and locked the door. The room was small, enough space for a set of narrow bunk beds and not much more. It had a window overlooking the waves. AJ was sitting on the bottom bunk. Deen sat beside him and lit a cigarette, while AJ prepared the foil. He grabbed a can of deodorant from AJ's duffle bag and sprayed the room copiously to disguise the stench that would soon emerge. He felt guilty knowing Parvez was up there, but he consoled himself with the memory of Parvez's promise to never chase again.

AJ lit a candle, popped a coin in his mouth and led the tilli under the smack, inhaling the fumes.

Whoooooooosh.
Whoooooooooooooosh.
Whoooooooooooooooooooosh.

The stench filled the room, mixing with the stifling deodorant, creating a fog that was difficult to breathe in. AJ handed the foil to Deen and continued to lead the flame underneath. Deen inhaled the smoke, dropped the coin, took a drag from his cigarette and let the twin fumes out at one go.

Instantaneously his head congestion cleared up and his body relaxed. AJ stuffed the foil into the bag and handed Deen a bottle of wine.

Deen returned to Maria's side, ready to enjoy the night. Anusheh was singing already...

> *Carry me to the shore,*
> *I'm in no state to make the crossing.*
> *O Merciful Friend, I alone await the ferry.*
> *No one but you can save me.*
> *I've neglected all my prayers*
> *And never followed the Friend of the Fallen,*
> *That's why I crave your mercy.*

It was a devotional song about pathways to the heart. The journey inwards, across the turbulent sea, to the shore of faith. Deen hummed along into Maria's ear, but something was missing. His tone sounded empty. Lacking conviction. Had people forgotten how to pray? Had they lost themselves in material greed and given up on spiritual pursuits? Were they drowning in suffering because God didn't hear their insincere prayers? Were they submerged in man-made problems because they were too selfish and disconnected? Strangers to themselves, unable to find God within?

The next song was about crying alone by the banks of the river. An intense loneliness swelled up within Deen as Anusheh sang. Her voice ululated with the waves and pulled at his heart. He noticed the river in the moonlight, the river Lalon had written about, the river that had devastated whole villages during the monsoons, the river with broken souls and drowned spirits strewn across its muddy floor, the river that both gave life and took it without once thinking of the consequences.

A breeze passed through the boat and intoxicated the musicians, altering their tempo. The next song was about love. The truth of the song rose up before Deen, almost palpable: only love mattered. It struck Deen like an epiphany. Love for God, love for those in your life, love for life itself. The song spoke of kindness and acceptance, not Judgement Day or crowns of thorns, not guilt, not sins, not expectations, not demands. It spoke of being connected to the higher being at all times, energy in sync, staying in tune with joy. Deen gave Maria a hug. Life was sweet.

He stared at the phosphorescent waves in a dazed, helplessly amazed state. He marvelled at the revelations. Each song seemed to speak about something profound and relevant. Deen wondered if Anusheh was singing just for him or if everyone on the boat was under her spell, tuned in to the same wavelength to receive messages. Messages, like blessings, come to you, if you're at the right place at the right time and you're open to receiving. Deen felt blessed. God was shining on him. Tonight, for some reason, he was not God-forsaken.

Deen saw a shooting star and wished for inner peace. He pointed out the sky to Maria who looked upwards eagerly. Then she caught a glimpse of one too. Then another. Then another. Then suddenly everyone on the boat was whispering and pointing at the sky and together they witnessed a meteorite shower, making wishes left, right and centre, as the night exploded.

Late in the night, Deen and Maria made their way down the roof ladder, down the spiral stairwell and into a room of bunk beds. They locked the doors and kissed passionately. His fingers lingered up her skirt. She moaned as their bodies touched. He lifted her up violently and placed her on the top bunk, pushing her skirt up her legs, planting kisses on her calves, then her knees, then her thighs, till he reached her warm, wet, welcoming juncture, and then he began licking, slowly at first, exploring softly, and then frantically, desperate, passionate long licks as he tried to get deeper and deeper into her, sipping her juices, sweet and salty, and he felt reborn as she danced.

Outside, the waves beat against the boat in rhythm with the lovers. When finally she screamed with ecstasy, he pulled her off the top bunk and threw her onto the lower bunk, ripping off her shirt. The frame of the bunk created leverage for him to push himself deep into her and she in turn held on and pushed and pulled against his body, and they pressed against each other and they moved with hot, rising urgency, and nothing else existed except that moment, till finally they reached the glorious climax they were searching for and they were released. They collapsed into each other's bodies and Deen knew for a moment that LOVE was the answer and they were ONE, and then he drifted off into a disturbed sleep.

✦ THIRTEEN ✦

"Wahoooooooooooooooo!" AJ floored the accelerator of Shagor's Beamer. "Locker 31A, you make my mouth water!" He was tipsy and in a great mood. Shagor sat in the back, turquing hardcore. Deen sat shotgun, driving the music.

"I'm in awe of the complexities and contradictions of women," Deen stated. He pulled out the last cigarette from his pack. Last one lucky.

"It's simple. Give them diamonds and fuck them well, and you'll be taken care of." AJ was cheeky about women. He had slept with the finest models in Dhaka and now he had Sundari.

"My daddy's not a millionaire, dosto," replied Deen. "I ain't no fortunate son."

"That's right. Money's not your thing. Capitalistic bullshit. Save the oration. Anyway, with a face like yours, you can pull the ladies in without diamonds in your pocket. Just please them in bed. Who's keeping you up?"

Deen dragged in deep and exhaled a round of smoke circles. "Maria's moving to America."

"Maria! You're still into that babe? She's a man eater, Deen. Don't let your heart into the matter. Bad trip. Crash end.

Doomed. Move on to the next lay." AJ sped up to 120 mph and fishtailed through the trucks on the highway.

Deen pushed in a CD of Ravi Shankar. He pumped up the volume and let himself soar. He was on top of the world as they headed to Tongi, high already at the mere thought of smack. "Vaah!" cried Deen, in approval of the maestro.

"Change the CD," said AJ, suddenly sombre.

"Why, man? Shankar rocks!"

"Change the fucking CD," said AJ angrily.

"Ok, dost, after this track?" *How drunk is AJ?* Deen wondered.

"I said change the CD." AJ pulled out a pistol from the side pocket of the car and held it to Deen's head.

"What the fuck?" screamed Deen.

"Change the fucking CD," AJ said again, his eyes still on the road, the gun aimed straight at Deen's temple.

"What the hell are you doing?" Deen pushed the gun away from his face.

AJ stared at Deen, solemn dark eyes, then melted into peals of laughter. "I had you going there, dosto, didn't I?" AJ waved the gun in Deen's face. "Isn't it awesome? An original 9 mm Beretta. Made in Italy!"

"Stop waving that in my fucking face!" cried Deen.

"Chill," said AJ. "The safety latch is on." He tossed the gun onto the dashboard and laughed. "Shagor, did you see his face?"

"Huh?" mumbled Shagor irritably. "Oh ya, the gun. Deen, we shot a crow on my roof."

"We?" interrupted AJ. "Shagor wasted three bullets. I got it on my first shot. You should have seen the thing explode."

"It's deadly," said Shagor.

"If you can aim," said AJ.

Deen took the gun in his hand. Black shiny metal, a wooden butt with a golden bow and arrow engraved on it. The weapon was solid. It could inflict serious damage even if it was used to bang a man on the head rather than blow a hole through his skull. How fragile life is. Nine months in the womb before it even begins, endless amounts of protection, nourishment and love to survive, and then one slight flicker of a finger on a trigger could blast it all apart in an instant.

Deen wondered if anyone would miss him if AJ shot him right there in the middle of the road. Perhaps his mother would. Though she may have more peace of mind for the rest of her days. Maybe Maria would. For a few months. Until some university kid started buying her flowers and drinks. Nobody else would care. "Where'd you get this?" Deen asked.

"Raj Gopal! Would you believe it? The King gave me a gun to protect his precious rocks. Rocks the size of my balls!"

AJ parked in front of the tea stall. They helped Shagor out of the car, practically carrying him on their shoulders.

"Have you got cash?" asked Deen.

"Don't worry, dost," said AJ. "I've got a plan. I'm gonna sell my diamond. Javed blai will buy it."

Kala was at the stall with friends. He saw the boys and came running forth. "Deen bhai, we've been given a warning, there's going to be a raid today."

"How do you know?" asked Deen. Some peddlers were connected to politicians who paid dirty cops to tip them off before raids, but Kala was not in any such security net.

"Majid got the news when he was in town," explained Kala. "He was picked up by the cops yesterday. They beat him up then gave him the warning."

"That's unlikely," remarked AJ.

"You should see him, AJ bhai," continued Kala. "He had to go to the hospital, he was broken all over. Those cops have no respect for our people. They think we're dogs. I guess we are. We're khors. Don't even respect ourselves. I'm quitting."

"You've been saying that for years, Kala," said Deen.

"No Deen bhai, I'm serious this time. I need to get a job, my dad's too old to work and my mother can't support herself. I have only one brother. He's retarded, you know, ever since he had typhoid when he was four. Can't even feed himself. They need me desperately. And I need to do it for myself too. I can't afford this anymore. Most of the time I'm turquing. It's poison. I've wasted too many years."

Shagor let out a groan.

"Let's go," said AJ.

"Falani got rid of her stuff," said Kala. "She's keeping a low profile, we all are."

"Let's go to Musa's shack," suggested AJ. Deen nodded. The boys ignored Kala's protests and crossed the road, with Shagor balanced in between them.

"We have to clean up our shit," said Deen.

"Why?" said AJ.

"It's self-destructive."

"You tried rehab, dost. It was prison, you said so yourself."

"Waste of time," Deen agreed. His father had sent him to a rehab in Calcutta. It was the worst experience of his life. The rehab was run by a group of Christian monks who had their own rigid ideas about breaking addictions. They gave him medication to ease his withdrawals and kept him locked up at night. There were no girls, only vegetarian meals, the bathrooms were filthy. They made him repeat verses from the Bible on Sundays. Deen learnt some tricks from the other patients there, like how to shoot up with a needle. After three months of shooting heroin, Deen returned home more messed up than he had been to begin with.

"Rehabs are for quitters," said AJ. "This is my life. No one's gonna tell me how to live. It's about freedom."

"It kills grey matter," said Deen.

"Dost, you read too many books. You don't spend enough time chasing pussy. Don't give me that grey matter shit. It's about having fun. Chasing the dragon is as good as pussy. Would you ever stop fucking? No. Cuz you're a bloody romantic."

"But Chinx is in a coma," said Deen.

"You're watching too many hospital dramas," said AJ, as they wove through the narrow alleys towards Musa's shack. "So what if Chinx is in a coma? He's in a coma cuz he's a fucking pussy. He doesn't have any balls. Are you a pussy? Because if you are, you should grow some balls. Do you have balls? Are they the size of fucking marbles? Men have balls and we quit when we want to. Am I clear?"

"Crystal," said Deen, at the doorstep of the shack.

Inside, Musa, his praying-mantis brother, and two men they had never seen before, were playing carom. Majid was lying on a cot behind them. His eyes were puffy, his lips were swollen, a cotton gauze was plastered to his nose.

"What the hell happened to you?" growled Shagor, hiding his withdrawals.

"Cops," Majid mumbled.

"Damn," said Shagor, who wasn't really interested in the story. "Musa, hook us up with a line." His poker-face was well-trained to hide the desperation brimming within him. He knew not to let on how badly he needed a hit.

Musa stated his price and the boys agreed without argument though no one had any money. Musa retrieved a small bag from the inner room of his shack and pulled out the stuff.

Shagor shoved a coin into the roof of his mouth and inhaled the fumes as Musa dragged the lit tilli under the smack. *Clink.* The coin fell out. Shagor took a drag from his cigarette, and let out twin fumes.

AJ chased next, then Deen. The three of them sat back and smoked a cigarette, enjoying the feelings. When they got up to leave, Musa asked for his payment.

"Give it to us on credit," said AJ. "We'll pay you by the end of the week."

"No cash means no smack. You better pay NOW," said Musa.

"We can't," AJ argued. "Couldn't even if we wanted to."

"Pay. Me. Now." Musa continued, slow and angry.

"What the fuck do you mean by NOW?" asked Shagor.

"The rule is simple. No cash, no smack. I stated my price before. You have to pay me NOW."

"Do you KNOW who the fuck we are?" said Shagor. "DO YOU KNOW WHO THE FUCK WE ARE?"

"No. I don't know who you are. I don't care who your daddy is, pretty boy. You owe me cash and you better pay up now." The other basti men silently exchanged heated looks. They hated Shagor and his type. Rich, arrogant junkies. They needed his money to survive, plain economics, but they hated his type.

"We'll pay you back, we always smoke on credit. It's no big deal. We're known in this area," Deen reasoned.

Musa kept his angry eyes on Shagor. "I don't know who

the fuck you THINK you are. You smoked MY smack, in MY house. You pay me now."

Shagor pulled out AJ's pistol from inside his pants and pointed it directly at Musa's face. His eyes were watery and red. "We're not paying anything. Not now, not EVER."

"What are you going to do?" Musa challenged. "Shoot me? So shoot me!"

Shagor glared at him. The basti men shuffled uncomfortably. Deen and AJ looked on in hidden disbelief. Majid remained motionless, eyeing the gun with cautious interest, eyeing Shagor with lazy disdain.

"Your fucking father can pay for this trip," said Shagor. With cold, calculated aim, he shot Musa in the foot.

Musa screamed in pain and doubled over. Shagor stood frozen, shocked at the sight before him.

"Let's get out of here." Deen pulled Shagor out of his trance.

Shagor pointed the gun at each of the basti men in turn, his hands shaking. "Don't try to follow us," he warned.

Musa cursed as a dark red pool spread across the floor. The smell of gunpowder, unsettled dust and fresh blood mixed with the smell of burnt heroin.

"Go!" Shagor said to his friends. AJ and Deen hightailed through the alley towards their car. Shagor trailed, waving the gun behind him like a madman. "Go, go, go!" he shouted.

"What the hell? Why'd you do that?" screamed Deen as they jumped into their car.

Shagor laughed and revved the accelerator. "Waaahooooooooooo!" he screamed.

"You're nuts, dosto! That was so unnecessary!" Deen was shaking in disbelief.

"It all happened so fast!" shouted Shagor in excitement.

"That was Raj Gopal's gun," said AJ.

"You could get us in a lot of trouble, it's not a toy," Deen shouted.

Shagor grinned, high on smack and adrenaline. "Did you see the look on Musa's face? The coward didn't even try to stop me!"

"Of course he didn't," snapped AJ. "You had a GUN. Who's going to fight a man with a gun for a few bucks? But that was Raj Gopal's gun, who the fuck said you could touch it?"

"It felt good to pull the trigger, but his toe didn't explode."

"You think he's going to let this go? The entire basti will be after you like a mob. They'll be after *us*!" said Deen.

"Nah, man. Basti folks are chicken," said Shagor. "Farmers, not fighters. No one's going to mess with us. My dad will have them thrown in jail if they try."

"Ya, that's good news. Pick on those who can't fight back. Great job, dosto, "grumbled Deen.

Shagor accelerated and they sped off into the future.

* * *

Deen arrived at AJ's place and found him on the way to euphoria.

"What're you flying on, dosto?" Deen asked.

"Oooohee, you're going to love me!" AJ said.

"Don't turn gay on me, man," Deen said wryly.

"You are going to kiss my feet. I am about to make your day."

"Did you convince Maria to marry me?" Deen asked.

"You want to marry Maria?"

"I dunno. Maybe."

"I've got you something million a times better than a lady's snatch!" AJ chuckled.

"I seriously doubt it."

"See this?" AJ held up three white pills. "Lucy! Pure white Lucy."

"No way, dosto!" Deen scrambled to take a closer look. "Where'd you get that?"

"I have my sources." AJ grinned.

Deen and AJ swallowed the pills. AJ pushed Led Zeppelin into his stereo and lit a cigarette. Deen pulled out his pack. Last one lucky. "Do you have a light?"

"I got some whiskey too." AJ passed him a box of matches. "To lighten our ride down."

"You started without me?" Shagor waltzed in, with a stolen cell phone in his hand.

"Chill, man. Here's yours." AJ tossed him a pill. "We just popped, it hasn't hit yet."

Shagor examined the pill for a moment then gleefully swallowed it. "Wow, I feeeeeeel it!" he shouted.

"Ya man, sure you do." AJ laughed.

"It's like an orgasm!" Shagor continued.

"Shaddap." AJ cut him off.

"Ok, ya, how long does it take to hit?" Shagor asked eagerly. "Want to buy a phone?" He waved the phone in their faces.

AJ shook his head. "Let's go have tea?"

"*Sweet tea,*" Deen sang out. The roadside tea stall where they hung out was their favourite not only because it was conveniently located next to Falani's basti, but also because it served the best tea in the country, thick with condensed milk and always soul-soothing. Perfect when high.

AJ grabbed his CD case and they piled into Shagor's

Beamer. Deen, the music navigator, pushed in a *Doors* CD.

"Do you feel tingly shit in your legs?" Shagor asked excitedly.

Deen felt pins and needles all over his body. He enjoyed it in spurts. It travelled through him in concentric waves, sometimes a funny numb feeling, sometimes like a convulsion. He wondered if his shakes were real. The others didn't say anything so he concluded the sensations might all be in his head.

"Waaahoooooooooooo!" AJ rolled down his window.

"I'm going to race this guy!" Shagor announced, speeding up next to a blue truck.

Deen pumped up the volume. GLORIA blared on the speakers. The boys got into the beat and sang along, Glooooria! G-L-O-R-I-A (strumming air guitars) Glooooria! G-L-O-R-I-A (screaming as the music took over) Glooooria! G-L-O-R-I-A (laughing with their heads out the windows) Glooooria! G-L-O-R-I-A.

"Hey! Maaaaria!" AJ shouted. "M-AA-R-I-A!" he sang, stretching the A to make it fit. Deen laughed and joined in. Maaaaria! M-AA-R-I-A. Maaaaria! M-AA-R-I-A. Maaaaria!

The wind blew through his hair, blending in with the tingles in Deen's body. The trees and cars outside were morphing into odd shapes as his vision pulsed in and out of animation, along with the beat, turning the horizon into a strange tie-dye abstract piece of art that seemed alive. Next to him, Shagor laughed hysterically. AJ was still singing, oblivious to the rest of the collapsing world.

"Do you guys see what I see?" Shagor asked, in between giggles.

Deen looked up and shook his head to throw out the hypnotic wind trance.

"Look right out there." Shagor pointed to the rear view mirror. "Space fireballs with monkeys riding on them!"

"Oh ya?" said AJ.

"How do those hairy little fuckers hold on?" said Shagor. "It's amazing! Just look!"

"Man, it's hitting you hard." AJ laughed.

"Ya, I know they're not real," said Shagor defensively. "But don't they look so real? Deen?"

"I see what you mean." Deen offered. His arms dropped like heavy weights in an eerie mind body disconnect. He tried to command his arm to lift. It obeyed, but it lifted in a wave-like dance motion. Deen smiled, amused with his own body. He repeated the process with his legs.

"Reality walks a thin line," AJ announced. "It's not always like, if you see it, it's real."

"There's a pagla near my house," Shagor piped in. "His eyes will fix on a tree or a car or some shit like that and he'll stare at it for days, but he's really in another dimension. He says things that are oddly wise. I don't think he's really mad, it's just that he can't communicate with our world any-more."

"*Our* world, meaning yours and mine?" AJ jeered.

"Madness is relative," Deen mumbled.

"Relative to reality?" said AJ.

"Relative to the dominating knowledge system that decides what's right and wrong," said Deen.

"Ya, like the government," said AJ.

"Like the President of USA," echoed Shagor.

"Like the Pope," added Deen.

"And the army," said AJ.

"Eradicating mind-altering drugs," said Deen. "Ever won-

der why? Alters the mind, opens up other dimensions of reality, where rules and borders don't exist."

"Sometimes, when I'm tripping my ass off, I feel like I
may be mad. In my own head, I mean," Shagor interrupted.

"That thought's crossed my mind," AJ teased. "You are mad."

"No seriously guys, I think I may be going mad," said Shagor
with increasing agitation. "Do I seem normal to you, Deen?"

Suddenly Deen thought Shagor seemed more like a ptero-
dactyl than a human. He had razor-sharp talons and a deadly
beak. Deen pulled back in fright. Before he could reply, AJ
said, "No man, you seem mad."

"No seriously, what would happen if the high, say this one
time, didn't wear off, and you got stuck forever in the rabbit
hole?" Shagor laughed uncomfortably. "It happened to Rob.
He went on an acid trip and never became quite normal after
that. It happened three weeks before he OD-ed."

"Shut up man! Who the hell talks about ODs when they're
tripping? Don't talk shit, you're killing my buzz." AJ shot
out.

"Are you scared?" Shagor jeered. "AJ is a bheethoo, you
hear that Deen?"

Deen had zoned into the bass guitar and the rhythm seemed
to be vibrating within him, in his heart, his bones and every
organ in his body. He could feel each note pumping through
his blood cells as it traveled through the arteries in his legs. He
was conscious of his *being* on a molecular level and it too was
in sync with the guitar. Every unexpected note sent a lightening of colour through his field of vision, so that he could not
only hear the music, but also see it.

"Where's the goddam tea stall?" Shagor demanded, searching for a familiar landmark along the unlit street side. "Where are we?"

All they could see for miles to come were silhouettes of haystacks in paddy fields.

"Pull over at the next sign of civilization," AJ suggested dryly.

Eventually they arrived at a strange building covered in neon green fairy lights that were flashing Las Vegas casino style. It was a budget restaurant serving Bangladeshi food, with blaring Bangla songs on the radio. There were a hundred aliens scattered around cluttered tables, as if it were midday lunch on Mars. Varieties of species, some green, some slimy, some with egg-shaped heads, chatted away in shrill Bengali, while eating biriani and chicken.

Shagor spoke to a helpful waiter and discovered they were in Kumilla, three hours away from Dhaka. It felt like only minutes since they had left AJ's, but time does strange things when you're not looking.

They were drinking tea, tripping off acid, when simultaneously all three cell phones beeped. Deen looked at the message on his phone. Rahul had sent them a mass text. Sent out to some group list. Casual as hell. "Chinx is dead. Janaza at noon."

✦ FOURTEEN ✦

Deen and AJ arrived at the mourning house a little before noon. There were forty cars parked along the street. Deen rang the doorbell.

"*Salam'alaikum*," said a sad eyed lady. "You must be Chinku's friends. I'm his mother."

"*Salam'alaikum*, aunty," they said in turn.

"I watched my baby kill himself, right before my eyes." She clutched the end of her sari. "Come."

The house smelt of death. There were sheets laid out on the marble floors and baskets of rosary beads scattered around. Leaning against the walls were silver haired ladies in white saris and aunties with children, counting prayers on the beads, sharing memories in between sobs. So many deaths one must face in a lifetime. In the living room, bathed already, wrapped in white cloth, was Chinx. Chinx's father, brothers, uncles, cousins, grandfathers, in white kurtas, stood around, stoic, mostly silent. Their grief stabbed into the emptiness in Deen's gut.

"Here," said Chinx's mother. "Chinku's friends are in here."

Deen stepped into a room full of ratty-faced junkies. Khors, most of them sober, in white kurtas, downcast eyes. Rahul.

Shagor. Monwar, the quiet smackie who knew a lot about religion. Asha, who was once a classical dancer but now looked like a skeleton. Farhan, the con artist. Deen knew them all from school, they were one year junior to him. English-medium school rich kid junkies. They partied together once in a while.

Chinx's room had red walls, a Darth Vader poster, a bamboo lamp on the floor. On the other side of his bed were his neighbourhood friends. Bangla-medium school kids. Deen knew most of them too, all junkies. Raihan and Rubel, brothers from St. Josephs, played football back in the day. Fazle, aggressive, macho yabba khor. Naved, the prick.

Deen and AJ sat on cushions propped up against Chinx's closet.

"It's crazy. I can't believe this happened." Rahul pulled up a cushion next to Deen. "I hung out with him last week."

"I feel hollow," replied Deen.

"He wasn't fine," continued Rahul. "But he was doing better. He was in rehab you know. They had him on largatrine."

"No one prescribes that shit anymore," said AJ.

"It's not a cure," continued Rahul. "Blocks neural pathways to ease withdrawals, but what about the habit? Chutiya doctor. What was Chinx going to do with his urges? The minute he got drunk he went and chased. Couldn't stop himself, he was a khor. With blockers in his system, his body couldn't handle the smack. Fucking doctor doesn't understand addictions!"

Deen had known Chinx since primary school. He aced his classes, teachers loved him. He dated a girl named Nadia whom he adored. He always offered rides and went out of his way to accommodate his friends. He had become a recluse over the past few years, caught up in the chase. Now he was Dead. For maggots under the earth. For heaven, maybe, for hell, maybe. For an eternity of NOTHING ELSE, maybe. Bones in the graveyard. The end.

No more addas with friends, no more mornings, no more dinners, no more music, no more long drives, no more hot showers, no more tea, no more rain, no more love, no more kisses, no more sex, no more late afternoon naps, no more movies, no more parties, no more football, no more highs, no more lows, no more chasing, no more withdrawals, no more vomiting, no more stealing, no more lies. . .

Shagor interrupted, "Hey man, I'm turquing," he whispered. "Let's go to Tongi?"

Deen felt disgusted. "No man. The guy just died. I don't feel like chasing."

Deen stepped out of the room and into the verandah to catch his breath. Chinx's younger sister was sitting against the wall. She had grown up since Deen had last seen her, she had become a woman. She looked beautiful, even in her mourning kamiz and sad eyes. Deen sat down next to her. "I wish I could have helped him," he said.

"You? Ya. You and all his other friends." She smiled bitterly. "How could you help? You can't even help yourselves."

Chinx's mother hurried into the veranda. Deen could hear howling sobs from the living room. "They're taking his body," she said. "Come."

Deen stepped into the living room. Chinx's cousins were carrying his body in a wooden khatia, from the living room, through the corridor, out the door, into the car, off to the graveyard and into the ground. Forever. *Chinx's Last Journey.*

"Are you going to the graveyard?" Chinx's mom asked Deen at the doorway.

"Ya, aunty, of course," replied Deen.

"Ok, but promise to come back here again. Anytime. Come as if Chinku were still here. Come spend some time with me. We can talk about Chinku. He was a sensitive boy. Before the drugs. I tried to help him. I've been begging him to go for treatment for over six years, ever since I found out about his addiction. I sent him to America, I thought that might make him happy. He came back with more problems. I found a doctor in Bombay who runs a rehab known as Land. He heals addicts through love, none of those chemical blockers, no drugs to stop drugs, just positive energy. It was the answer to our prayers, but Chinku refused to go. He was in denial. Then I sent him to the rehab here. It was my fault that he went. I sent him."

The male relatives stood queued at the doorway, waiting to get past Chinx's mom, out to their cars. Not ready to let Chinx go, she stalled, dragging out the conversation with Deen for as long as she could. Finally, Chinx's father took her in his arms and led her back into the house.

Deen got on the bike behind AJ and they followed the procession.

It reminded Deen of his father, he was buried in the same graveyard. Deen was at a party when his old man was rushed to the hospital in the middle of the night. By the time Deen had sobered up enough to join him, his father had already lapsed into a coma. Deen wondered what he might have said, had he arrived in time to catch his last words. Deen thought about the Bombay rehab, Land. Neverland. Never do drugs again Land. *Need to google it*, he thought. *Maybe I can quit. Move to America with Maria.*

"Dosto," interrupted AJ, "I can't find the gun."

"What?"

"I can't find the Beretta!"

"What do you mean?" asked Deen.

"Raj Gopal is going to kill me, I mean really, kill me. You'll have to come to my janaza next."

"Calm down, dost. Try to remember, where did you put it?"

"I left it in the glove compartment of Shagor's car, but I went to get it yesterday and it wasn't there. He doesn't know where it is. We searched the entire car."

"You think he sold it?" asked Deen.

"No. He says he didn't."

"Maybe it's at your apartment."

"I looked. I'm so screwed. Ronnie won't pay me. I owe Quader bhai money. And now Raj is going to kill me," grumbled AJ.

Raj Gopal was Bangladesh's most feared, revered mafia Don and AJ had lost his gun. Deen wondered how far AJ was from the deep end of the black sea.

They buried Chinx in the Banani graveyard around 3pm. Chinx's friends and family took turns with the shovel. *Bury your beloved*, thought Deen as he dropped dirt over his friend's bones. He wondered who would do this for him when he died.

* * *

Deen almost stepped on the body. He was stoned out of his mind and his thoughts were traipsing about the intangible universe. It was late already and the last thing he expected was a body sprawled out face down in his path. Deen stopped abruptly and AJ, who was tailgating, bumped into him.

"What the hell, man? What happened?" AJ asked.

"Dost, there's a man lying in the middle of the road," said Deen.

"Step over him, what's the problem! Go, go, go!"

"Dost, he's lying twenty feet from Falani's shack. Don't you think this is kind of risky?"

"Why the hell would it be risky?"

"Do you think he's dead?"

"Who cares? Don't touch him, then it'll become risky. They'll pin the blame on you. Say you killed him or some shit. This is Falani's problem, not ours. Go!"

Deen knelt down beside the man. He wasn't dead yet. "He's breathing . . . barely."

AJ crouched down next to Deen with his lighter out, shining a flame on the man's face. "He's passed out?"

Kala trudged up behind them, a lantern swinging in his hand. "Deen bhai, leave him. Don't worry, he's a local. Just really smacked out."

"What do you mean? He's about to die. Does Falani want a dead man on her doorstep?" Deen was alarmed.

"His name is Borkat," said Kala. "He was a rickshaw walla Chased at the end of the day to relax his aching muscles. Came here occasionally to buy stuff. Never bothered anyone. Never smoked here. Got stuck in the spiral though. Hasn't been cycling for a month. He's completely run out of money and he's turqing. I think he hasn't had smack in two days. He can't eat or sleep. He came to Falani for a handout, he could barely speak. Shagor bhai was smoking in the room and Borkat nearly fell over him. Knocked his foil out of his hand. Shagor bhai was pissed off and beat the crap out of him. Threw him out of the house. I think he passed out right after that." There were tears in Kala's eyes.

Deen looked at AJ.

"No way man, I need to chase," argued AJ.

"Let's try it this way." Deen pushed the body into an upright position. "If we carry him in like he's sitting, we'll be able to get him around the bend and to her door."

"Deen, what are you, some sort of saint?" AJ asked. "We should leave this bastard and go for a hit. You want me to break my back? For a stranger?"

"Kala, hold his waist." Deen positioned the body. He motioned AJ to lift under the arms while he prepared to grab the legs.

"All right, on three. One, two, three." They nearly fell over, Borkat was so light. Kala, though skeletal himself and a foot shorter, was almost able to carry him alone.

"You think there's any cash on this guy?" AJ asked as they navigated the body into Falani's shack.

"No, no, no!" Falani cried. "What are you doing? Shagor bhai will kill me." She stole a terrified glance at Borkat, then looked pleadingly at AJ. His hardened face made it clear he wasn't about to move Borkat again. She shifted her gaze to Deen.

"You have to give him some smack, Falani," Deen said urgently. "He won't last much longer otherwise."

Falani sighed. She fetched her peacock-purse from the back room. Kala stood ready with a foil and a pipe.

"Deen bhai, let's prop him up," Kala said. "He doesn't have the strength to sit."

Deen grabbed Borkat and leaned the body against his knees. "I've got him. I'll hold the pipe in his mouth and you run the smoke. AJ, grab him from behind."

Falani had the spit can ready. They knew what would follow. Deen held the pipe to his mouth. Kala ran a flame under the foil. In silence, they watched the smack melt. The smoke reached Borkat's nose. The boys braced themselves.

As soon as Borkat smelt the fumes, his eyes popped open. He took a long drag and dropped the pipe from his mouth. He leaned forward for the cigarette in Deen's hand. Deen put it to his lips. Borkat inhaled, but before he could let anything out, the retching began. AJ held him over the spit can. Deen's stomach cramped up as Borkat convulsed, groaning in pain. Nothing came out, just saliva. Empty system, nothing left to give. He heaved for five minutes then collapsed in a huddle.

Slowly he opened his eyes and stared at Deen. "Give me another drag." He could barely get the words out. AJ propped him up. Kala lit the flame. Deen passed him a burning cigarette. Last one lucky. Borkat chased once and passed out again.

The boys took a hit of the remaining smack. After about ten minutes Falani asked them to leave. "You shouldn't stay. It's getting late. I'll take care of him then send him on his way."

* * *

Deen and AJ returned to the basti the next day as usual. They crossed a group of basti boys sitting in front of the mosque, staring at them with disgust. They reached Falani's shack and found Borkat lying in his own vomit. He wasn't breathing. Deen thought he looked peaceful, none of that hungry dissatisfied look of a smackie. Now he seemed content.

Falani came out. "We did all we could bhaiya, he was in bad shape, couldn't take smack in properly. Shagor bhai came by at night and threw him out again. He's been lying there since. Kala tried to wake him up to feed him. He couldn't get up."

"So ends another smackie," said AJ with sincere grief.

"I found him in the morning," Falani continued. "He was already dead. I didn't know what to do so I left him there. The neighbourhood boys came by earlier, they said I have to bury him, I can't leave him lying here. They're really upset too. What am I supposed to do?"

Poor Falani, caught in the web. Deen's heart broke. Two deaths in one week. Smackie Fate. He'd probably end up like unloved basti Borkat. Alone and pathetic, with no one to bury his bones.

* * *

Deen got off AJ's bike at the tea stall. He lit a cigarette and noticed a Range Rover parked on the other side of the road.

"Is that Parvez's car?" Deen asked.

AJ peered over, "Ya maybe."

"What do you think it's doing there?"

"I dunno."

"Do you think he's come to score from Musa?"

"I dunno."

"Dost, come with me, let's check it out," said Deen. Had Parvez broken his promise? Had he come to chase? Was he sinking into the black sea? Deen felt responsible for his friend. Parvez looked up to him, followed in all his interests: music, soccer, and now drugs? This was all his fault.

AJ scowled. "We aren't going in there, not after what Shagor did, so forget about it. Let Parvez live his life."

In her shack, Falani and her girls were gathered around a game of Ludo. Majid watched, drunk. Falani greeted the boys with a stained smile and sent her girls to the inner room to play.

"There's going to be a drug bust in this basti," Majid slurred.

"How do you know?" asked Deen.

"Falani, hook us up with a line?" said AJ, ignoring the drunk. "Where's Kala?"

"I don't know bhaiya, he hasn't been here in a few days, not since Borkat died," said Falani.

"Maybe he's gone home," suggested Deen.

"Maybe," sighed Falani. "He's been saying he wants to quit. Maybe he has . . . " Her voice trailed in hope.

"Our basti is screwed," said Majid. "Sergeant Allaudin Akbar is onto us. The worst of the crackdown will fall on the ped-dlers."

Deen looked at Falani. "What are you going to do?"

"I'll be fine," she replied. "What can I do? If I stop selling, we'll have nothing to eat. I'll have to take Runa out of school. How will we survive?"

"Falani will be arrested," warned Majid. "We are all at risk till we kill that sergeant!"

"Ya Majid, you kill him," said AJ laughing. "Do us all a favour. Kill the sergeant who's after this basti and who told you so because he loves you."

"They won't arrest me," said Falani bravely.

Deen could see her face had shrunk. She pretended Majid's prophecy didn't bother her. Doe eyed Falani. She had helped him through many hard times. He felt a stab in his heart. She looked so hopeless. "I'll do it," he said, suddenly.

"Do what?" asked Falani.

"I'll kill the sergeant."

"What?" said AJ.

"I'll kill the sergeant," Deen repeated slowly.

"I can get you a gun," urged Majid.

"I can't find *my* gun," accused AJ. "How are you getting a gun?"

"From the guy I buy smack from," replied Majid indignantly.

"Ya, ok," continued Deen. "Give me the gun."

"It'll be easy for you. You can walk right into the sergeant's office. They won't stop you, you look like a gentleman." Majid was excited. "I'd do it myself, but I can't get close to him."

"Are you guys even remotely serious?" asked AJ. "This is ridiculous. I've never heard of a more hair-brained idea. Deen, you aren't going to shoot a fucking sergeant."

"Yes I am," said Deen, brimming with regrets. He could not do anything right. He could not keep his friend away from junk, he could not keep his lover happy, he could not quit smack. He would save Falani, even if it was the last thing he ever did.

✦ FIFTEEN ✦

Deen lay on his floor staring at the ceiling fan rotating slowly, creaking with each cycle. Today he would do it. He would quit once and for all. Quit and be free! The last two deaths had shaken him up. His garbage can was by his side. The urges had started already. His arms were itchy and his legs were numb. He dreaded the oncoming withdrawals and he was ready with a stash of minor drugs to help him survive the pain.

He had tried to detox in the past, in Virginia, when he had gone to visit his uncle. He had boarded the plane with a lump of sugar on a foil neatly folded and stuffed into the lining of his cigarette pack, his pipe hidden in a hollowed out cigarette. Avoiding smoke detectors was a tricky manoeuvre, but he tried it, three hours into the flight, in the air above Afghanistan. In the airplane bathroom, he lit up the brown sugar and inhaled, lit his cigarette and inhaled, cut off the burning tip of his cigarette, dropped it into the toilet seat, then, relaxed for a moment, sprayed his deodorant and exhaled one smoky, de-odorized puff, into the flush of the toilet. He only had enough sugar for one chase. When the plane stopped in London, he was already sniffling. He couldn't sit still. By the time the plane took off over the Atlantic, he was turquing hardcore.

He tried to sip a glass of whiskey, but vomited it out, to the horror of the passengers sitting next to him.

He reached Virginia in a state of complete disintegration. His uncle arrived at the airport to find him sprawled out on the sidewalk, puking. He spent the next three days in his uncle's guestroom. He didn't leave the room even once. Excruciating pain, uncontrollable shakes, gut-wrenching retching all week long. Unable to eat, unable to sit, unable to breathe at times. Sweating then shivering, complete imbalance. Lying in bed with a blanket around his head, trying to fight off the urges, the psychologically demented, mind altering, obsessive need that howled inside his brain. The detox worked though. He was clean for three months, but then he returned to his life in Bangladesh.

His pathetic, waste of space life. He needed to do more. Make a difference. Reach out. Contribute. That's what his father had wanted. He needed to take care of his mother. She was so alone.

AJ would probably call soon, it was high time for them to chase. Deen locked his door and turned his phone off, determined to block out temptation, but how long could he resist? Even if he stopped for the day, or the next three days, the moment he left his room, he'd walk back into his life. He'd see the road to Tongi. He'd see the emptiness around him. He'd see AJ.

Damn AJ, lousy bastard. He could avoid AJ for a while, but what would he do instead? He couldn't imagine life without smack. Watch TV? Read books? Play ping pong with Parvez? If Parvez was still clean which he probably wasn't, since Deen had let him down.

He had let everyone down. He was a failure. Failed friend,

failed lover, failed son. He was a pathetic junky moth spiral-
ling in towards doom. He would die alone, like an unloved
basti boy, with no one to bury his bones.

Deen admonished himself for wallowing. He needed to
stay positive. He tried to regain composure by meditating.
Om. . . He shut his eyes and slowed his breath. With each
exhale he tried to hold off from oxygen for longer, as if he
were under water. Soon he wasn't sure if he was breathing at
all because his chest wasn't moving, and then he thought of
Chinx, wrapped in white cloth, with no chest moving.
Dammit. Why did his thoughts always drag him to the low-
est valleys of his past? Or was it that he had no good memories to be dragged to?

Deen lit a cigarette. This time things would be different.
He would complete the detox and then leave Bangladesh for
good. Go to America with Maria. Get a job. Live a clean life.
Maybe a few beers in the evenings, with the band. Be a normal guy. Normal appetite for meals. No mouth sores. No
nausea. Invigorated taste buds ready to savour delicious meals.
Lots of juicy steaks. Mind blowing sex with Maria. No
smacked-down sex drive. Walks in parks, candle lit dinners
and more sex. No fights, no disappearing, no secrets.

Deen felt guilty that Maria knew nothing about his addiction. He wanted to tell her, to unburden himself, but she was
too fragile. Perhaps she didn't want to know.

M-AA-R-I-A. Maaaaaaaaria! She made it all worthwhile.
She made it sunny at night. He needed her to help him over-
come the withdrawals. She was his shelter from the storm.
She was his lighthouse. With her by his side, he could reach
the shore.

Deen felt weak. He couldn't do it. He wouldn't be able to

hold out against the pull of *H*. He couldn't clear it from his mind. He wandered to visions of Falani's shack, of AJ's wild eyes when he had cash for their trips, of Kala pulling the tilli under the panni, the disgusting stench and the feeling in his head the moment he inhaled the fumes, the way his sinus and aches cleared up in the instant, the very instant, that the smack entered his system.

Deen thought about the Neverland drug doctor, but he didn't need help. He could quit on his own. He had done it once before, he could do it again. He just needed to detox himself, then his life would be back in control. He wasn't like Chinx or Borkat. They had real problems. He was just head fucked. He just needed to stop chasing for a week to clear his mind. Then he'd sort out his life. He'd play football again. Score a few goals. Get high on field ego. Buy a guitar. Jam with friends. Write a couple of perfect songs. Make music all night long.

Be ALIVE!
Dancing!
Singing!
Loving!
Living!

Not half dead. Not zombied out. Not weak and desperate, too exhausted to survive. He could quit as soon as he was ready. Was he ready?

The sound of a distant train drifted in through Deen's window and yanked at his heart. The tracks were only two streets away and he could hear the northbound train when the wind was right.

Dhug-dhoog, dhug-dhoog, dhug-dhoog.

The rhythm matched his heartbeat. It lulled him back to memories of his childhood, when he spent hours by the tracks watching the blue and yellow compartments pass by, with people from all over Bangladesh hanging out of the cabins, clinging to the doors, sitting on the rooftops, silhouetted by the sky. He was fascinated back then by the multitudes of people cramped together despite the diversity of their thoughts or experiences, travelling, each with a different purpose, running away from something, or running to something, in search of something, somewhere else.

He had dreamt of running away too, to explore distant countries, to taste foreign cultures, to discover women of all races, to feed his insatiable curiosity, to travel like Ibne Battuta or Uncle Oswald, to write and make music and find deeper meanings. Those dreams had dissolved into a muddy sequence of other smaller dreams, shrunken dreams to suit his collapsing ambitions. The dream to run away to Afghanistan in search of the source, to run away to a remote village to become an undisturbed khor, to run away to Tongi to Falani's shack. Deen longed to be in the train now, running away from the impending withdrawals.

Deen laid his stash out, a bottle of cat, two inoctane pills, some weed and a little whiskey. Temptation to smoke the joint beckoned, but he had to ration his supplies. Soon the pain would be unbearable, then he would need to dip into the stash sparingly, to make it last him through the journey down to Hades.

Last dance with Mary Jane. One more time to kill the pain. I feel summer creepin' in and I'm tired of this town again. He hummed to distract himself. Why couldn't he be a normal guy? Why had his father died? Why had he been summoned by smack? Why had everything gone wrong? Was this his kopal? His kismet? Destiny? Was he living out life as it had been ordained for him? Was this his path? God's will?

God, he thought. *Please. Please help me. Help me find myself. Help me recover. God!* Deen prayed with all his might. *God, hear me! God, give me redemption! God, free me from the scorpions in my mind: the unstoppable urges, the agonizing regrets, the guilt on my shoulders, the precious time wasted. Forgive me, if you are punishing me. Remember me, if you have forsaken me. If you are testing me, I'm failing, God, save me!*

Ya right. Pleading in vain. As if God would hear him now, after he had ignored Him for a lifetime. *Fuck off, my son.* Deen mused in a thunderous voice. *Fuck off.*

Deen's thoughts were interrupted by a knock. He pushed his stash under the bed and unlocked the door. Maria stormed in, white shirt, thick kajol on her angry eyes, hair tied up in a bun.

"I called AJ to find out where you live. Your phone's off. Are you trying to avoid me?" she charged. Her eyes were wild with insomnia, her breath heavy with whiskey.

Deen swallowed hard, *why's she here?*

"What am I doing here?" said Maria indignantly. "I could be with kings. Do you know the men who are interested in me? Good backgrounds, rich, handsome. They are rare to come by, but I've got a few to choose from. They call me back when I call, Deen. Every time I go to parties, they're eyeing me, but you wouldn't know. I'm a fool, stuck in a relationship with a guy who doesn't even care if I'm dead or alive."

"I do care," said Deen softly.

"Deen!" Maria threw herself into his arms. He held her close, breathing in the smell of her citrus hair, feeling her warmth in his embrace. "I thought you would have called." She looked up with glossy eyes. "It's been ten days since the concert. You disappeared. What did I do to deserve this?"

Had it been ten days? Deen felt lonely. He wanted her to understand him, but then he'd have to tell her about everything: Borkat, Chinx, the detox. He loved her, he couldn't disappoint her with the truth. She was too vulnerable, she might have another breakdown. What if he quit? Then he didn't need to tell her, it would all be in the past. What if he couldn't quit? Deen couldn't bring himself to admit his addiction and his defeat in one deflating moment so he downplayed the situation. "What do you mean? I was right here."

"Deen, I needed you. I'm so depressed. I want to kill myself. I have visions of hanging myself from the fan with my orna." She buried her face into his chest. "Deen, you're all I've got!"

Deen gently kissed her tear soaked eyelids, repeatedly whispering that he loved her. Maria was the most precious element in his life. He tried to stifle his sniffling. His head cold had begun.

"I didn't get into the journalism programme," said Maria.

"Their loss, you can apply elsewhere." He tried to draw his attention away from the urges creeping into his conscience. *Focus,* he told himself, and lit a cigarette.

"I didn't apply," she said. "My dreams are ruined. It doesn't matter, I don't want to live anymore, I need euthanasia. It's not the weight of our fears that keep our ideas from growing wings and soaring in the sky, it's concrete reality hitting us like a wall."

Deen touched the side of her cheek, lightly dragging his

fingers over her lips. His heart caved in. Why did she have to look at him so helplessly as if he were her only flicker of hope? He couldn't save her from her demons. He wished he were a stronger man. He spewed banal consolations, unsure of what else to offer. "From our lows we learn to appreciate our highs."

"It's all downhill now. I've never felt this undone. I don't know what's wrong with me."

"You have to enjoy the little things." His words sounded empty. What little things? He watched tears roll down the slopes of her cheeks.

"I drank again last night. I can't stop myself anymore."

He knew she'd been drinking. Probably all night. He took her hand in his and squeezed it.

"I feel so alone," she sobbed. "Disconnected. And it's not just my life I hate. Everyone seems pathetic. No one is happy. No one's found deeper bliss or any *reason* for living. People like to dwell in their shitty little lives out of *habit*. Even you, Deen, your life is a waste of time."

Deen wanted to caress her hair but it was tied up tight in a damn bun. He hated how she became when she was in these moods. Vicious in her despair. Casually shredding him apart on the side as she destroyed herself. *Hell hath no fury like a woman scorned*, though he doubted anyone had ever scorned her. She was too beautiful, too dangerous, hot chilli pepper temper. Her fury was born of self-scorn, erupting like a volcano from within the peaks of her own insecurities. Her mind was exploding with negative thoughts and she was chemically imbalanced, depressed as hell, maybe bipolar. "Maria, lighten up." *Take it easy, take it easy. Don't let the sound of your own wheels drive you crazy.*

"I can't lighten up, my life is shit!" she snapped. "Your problem is that you're too chilled out." She paced Deen's room for a minute. Finally she smiled and said, "There's a party. That first-year you hang out with, Parvez, he's throwing it. At an apartment in Uttara. Let's go?"

Deen's stomach growled and the dream jealousy reawakened in his gut. Why did Maria want to go to Parvez's party? To meet eligible men? What would he do there, watch? He had no desire to go to a party. All he wanted to do was go to the basti, but he wouldn't go there either. He wouldn't go anywhere, because he was quitting. Forever. He would not submit to his urges. Deen mumbled, "I have to stay home."

"What? You don't want to spend time with me?" Maria burst into a fit of sobs. "I'm sorry. I don't mean to cry. I'm having a bad day," she whispered, choking on her tears.

Deen pulled her into his arms. He admonished himself for feeling jealous unfairly. Maria had done nothing to deserve his mistrust. He suddenly wanted to comfort her, to give her the love she craved, to take her love and fill the potholes in his heart, to distract himself from the stray thoughts that were piss-sniffing their way back to smack. He wanted to go to the party, Maria needed him. There'd be booze, he could drown out the aches in his body, it would help him detox. Tongi wasn't too far from Uttara. He could make a quick trip to the basti to ease the withdrawals. *If you got bad news, you wanna kick them blues – cocaine. When your day is done and you wanna run – cocaine.*

Deen shook his head to dislodge the devil's grip. His urges were playing mind games. "I can't go," he said. "There are important things I need to sort out."

"What important things?" Maria asked. "Please tell me. What is so important?"

"I can't talk about it," he replied. His arms were itchy. He desperately needed to scratch.

"Ya, Deen. You have important things to do, like watch the flowers in your garden grow, like count the cigarettes in your ash tray, like have gay sex with your lover, AJ. I'm on the verge of a breakdown and you can't come out for the night to be with me? Forget it, Deen, you've made it pretty damn clear that this is over. I'll find myself a real boyfriend tonight." Maria stormed out.

Deen watched Maria's hips as she left. They swung from side to side accentuating her shapely ass. He missed her immediately. He hadn't meant to fight, but how could he tell her the truth now? He had come too far with the lies. Deen wondered if he had lost her this time. Would she really find herself a boyfriend? He needed to go to the party just to keep the slutty men at bay. He saw the way they looked at her, those hungry bastards. He wanted to rip off their balls and stuff them in their mouths and pour kerosene on their sweaty faces and strike a match.

His rage surprised him. He wondered if the heroin was to blame. It wasn't just the smack though. It was Maria pushing him into the deep end when he was already low. His urges were worse now and it was her fault. She had driven him to this state. All she wanted to do was fuck better men. Fuck fucking kings! That's why he needed his only solace, her Highness. Deen groaned. His stomach cramped. Urges were conquering his will power. He had to stop himself. He had to protect his sobriety. He couldn't leave the room in the middle of his detox, even if it cost him Maria.

Redemption comes at a cost, he reasoned with himself. You have to want it bad enough. Bad enough to fight off the parasites inside your veins that possess you and make you need heroin, just heroin, an obsessive need that claws at your guts and the inside of your skull and leers at you and lures you in like a pied piper in the storm of your life and all you can do is tie yourself to your bedpost to keep from throwing yourself in front of a train and still you are alone with that damn boa constrictor around your intestines, alone with no one else to carry your cross, and you can't give up though your mind is twisted and negativity grips your ankles and drags you into a sunless world inside your head and you sit on your bed contemplating the value of your life and there's nothing there to account for it, so you wonder who'd miss you if you disappeared, who'd bury your bones? If only you could, for once, take the reigns, regain positivity, peace and love. Deen tried to hold on to the ephemeral feeling of freedom that flickered through him, but it slipped away. He was too exhausted. Was it because he had forsaken God? Blood rose to his head.

Feeeelings.
Easy slip.
Red eyed.
Madness.
Psychosis.
Empty lot.
Stranded.
Night train.
Where are you trying to go?
GOD and GOB.
Don't take it personally.
Don't fall from grace.
It's so hard to stay afloat.

Downward spiral.

Last one lucky.

There was another knock at the door. Parvez stepped in wearing a dressy blue shirt, his hair gelled up like Deen's. "I was on my way to Uttara, I thought I'd pick you up."

"Thanks, kid, but I'm not going."

"You were going to help me with the music, remember?" said Parvez. "It's the first party I'm throwing. It'd mean a lot to me if you came. There'll be lots of booze."

"I can't. Not today." Deen lit a cigarette.

"Nina said she'll try to come."

"Nina?"

"Her parents are ultra conservative and strict but she'll sneak out tonight. She's sleeping over at Maria's. Maria will be at the party, too. Come on, you should come."

"Who else is going to be there?" said Deen. The jealousy in his gut was still raw.

"Tons of people. Bhaiya, I really like Nina. There's something about her. I think she's beautiful, you know, like a beautiful person inside. She cares about things."

Deen nodded. His arms were suddenly unbearably itchy.

"I don't know if she likes me though. I get mixed signals. She may be testing my devotion or something. Maybe she doesn't know what she wants." Parvez smiled. "Tonight I'll make her change her mind. Hey, bhaiya, you're sweating. Turn on your AC. It's hot outside. I bought thirty bottles of alcohol for tonight, to keep the guests hydrated!"

"Thirty?" Deen tried to sound casual. *Shit.* He was sweating profusely. He switched on his AC.

"Ya, four bottles of whiskey, four bottles of tequila, four

bottles of vodka, two are Sky, my dad brought them, ooof! Four bottles of Bacardi, four bottles of gin, and ten bottles of wine. All red."

"I like red," mumbled Deen, scratching his arms vigorously. *Red, red wine, makes me forget.*

"I think the boys are bringing some yabba too," Parvez added.

Deen's stomach cramped up again. "Yabba?" Sirens blared in his head. Parvez had promised to never try smack again, but yabba? Yabba was the devil too.

"Are you shivering now? Turn your AC down low. You turned it up too high, now you're shivering. It's too cold with the AC on really, just turn your fan on."

Deen turned the AC off and turned the fan on and lit another cigarette. His hands were twitching. "Yabba?" he asked, not knowing what to say. He couldn't concentrate on words. He wanted to save Parvez, but his intestines were wrestling within him. He tried to regulate his breathing. Inhale. Exhale. Inhale. Exhale. Inhale. Exhale.

"Oh ya," Parvez laughed, "Just yabba, not smack, if that's what you mean. Smack isn't really my thing. It's too intense."

Deen sensed something suspicious in Parvez's demeanor and defensive tone. A trace of sly spread through his fresh eyes.

"Are you ok?" asked Parvez. "You're seriously shivering."

"Upset stomach." Deen tried with renewed vigour to conceal his shakes. He needed to concentrate on the problem at hand. He needed to save Parvez from the black sea.

"All right, I'm off," said Parvez. "I've got a party to throw."

Deen breathed a sigh of relief and locked his door. He lit a cigarette and tried calling AJ. The phone rang but no one answered. Deen turned off his creaking fan and lay out on his bed with his eyes closed, blowing smoke rings into the emptiness around him. He didn't have the drugs they had given him at the rehab in Calcutta: the paracetamol for the fever, the Butapin for the stomach cramps, the Imotil for the diarrhoea, the morphine for the pain. All he had was a little cat, some inoctane pills, some weed and one shot of whiskey, one measly shot. There'd be booze at the party, to ease the ride down.

A muscle spasm ripped through his body like a claw. Deen writhed in pain. He curled into fetal position, trying to ignore the spasms. He could barely breathe, his nose was stuffed up. He had scratched the skin right off his arms. He lunged over his garbage can and began retching, rattling his entire body. Nothing came out. He had not eaten all day, there was nothing for his body to reject. He pulled out his stash and began preparing a cocktail of drugs for himself. He hoped he would be able to keep it in, otherwise he was doomed.

* * *

Unable to make sense of the chaos in his room, Deen stumbled onto his bed. His bookshelves morphed into unrecognizable shapes. His chair was a demon reaching out to tear off his limbs. He sensed hidden cameras, spyware planted to expose him. He forced his eyes shut, but then his head became a receiver for radio signals tapping into CIA messages, satellite broadcasts, cop walkie-talkies. He could hear their plans to reveal his secret, to arrest him and his dealer, to destroy the basti and burn all the sugar in Bangladesh.

Dhoom! He heard a crashing sound. He looked around but nothing outside him was disturbed. *Dhoom!* As if a bomb had exploded fifty metres away. He tried to hum to remind himself of what real sounds sound like. His voice quivered and emerged as a broken moan. He clutched his head in his hands, to squeeze in his temples and silence his brain.

He saw raving lunatics breaking in through his window. He panicked. What if they got in? He grabbed the garbage can. He wished he had something sturdier to beat them down with, but the can would have to do. He flung open the window. The wind lashed against his face. There was no one there. Of course, there was no one there. He put the can down and cursed himself. *Get a grip. This too shall pass.* He wondered how long it had been. He had no reign over his thoughts. He was falling into the abyss of insanity. Maddening madness.

His body shook uncontrollably. His heart pounded too fast. He slowed his breathing, then found himself gasping for air. His body no longer ran on autopilot. He had to concentrate to breathe. He had to concentrate to blink. He lay on his bed, focused on staying alive. He was heading towards a cardiac arrest. He wished it would happen quickly and be over with. He heard Maria call him. *Where are you?* he replied.

"Deen, it's not going to work out between us. You're a junky." She erupted into a cackle of laughter. Junky. Junky. Junky. The word echoed in his ears and flashed through his brain like comic book bubbles. BOOM. BANG. JUNKY! He tried to think of something else, but he couldn't change the channel. He was stuck on channel JUNKY. The voices became a softer, monotonous chant. Junky. Junky. Junky. The word collapsed into mispronunciations and gibberish. Occasionally he heard words he understood, but they made no sense in the midst of the garble. It was as if he were in a foreign country.

Deen's mother entered the room with a lady. "She's a counsellor," she explained. "She's going to help you." Deen eyed her with suspicion. She spoke slowly as if to a child, but he wasn't listening, distracted by the scarf around her neck. It was a red scarf with polka dots. Suddenly she screamed. She was covered in blood. Someone had hacked through her neck. Her head was almost completely severed, hanging onto her body by a few veins. Her spinal cord was splintered. She fell to the floor. Flies settled on the congealed blood around her neck. Deen woke up to find flies buzzing around him. He was covered in his own vomit.

AJ walked into the room. "What's wrong, dost?"

Deen was relieved. *Dosto, I'm totally screwed. Help me!*

"What happened?" AJ asked, concerned, inching closer.

I got some pills from a guy near here. Maybe they were laced. Deen looked at AJ and slow, sickening realization passed through him. It wasn't AJ. It was somebody else. Somebody dressed to look like AJ.

Who are you? Deen demanded.

I'm AJ, man. AJ! AJ! AJ! The man began to decay, his face melted into gangrene, his arms wilted at his sides. Deen was frantic. *It's in my head. It's only in my head. This too shall pass.*

The decomposing impostor reached out to choke him, grabbing his neck. Deen tried to ignore him, concentrating on staying calm. The bony fingers jabbed into his skin. He couldn't breathe. He was being choked by his imagination. Unable to bear it any longer, he grabbed the impostor's neck and pushed him off. His flesh was wet, full of pus and boils. Deen kicked him in the chest and felt his body crush under the weight of his shoes. The guy dragged himself out of Deen's room. Deen didn't try to stop him. *Let him go, he won't make it too far. No, no, no. He doesn't exist, that wasn't real. This too shall pass. God give me strength!*

A train passed in the distance and Deen was gripped by the urge to throw himself in front of it, to end the nightmare, once and for all, but he couldn't lift himself up off the ground. His head was spinning. His life flashed before his eyes, like snapshots on a disposable camera. Snap. He saw his first chase and the retching that followed. Snap. He saw strawberry and cream candies in his hand. Snap. He saw his mother weeping as she begged him to give up drugs. Snap. He saw the lumpy mattress at the rehab in Calcutta. Snap. He saw the sly in Parvez's fresh eyes. Snap. He saw Maria, beautiful and seductive, engrossed in small talk with a university kid. Snap. He saw Borkat lying on the ground, dead. Snap. He saw a syringe hanging from Rahul's arm. Snap. He saw Chinx's body wrapped in a white sheet. Snap. He saw a garland of white flowers. Snap. He saw smoke snap rising from a foil. Snap. He saw smack snap burning. Snap. He saw cops snap and cop cars. Snap. Snap. He saw blood. Snap. Snap. He saw his own feeble hands snap trying to lift himself snap off the ground snap and the puddle of vomit snap that he lay in. Snap. Snap. Snap. Snap.

✦ SIXTEEN ✦

Deen and AJ arrived at the basti as usual the next afternoon. They passed a group of children playing with marbles, a wrinkled woman hunched over a water pump, heaps of plastic bottles, piles of burning trash and faded clothes hanging out to dry. Deen wondered if he was ever going to break out of the cycle.

He noticed a little boy, bony like the rest of them, torn shorts, sun-kissed red hair, scratch marks on his legs. He was kicking around a deflated football, beaming a toothy grin. Twinkle in his eye. Oblivious to the cruelties awaiting him: the suffering that was his birthright, the basic needs denied, the dignities trampled upon. Friendless, penniless, hopeless, still smiling. Deen watched in awe: the innate joy in a child's heart triumphant over all else.

"The basti's quiet today. Where is everyone?" said Deen.

"At some goddam religious festival probably," replied AJ.

"Do you think there'll be a crackdown on Falani?" Deen asked.

"No. It was a load of shit."

Deen knew AJ was right. Majid couldn't be trusted. "Have you got cash?"

"Don't worry, man," said AJ. "I'll go to Javed bhai straight from here. He'll buy the diamond. It's cool."

The boys stepped into Falani's shack and stopped in their tracks. The smell of fresh blood permeated the room. What Deen saw next stabbed his heart and stayed imprinted in his mind until his dying day. Kala was sitting on the floor chasing smack with the stubs of his arms. His arms were bandaged and just below the elbows, his hands were gone. He clutched a pipe with his two bandaged stubs. Falani held the foil to help him chase.

His face was haggard, dark circles under his crestfallen eyes. "I must look ghastly," he said finally, finishing his chase. Deen held a lit cigarette up to his lips. Kala took in a deep breath then let out the smoke.

"What happened?" AJ helped Kala put the pipe down.

"I couldn't do it," Kala moaned.

"Do what?"

"I tried to detox," he said. "But I couldn't distract myself. All I wanted to do was chase. Withdrawals like I've never had before. I got really drunk. I kept cursing my hands for feeding me smack and killing me, killing me, killing me, and I thought, damn these hands. I was mad in my head, mad for smack, mad in pain, and drunk too, and I was turquing, and I thought, damn these hands, I'll get rid of them! I put my hands on the train tracks and I said, *take these hands, God, but let me be free!* I was in a bad state, bhai, a really bad state."

Deen was stunned. Sad, desperate Kala, chopping off his hands to save his life. Smackie Fate. The possibilities are infinite and most of them are ugly.

"It didn't hurt much. I had gone mad. I felt the rush of wind as the train flew past me." Kala's eyes glazed over. "But the saddest thing of all? I couldn't stop chasing. I spent two days in the hospital. My mother borrowed money from her brothers to pay for the surgery. Then I went back to her place. She had to feed me, clean me, everything. She's old, you know. She has Siraj to look after too. And I did this to her. What sort of a man am I? I make my mother suffer."

Deen watched flies gather on Kala's bloody bandages.

"The doctor said I should stay in the hospital," Kala continued, "But we couldn't afford it. Early discharge. I have to go back every day to get fresh bandages. I'm still bleeding. I used to sell blood at the hospital. One bag each month, I couldn't sell more, I didn't have enough. They won't buy from me again. This time, I had to *buy* blood, three bags. They knew me, but they wouldn't give me a discount. I'm in such deep debt, I don't know what I'll do. I should have thrown my body in front of the train, not my hands!" Kala sobbed. "And all along, bhai, I felt like I was dying. Not from pain, shame, guilt or regret, but from the urges! All I could think about was smack." Kala wiped the tears from his eyes with his bandaged stub, leaving a trace of blood on his cheek. "Here I am now, my hands lost forever, useless as a cripple, can't even chase my own sugar, and I'm still a junky."

AJ patted Kala on his back, "Let me know how much money you need," he said. "I'll help you out."

A panting boy stumbled in, interrupting the conversation. "Raid!" he shouted. "Cops all over the place!"

Falani disappeared into the back room. Deen grabbed the stash in front of Kala and stepped outside. He tucked behind the shack and contemplated throwing the sugar into the river, but decided against it. He was nervous and sweating as he dug a hole next to the krishna chura tree, to hide the stash. *Dig,*

dig, dig, he thought, *dig your grave.* He could hear the foot-
steps of cops approaching. He hurried to bury the stash. He
returned to Falani's doorstep, wiping his dirty hands on his
jeans. Several cops stood by her doorway with rifles in their
hands.

"Go away," yelled one of the cops. "Don't interfere."

"Those are my friends," said Deen, pushing his way back
into the shack. Inside, four cops were shuffling around in search
of drugs while AJ watched on with indignant red eyes.

"I can't find anything, sir!" whined a scrawny cop to the
sergeant by his side. The medals pinned on his green uniform
looked too heavy for his frame.

"What do you mean?" bellowed the sergeant. "Keep searching. I can still smell it!" He glanced at Deen and AJ with agitation, then turned to stare at Falani.

She was sitting on the bench, her hair hidden under the
achol of her sari, doe eyes filled with fear. She had her two
daughters tight in her embrace. The younger one was sobbing. Red dress, two little braids in her hair. The older one
stood biting her lips, doe eyed like her mother.

When the cops were certain their search was complete and
unfruitful, the sergeant ordered them to arrest everyone.

"Even him?" asked the scrawny cop, pointing to Kala.

"No," huffed the sergeant. "Leave him there. Did they chop
off your hands for stealing?" he jeered at Kala.

"What about her?" The scrawny cop pointed to Falani.

"Arrest her," shouted the sergeant. The scrawny cop hurried
happily towards Falani.

"Amma!" wailed the two girls. Falani tried to calm them.

"Leave her alone." Deen stepped in between the cop and
Falani.

The sergeant puffed his chest out. "She is under arrest," he bellowed into Deen's ears.

"Over my dead body," challenged Deen.

"Arrest them, too," ordered the sergeant, lifting his rifle into the air menacingly.

The cops approached Deen and AJ with frightened reverence. The boys were clearly genteel.

"On what grounds?" demanded AJ.

"You were in the basti during a raid," charged the sergeant.

"We have important friends," warned AJ.

"I'm sure you do," he replied. "Arrest them!"

The cops hesitantly cuffed Deen and AJ.

Falani whispered instruction to her daughters. "Behave and be brave." She sat them down next to Kala who acknowledged his guardianship over them. The scrawny cop placed Falani's dainty hands in cuffs. Her younger daughter whimpered while the older one tried to console her with a hug.

"You'll regret this," AJ warned. "There will be consequences."

* * *

Deen scanned the police station as he waited for Parvez. The green walls were soggy with humidity. The fan circled lethargically, making more noise than wind. Thick cobwebs hung from the ceiling. A frail lady in a ragged sari sat on a bench with a child in her lap. The bored child swatted mosquitoes, while she sat frozen, her harrowed eyes downcast. Beside her sat a hairy man chewing paan noisily. Next to the main room was a small office, the sergeant's office, and next to that, were several smaller rooms, temporary jail cells possibly. Deen shuddered at the thought of spending a night in those dreary holes.

Mintu chacha was a powerful minister. If he showed up and pleaded their case, no one would try to detain them. It was AJ's idea to call him for help. Deen protested, reluctant to drag Parvez into the mess, but a lack of other options pushed his back up against the wall. AJ convinced Detective Khan to allow them one phone call and Deen called Parvez. Parvez and his father arrived in a Range Rover, followed by two cars full of guards. Sergeant Akbar and Detective Khan tensed up at the sight of the minister.

"*Salam'ulaikum*," said Parvez's father. "I am Mintu Fazad." The introduction was unnecessary, they both knew who he was.

"I'm Detective Khan of the CID," began the detective, "And this is my colleague. . ."

"What happened?" interrupted Parvez's father.

"We arrested these boys because they were doing drugs," said Sergeant Akbar.

"No we weren't," said AJ.

Sergeant Akbar shot AJ a stern look.

"What happened?" asked Mintu chacha again.

"We were hanging out with friends in the basti," said Deen.

"*Friends* in the basti?" The minister raised a suspicious eyebrow.

Deen could see he was angry. No boy from a good family would be 'hanging out' in a basti unless he was up to something shady.

Sergeant Akbar cleared his throat. "This is my thana, you can direct your questions to me, sir. My name is Sergeant Allaudin Akbar. We raided the Tongi basti and found these boys there. Are they your sons? I have reasons to believe they are khors."

"What reasons?" challenged AJ, blood shot eyes.

"What sort of khors?" asked Parvez's father.

"Heroin khors!" bellowed the sergeant. "Drugaddicts!"

"He's talking shit," said AJ.

"In the name of Allah, the most merciful, I swear…" began the sergeant.

"Son, what happened?" Mintu chacha looked at Deen.

"Chacha, we were hanging out in the basti. The cops showed up and arrested everyone."

"But why were you there?" he asked.

Parvez interrupted, "Abba, let's get them out of here, we can discuss the details later."

"Release them," the minister ordered. "There's been a mistake. These boys are innocent."

"We need to question them," argued Sergeant Akbar, reluctant to let the boys go.

The minister handed Sergeant Akbar a thick wad of cash to lubricate the negotiation process.

"Were you drinking? I mean, hard drinks?" Parvez's father asked Deen, as the cops unlocked his handcuffs.

"Abba!" interrupted Parvez again. "We can talk later. Let's go."

"The youth these days," he huffed, "are corrupting our values."

"Falani's here," whispered Deen to Parvez, "Can you ask your dad to get her out too?"

"Her? There's a girl with you?" said Parvez's father in disbelief.

"Who?" asked AJ.

"Falani," said Deen again.

"Falani?" piped Sergeant Akbar, picking up on the conversation. "Falani cannot be released. I have to keep her for questioning."

"Questioning for what?" glowered Deen.

"Here." The minister handed the sergeant another wad of cash.

Before the sergeant could decide what to do, Detective Khan ordered the scrawny cop to release Falani. Sergeant Akbar glared at the detective, but he dared not argue with the wad of cash clenched in his fist.

Mintu chacha frowned in disgust when the guards brought out Falani. She was a basti girl, not one of Parvez's friends, not worth the money he had just spent to have her released.

"You ok?" Deen asked Falani as they walked out of the station.

"Thanks for getting me out of this, Deen bhai," she said. Her face was exhausted and tear-stained.

"Did they mess with you?" he asked.

"I'm ok," she said. "The gun," she whispered, pulling him aside. "I don't think they found it when they searched my house."

"What gun?" asked Deen.

"The gun. Majid got it, you know, the gun he promised to get for you. The gun to kill the sergeant with. What should I do?"

Deen looked into Falani's imploring eyes. He could see it hurt her to ask him for help, even after all she had done for him. It broke his heart to see her so helpless. "Take your girls and get out of the basti," he suggested. "Find some other place to stay. I'll meet you at the tea stall, bring the gun. We'll stick to Majid's plan." He was surprised Majid had managed to find a gun. The rest was up to him.

* * *

Falani shuddered as she recalled the past two hours. The cops had touched her everywhere, pushed her out of the car and into the sergeant's office, tugged at her sari, fondled her breasts, squeezed her stomach, caressed her cheeks, patted her butt, pinched her thighs. The sergeant had watched with a satisfied smirk, then he ordered the men to leave his room and locked the door behind them.

She was damned to hell, he shouted, God would never forgive her. He grabbed her by the blouse and pulled her up close to him, his hand cupped her breast. She cried as he slapped her around, cried as he shook her violently, cried as he pulled her against his body. She could smell the garlic in his breath, she could feel the erection in his pants. She felt dirty and frightened. Then suddenly he released her, as if sickened by his own lust, and threw her against the wall. She crumbled onto the floor. He pulled her up again, pulled her hair with one hand, her blouse with the other, and violently unlocked the cuffs on her hands. He vowed to come back for her, to finish her off, *once and for all.*

What would happen to her girls then? Only Deen could help her. *Altruism is as rare as diamonds,* thought Falani. Deen was unlike the other boys. He was a sensitive soul. For her, he was going to kill the sergeant. The thought made her shiver. No one had ever cared for her enough to help her out before.

Falani wondered where she could leave her daughters in the meantime. Majid did not have a place and her other brothers had turned her out of their homes years ago, crushed by their own poverty. She did not know where her husband was. Her father was a two day journey away, in Mymansingh, and he could not afford them either. Maybe they'd be safe at home. Maybe the sergeant would not come back for her. Maybe he was bluffing, his strategy to terrorize her into submission. She knew she was lying to herself, but what options did she have? She laughed at her life. She never thought it would end up like this.

* * *

Sergeant Akbar rubbed his hands together gleefully. His men had found Majid wandering around by the tea stall during the raid. It was the will of Allah, the most merciful, no doubt, why else would the khor have shown up in their path at just the right moment? He was on his way home, when the cops spotted him. He escaped them for a strenuous ten minutes, but after that, the chase ended. He was a weak junky and there were three cops on his trail. Even if he knew the maze of alleys better than any of them, physically he was no match.

Luckily the damn detective didn't know about the arrest. Allah, the most merciful, had strange ways of revealing himself. Today, in the form of the khor's confession, would come the path to justice. A justice that he, Sergeant Allaudin Akbar, would mete out himself. Good-bye, goddess of gloom.

✦ SEVENTEEN ✦

AJ arrived at Sundari's apartment to find her taking an afternoon siesta. He undressed and slipped into bed next to her, spooning her warm body. She smelt freshly showered. She felt buttery smooth. She lifted his spirits in an instant.

"Hi AJ," she whispered drowsily.

He nuzzled into her neck.

"How have you been?" she asked, turning to face him.

He kissed her chin. She tasted like liquorice. Or alcohol. Suddenly AJ was livid. He pushed her away and shouted, "Who did you screw last night, you whore?"

Sundari smiled, all too familiar with his moods. "Don't be silly. You know I didn't screw anybody."

AJ glared at her, then retrieved a pack of cigarettes from the pocket of his jeans. He lit it up and wrapped his tongue in smoke.

"What's wrong, why are you upset?" Sundari sat up to rub his shoulders. "What's on your mind?"

"Nothing," AJ grumbled. He thought about Raj Gopal slouched in his couch like a king. With a ten inch cigar in his mouth. With ten Benzes in his garage. With packets of '10s' littering his bedroom. With ten thousand men at his beck and call. Unfuckable Raj. AJ wondered if he could ever attain such glory. Command an empire like Shah Jahan, not perpetually stuck in petty troubles. His mission to fetch the precious pouch in locker 31A was messed up, someone had stolen his gun. He couldn't keep his insignificant bit of life straight. He was not in control. He had become a puppet, moving to the whims of a ruthless marionette. Even Hasan knew it.

"Tell me what's wrong," coaxed Sundari. "You need to trust me. Stop putting up a wall between us."

AJ grunted and pulled Sundari into a fevered kiss. Was he putting up walls? Afraid of intimacy? Afraid of being vulnerable? Afraid of abandonment? Not really. He had bigger things to worry about. Like where to find some money. AJ tried to focus on the kiss.

Sundari stroked his chest and pulled him close to her. "Things don't have to be like this, AJ. You can quit smack. I can sell my diamonds. We can start fresh."

AJ smiled, wondering what he had done to deserve such affection. "I don't want to leave my life." He just needed a bit of money to solve his problems. He'd figure something out. "Don't sell your diamonds. They look good on your pretty neck. It drives the crowds wild, you like that, don't you?" he sneered.

"Take ownership over your actions, AJ. Stop feeling like a victim. There's more to life."

"Is there? Life's over so soon, who cares really how it passes by?" AJ was in no mood for a lecture.

Sundari dragged her finger over the scar on his cheek. "What about happiness?"

"What about happiness?"

"Happiness. Shanti. Health. Key ingredients, don't you think? Isn't it time to make some choices that might lead you to a better future?" She absent-mindedly touched her stomach.

"Don't nag," AJ growled. What did she know about happiness? Money was the key ingredient. Everything else was flavouring.

Sundari bit her lip to keep it from quivering and immediately AJ regretted his harshness. She was trying to help. He pulled her into his arms and began kissing her again. There were some things she would never understand. Not until she had lived his life and experienced what he had been through.

* * *

Falani fingered the cold gun in her purse. She arrived at the tea stall ten minutes early. It was deserted, as one would expect at 2:50 am. Broken glass, plastic bags, stale food and flies littered the ground. Falani examined the gun. Black shiny metal, wooden butt with a golden bow and arrow engraved on it. It was heavier than she had imagined. And beautiful, in a sinister sort of way. Smooth, like a sculpture, not a weapon, like a piece of art. Majid had borrowed it for this very purpose, but was she ready to hand it over?

The night felt cooler than usual, kal boishakhi storms were approaching. Falani rubbed her palms against her bony shoulders to create some warmth. She wondered if Deen would remember the plan, it had been a crazy day. She thought of the hatred in the sergeant's eyes. Was it hatred? The moon was indecisive behind scattered clouds. She wished they had chosen a different place to meet. Or maybe a different time. She wished she were living a different life.

A soft whistle emerged from the darkness.

"So you've come. I wasn't sure if you would. Maybe we shouldn't go through with it. Deen bhai, how can we kill him? He has a daughter. I saw her photo in his office." Falani's words poured out with a breath of relief.

"Murder is never pretty, Falani. Hell, my conscience will probably explode, but you can rest assured that fat sergeant will come for you and when he gets you, it's going to be ugly."

Falani's doe eyes widened for only a moment before she pulled them tightly shut. The flies incessantly pierced the silence and the night seemed to grow a little wild. After three dark minutes, Falani opened her eyes and smiled. The worry lines above her furrowed eyebrows parted, serenity came about her face. She reclasped her peacock purse and whispered with resolution, "No bhaiya, Allah will protect me. I'm sorry I asked you to do this. Forgive me. I have some sugar for you. You want a hit?"

"You've got too much love for humanity," Deen sighed, and followed her into the basti to ride the night.

* * *

Sergeant Akbar was amused at how quickly Majid had squealed. Selfish rats, don't even stick up for each other. It took only three electric shocks to get Majid to confess for the tape recorder. He was surprised though that the khor really believed he'd be set free if he complied. Why would the sergeant set him free? Once he had the confession, Sergeant Akbar happily threw the khor into the fire where he belonged. When the khor screamed and begged for mercy, Sergeant Akbar felt wise as he said, "Pray to Allah for mercy, lest you burn for all eternity!"

The live wire Sergeant Akbar had pulled into the hidden chamber adjacent to his office was illegal, no doubt, but he could always say it was there for his radio. The live wire left no scars if he was careful to hold it against the sweat under a bushy patch of hair. He would say the vermin had died of natural causes while in captivity. Heart attacks happen to everyone, the most popular ailment of modernity. No one ever questioned him though, nobody missed the basti folk.

Disposing of the body was more of a hassle than a challenge. Sergeant Akbar had his men take the body to the incinerator where Hindus were cremated. Regular practice, pay them 10,000 taka to take care of the whole mess. The only thing that disturbed the sergeant was the repulsive smell of burning flesh. He could not get rid of it no matter how much lemon air freshener he sprayed in the room.

Now Majid was dead. One less drugaddict to worry about. He would wipe them out, one by one, if that's what it took! The sergeant sat down to replay the confession. He dipped a piece of roti into the cold gravy leftover from the curry he had eaten in the afternoon. His oily fingers left a residue on the tape recorder which spread as he tried to wipe it off with the back of his sweaty sleeve. The sergeant called for his tea boy.

"Samad," the sergeant announced to his eager apprentice, "that khor has given me a confession!"

"What con . . . con . . . con-isnession, sir?" asked Samad dutifully.

"The confession I shall use as evidence, ev-i-dence, to bust the entire drug ring in the north Dhaka basti. Isn't it splendid, Samad?" said Sergeant Akbar.

"Very good, sir."

"I will be a hero, Samad, the headlines will splash my name. 'Sergeant Allaudin Akbar rids the streets of vermin!' 'Akbar the brave!' 'Akbar the great!' Once again an Akbar shall receive glory in the battle against evil!" shouted the sergeant.

"Very good, sir!" shouted Samad in equal excitement. He craned his neck to catch a glimpse of the tape recorder the sergeant was flailing above his head like a trophy.

"This hair," said Sergeant Akbar, pulling out a single strand of hair from his balding, patchy scalp. "See how fine it is?"

Samad nodded vigorously.

"This is how fine the line between Right and Wrong is, Samad, the line between Right and Wrong. Someday you will have to make decisions and you will know deep in your heart where the right decisions lie, on which side of the fine line. Choose wisely, Samad," chuckled Sergeant Akbar self-righteously. "Choose wisely and someday you too shall be a hero."

❖ EIGHTEEN ❖

By evening Deen and AJ were in a tired lull from an afternoon of random substance abuse. Deen had convinced AJ to skip smack for the day so instead they had each downed a bottle of cat, snorted sixteen amphetamine tabs and smoked copious amounts of ganja in preparation for an evening of dancing at Parvez's boishakhi booze fest. AJ had swapped his bike for Shagor's Beamer for the day. He and Deen were on their way to Nina's place in Uttara, to pre-party.

"Typical." AJ pulled the car to a reluctant halt at the railway crossing. A sluggish train chugged by. "Can't afford to buy myself a Beamer, can't find an empty road to rev on, can't find Raj's gun, can't find Ronnie. Everything is fucked up."

Dhug-dhoog, dhug-dhoog, dhug-dhoog.

"Did you ever wonder," asked Deen, "What it would be like to jump on a train and go off to a new life? Just go, with nothing of this life on you, and start again fresh, some place far away."

"Some things you can't escape from no matter where you go."

Cynical AJ, thought Deen. He watched the northbound

train move forward into the afternoon, away from him and his life, off into the distance. The lights turned green, but they could not surge forward, stuck in a traffic gridlock.

Deen pushed in a *Joplin* CD and pumped up the volume. *Summertime* wailed on the stereo and Deen wished the Bangla New Year would arrive quickly. The current year was a stale failure and he was eager to move on.

Mutilated beggars, stub man, trafficked children and toothless woman, gathered around the car. Deen felt claustrophobic. He stared out his window, above their heads, at the dilapidated bus next to them. It tilted to one side precariously. The front windscreen was a web of cracked glass held in place with masking tape. A green scooter shoved in between the bus and the Beamer, dangerously close. AJ rolled down his window to yell at the scooter walla. His voice startled a bunch of goats in front of the scooter. They bleated unhappily. Their shepherd boy was a bony, little kid. He patted their noses to calm them down, then resumed his search for cracks in the traffic.

A street vendor holding a dozen live chicken by the feet rapped on AJ's window. A rickshaw ferrying an oily-haired couple squeezed in next to their car. A feather from the flapping chicken floated through the smog and landed on the oily-haired woman's head, but she didn't notice. She was busy sipping the juice out of a coconut with a pink straw. A spindly man struggled to maneuver a two-wheeled cart, piled high with bamboo, in front of them. *No space for people to breathe*, thought Deen. Takes an hour to make a ten minute journey. Even in a Beamer.

Dhaka wasn't always cramped, cluttered and polluted. It was once a magnificent city. Parks, rivers, high-ceiling houses, sidewalks lined with banyan trees. Under the British rule. The exploitive British rule that inferiorized the colonial mind and stole the Kohinoor. And what since then? Rulership had exchanged hands. The poor remained poor, the rich got richer, and GOB let the city go to hell. They could have laid down electricity lines and water pipes, highways leading out to other places, infrastructure for a second city, maybe Kumilla, and then a third, perhaps Mymansingh, instead of piling everything into the little space of Dhaka. Corrupt pigs.

With the rest of Bangladesh neglected, Dhaka became the inevitable cesspit of all the maddening crowds, greedy businessmen, powerful politicians, desperate beggars and the oppressive upper class. Rapid, ill-planned urbanization. Open sewers and bad energy. Multistoried buildings rose from the ashes of once majestic houses, parking lots replaced parks, rivers were strangled down to stinking sewers full of toxic shit. Every inch of the city was overcrowded. All the electricity lines were overextended. Blackouts everyday. Even that, only IF you were privileged. No electricity in the bastis, periphery of the city, who cares? Deen was disgusted with Dhaka's state of disgrace. He longed to feel patriotic but instead he felt betrayed.

An armless beggar knocked at Deen's window and drew him back to reality. Deen did not for a moment feel like he was unfortunate, not in Bangladesh. He was lucky for sure. One of the luckiest sonuvabitches. Still he was angry. Bangladesh could have been so much more if it weren't for greed. Not that he was doing anything about it. At least he wasn't a hypocrite. It wasn't his job to represent the people. He wasn't the one letting the nation down. He just lived his life, minding his own business. And yet he was the one persecuted, on the run, always worried about cops. *Hello, arrest the PM*, he thought.

And what about you, God? he wondered. God, don't you hear their prayers? Where's the love? *Thomar dil ki doya hoi na?*

Bangladesh never had a chance really. What with the English oppressing the Bangla conscience for so many years. What with the Pakistani army wiping out the entire intelligentsia on the eve of Bangladesh's independence: all the doctors, professors and scientists. What with the Americans emitting carbon and fucking the climate, triggering floods and cyclones in Asia. What with the Indian government channelling floodwater south, draining their problems, submerging Bangladesh. What with the Middle East funding thousands of madrassahs where boys were educated to be illiterate sheep with no skills to market in the economic sphere, leaving them desperate and brainwashable. GOB had a tough job going for it, even if it was concerned with the welfare of the country, but it wasn't. Swiss bank accounts to fill before the next elections. Goons to arm. Porsches to purchase.

The traffic cleared up as they reached Airport Road. "Wahoooo!" shouted AJ, flooring the accelerator. "Nothing beats this rush!"

With the speed of the car, Deen's excitement picked up, the lingering drugs in his system reawakening for Round Two. Tonight would be good. Dancing, boozing, smooching.

Suddenly the car screeched as AJ pulled a hard brake, just barely missing a grey cat. It shot them a fierce look with piercing green eyes, then darted away.

AJ heaved a sigh of relief and accelerated again, the speed

picked up, then WHAM! They rammed into a second cat. A black one. The cat hit the car fender with such force, Deen felt the *thud* in his heart. AJ slowed down. Both boys were shocked, the feeling of death reverberating in their souls. Crash ending. Over in an instant. Nothing more.

"Cat chase?" asked AJ. "You think blacky was trying to bite off ol' grey boy's tail?"

"Maybe they were lovers?" replied Deen. *Or mother and child?*

"I didn't see him coming," said AJ remorsefully. "Just what I needed, run into a fucking bad luck black cat."

The boys drove on silently, their hearts heavy with the guilt of the cat death. When they reached Nina's place, AJ got out of the car to check the damage. "Nothing," he remarked. "No blood, no fur, no dents. As if it didn't happen."

* * *

Nina greeted them at the door. "Welcome to my home," she said. "Enjoy, because this may be the one and only time you're here. My parents get back from London tomorrow." Her short hair was slicked down, hip for the night.

"Haven't seen you since the concert," said AJ. "You look good."

"I can't believe I'm finally going to a party!" she said, giving them both a hug. "I hear they're fun." Nina smiled, dimples on her cheeks, and led them into the house.

Lamps lit up the living room. Deen noticed the artwork on the walls. Large canvases done by masters. Shahabuddin captured the power of a tiger's pounce. Fireworks of colour burst from a musician by Ranjit Das. Shakoor depicted the beauty of a woman at peace. Deen was awe-struck.

"Bhaiya! What's up?" Parvez interrupted. "Glad you're coming to this party. We missed you last time."

"How've you been, kid?" he replied. He was glad to see Parvez. The boy was tipsy, but he seemed to be back to his old self. Deen wondered if he had imagined Parvez's Range Rover parked outside the basti a few days back. He was beginning to lose faith in his senses.

"Deen, darling!" Maria rushed up to hug Deen. "Tonight's going to be an unforgettable night, I can just feel it." She had a thick layer of maroon smeared on her lips and an orna draped over her lacy dress.

The doorbell rang and Shagor entered. "I've got a bottle of whiskey," he announced, wide-eyed and wired, high on yabba. It was a Thursday night and he was ready to party.

Deen put Paul Van Dyke on the speakers and poured himself a whiskey on the rocks. He sidled up next to Maria. "My lacy lover, let's move to Manhattan."

Maria laughed. "Ya, let's go next month."

"Next week!" He and Maria drifted into dream revelry.

After several shots of whiskey, Shagor announced he was leaving. He and AJ swapped keys again.

"I'm meeting a girl named Laila for dinner," Shagor said as Deen walked him to the door. "She's hot and she digs me. I'm getting laid tonight!"

Deen returned to the living room and found that the group dynamics had become odd. Maria was pouring drinks for everyone, including herself, stumbling around in her stilettos, drunk already. AJ was flipping through CDs, looking stressed out, probably worried about the gun. Parvez's friends were wasted, laughing like hyenas, watching music videos on mute. Parvez was aggressively flirting with Nina, latched on like a leech, as she tried to socialize with the others. "I've written a song for you," Deen overheard him say to her. Nina grimaced. Deen wondered why Parvez was being annoying, was he drunk? Nina seemed more charmed by AJ.

"I need to pick up keys from my aunt's place a few blocks down," Nina announced. "Can someone give me a ride?"

"I've got my bike," offered AJ.

"I've got my jeep," said Parvez. "I can take you."

"I've never been on a bike," said Nina, smiling at AJ invitingly.

"It's not safe," Parvez insisted, "My jeep's outside, let's go."

Nina reluctantly accepted the offer. "Thanks Parvez."

AJ shrugged.

"We should get going too," said Deen. They had to score some pills from a guy who lived near Nina. "We'll see you all later tonight." He planted a farewell kiss on Maria's maroon lips and headed out with AJ.

* * *

The party was in full swing when Deen and AJ arrived. Strobe lights, turn tables and a dry ice machine filling the room with smoke. Expensive bottles crowded the coffee table. Plastic cups littered the floor. The place was full of familiar faces from university; scantily clad women and men in sleek shirts. Everyone was wasted.

"Finally you're here!" Maria pulled Deen onto the dance floor. "I missed you!" She was drunk and exuberant.

Deen took her face in his palms and juicy smooched her lips. As they danced, Deen scanned the room. The Finance Minister's son, looking like a pimp daddy. The four largest garment factory owners' sons, earning over 500 million USD a year, smoking in a group. A shrimp industrialist's son, shirt buttoned down, oozing arrogance. Three sexy sisters, daughters of the Agriculture Minister, all piss drunk. Hippies, children of architects and zamindars, underachievers and drifters, scattered among the crowd.

Deen pulled Maria in closer. They danced with their bodies pressed together. He could smell the citrus in her hair. The music was not great. The sound beat against the wall in an acoustic atrocity, but Deen was starting to zone it out. Maria looked beautiful and he felt on top of the world.

The room filled with dry ice and Maria cursed the machine. "It makes the room so smoky."

"Gives us privacy." Deen placed his teasing hands on her delicious bottom.

Maria gyrated her hips around his groin.

"Shake it Salome!" said Deen in appreciation.

They danced on and Deen felt warm with love.

"I think Nina's stuck in the bar room," Maria interrupted. "Parvez's cornered her. Hasn't left her side since we arrived. We need to save her."

"Why? Let the man make his moves."

"No," Maria insisted. "She's not into him, Deen. He's being a pest. I'm sure she wants to dance, but not with him! She's too shy to say anything. Could you ask AJ to dance with her? She's not used to parties and Parvez's being a terrible host."

Deen found AJ in the next room smoking a hookah with Rahul, Shagor and a girl. Shagor had his arms all over her. She seemed into him too. She was attractive, with thick lashes and hair down to her waist. She drew her eyes away from Shagor for a moment, to meet Deen, when Shagor introduced her. Rahul began recounting how many shots he had consumed over the past few hours. Deen took in a drag of the hookah. Apple flavour. In the corner of the room he could make out two bodies in a drunken embrace. He wanted to return to Maria.

"Hey AJ," said Deen, pulling him aside. "Can you hang out with Nina for a bit? She needs some cover."

"Why?"

"Parvez's drunk and on her case. It's funny, I thought he'd be more suave."

"Sure," said AJ. "Nina's hot. I dig those dimples."

"Give me a minute to distract him though," suggested Deen.

Deen entered the smoky bar room. The music was less intrusive, but still it drowned out most conversation. Parvez and Nina were sitting at a table, engaged in drunken banter. Deen pulled up a chair next to them and said hello.

"You having fun?" slurred Parvez, excited to see Deen. He was roaringly drunk and reeking of whiskey.

Deen nodded.

"I didn't know parties like this existed in Bangladesh," slurred Nina. Deen was surprised to see she was wasted too. He tried to assess her faint smile, was it discomfort?

"Everything happens in Bangladesh," shouted Parvez. "Behind closed doors."

"Why aren't you guys dancing?" asked Deen.

"She doesn't want to dance," said Parvez.

"Not in the mood," Nina explained. "Will you excuse me, I need to go to the washroom." She jumped at the opportunity to escape. As she walked towards the washroom, she stumbled.

"What's with the DJ?" said Deen quickly, to keep Parvez at the table. "Cheesy techno?"

"Aw, it's Jamsher DJing," replied Parvez.

"Let's go help him choose the next track," suggested Deen.

"That girl," Parvez slurred, "She's playing with my mind."

"She's not into you," said Deen gently. "Maybe you should leave her alone?"

"No bhaiya, you don't know the things she says to me when it's just the two of us. It's like she wants me to chase her. She has low self-esteem or something." Parvez stole a glance at the washroom door, waiting for Nina to return.

"Let's go to the roof," Deen suggested. The fresh air would do Parvez good. Parvez agreed reluctantly, too drunk to argue.

The night was windy. The roof offered a great view of Uttara. Deen handed Parvez a cigarette and lit one himself. "You can't force these things," Deen suggested.

Parvez frowned. "I love her, bhaiya. I've never felt this way before. I think she's my guardian angel. I wish she'd give me a chance. What's a guy got to do?"

"Give it time, let it be." Deen felt like a hypocrite. He knew what it was like to be stuck in an obsession.

"*Let it be, let it be. Let it be, oh, let it be,*" Parvez sang. "I wish I knew how to let it be."

A disapproving cloud expanded in the sky, casting a shadow over the roof. "Let's go back down?" said Deen. "It's going to rain."

"I've got some yabba." Parvez pulled two red pills out of his pocket. "Want one?"

Yabba was hardcore. It annoyed Deen to see the pills in Parvez's hand. "Why do you want to do that tonight?"

"*Y* not?" Parvez winked and handed him a pill. "Let's go!"

The night continued. Deen eased back into a good mood, dancing with Maria. The music was better. The dance floor was crowded. Strangers kissed in the dark. Old flames rekindled. Lovers met for the first time. Destinies were being shaped and reshaped.

Suddenly Parvez stormed onto the dance floor and pulled Nina out of AJ's arms, glaring at her with furious eyes. "What the hell are you doing?" he demanded. Nina tried to pry herself out of his grip. "Why are you dancing with him?"

"Relax, man." AJ pulled Nina out of the lock. "She didn't want to dance with you."

Parvez's furious eyes turned to AJ. He stepped up to AJ and slurred, "AJ you asshole, because you punk around the basti folk, you think you can rule over everybody else? If you touch Nina again, I'll cut you up and feed you to my dogs."

AJ pushed Parvez, almost knocking him over. Parvez drew his fist back to throw a punch, but Shagor caught him from behind and dragged him to the other end of the room. The space around them cleared as people shuffled off the dance floor.

Deen was shocked. He had never seen Parvez utter an unkind word. "Shagor," he said, "Take Parvez for a ride. Calm him down a bit."

Shagor was still holding up Parvez who was so wasted, he could barely stand. "Why don't *you* take this jack ass for a spin?" Shagor tossed Deen his car keys.

Deen was in no state to drive, but Parvez could not stay at the party, especially not if he wanted to pick a fight with AJ. Once AJ's ego was incited, there was no stopping him. "Kid, let's get some fresh air," Deen suggested.

"Ok, whatever, let's go." Parvez fumed. "Tell AJ if I run into him again EVER, I'll kill him." Shagor helped Parvez into the car. Maria followed, getting into the back seat, with her orna wrapped around her body.

Deen backed the car out of parking and noticed in the rear view mirror: two cats, one grey, one black, sitting on the driveway under a single ray of moonlight in the otherwise cloud shadowy night. Fierce green eyes stared straight at him. Cursing him? Bangladeshi folk tales spoke of djinns inhabiting cat bodies. Were they following him? The angel of death in the form of a feline? Deen wondered if it was an omen.

✦ NINETEEN ✦

The wind howled promises of an oncoming storm. Menacing clouds gathered in the sky. Trees bent back and forth violently, threatening to topple onto the road. Deen wasn't thrilled about leaving the party, but the night outside was striking. The boishakh season was beginning and with it, electric storms that could ionize the air and alter the energy frequency of the atmosphere, making everyone high. Storm high. Deen pushed *Riders on the Storm* into the CD player. "There's a different kind of energy during jhors," he said, driving down Airport Road. "A charge in the air. A buzz in your head."

"Jhors remind me of the frailty of man and the power of Mother Nature," said Maria, pulling her orna around her shoulders.

"Overdue rains, might fucking cool the city down a bit," grumbled Parvez. His head rested on the dashboard.

"Kid, why don't you check out the CDs in the glove compartment," said Deen. "Pick out a tune for us."

"You're good with music, bhaiya" said Parvez. "Why don't you choose the tunes and let me drive?"

"You want to drive?" asked Deen.

"Deen, he's really drunk," Maria interrupted.

"I'm fine, Maria," argued Parvez.

"I better drive, it's cool," said Deen.

"I want to drive." Parvez grabbed the wheel. The car jerked. An oncoming truck honked as it swerved to avoid them.

Deen tried to push Parvez away. "Sit down, kid, you're drunk," he shouted.

"Whatever, bhaiya, you're high on H!" screamed Parvez.

"What?" asked Maria.

"Shut up Parvez, let go of the fucking wheel." Deen struggled to pull over. Blood rushed to his head.

Suddenly Parvez let go of the wheel and jumped out onto the street. The car door swung madly as the car raced forward. Parvez hopped the highway divider and hailed down a truck full of pineapples going in the opposite direction. He negotiated with the driver and climbed on.

Deen sped up to the break in the divider, swung a u-turn and accelerated. Maria demanded more information about 'H'. Sirens blared in Deen's head. Shagor's Beamer was fast so he overtook the truck and hailed down the driver who stared blankly, tired and confused.

"Tell me where you want to go, I'll take you there," Deen reasoned with Parvez.

"Meghna ghaat," yelled Parvez, refusing to get out of the truck.

"Meghna ghaat? What the hell for?" Deen pleaded. The docks were over an hour away. "Let's go have tea!"

"Meghna ghaat is the place to be on a stormy night. You can see the fury of the river when the jhor begins!"

The truck started inching forward with Parvez still inside, so Deen grudgingly agreed to make the trip.

When they arrived at the docks, day was awakening. Maria

stepped out of the car and stretched out her arms. Trees rattled in the wind and anchored boats rocked furiously on the choppy water. Pellets of water tore away from the river and hit Deen's face like bullets.

"Sorry I was such an ass at the party," said Parvez, sobering up.

"No worries," said Deen. "Bad nights happen to the best of us."

Parvez pointed to a trawler with a Bangladeshi flag. It was tied to the ghaat a few metres away from their car. He made his way, against the wind, and climbed on board. They followed him on. Deen helped Maria climb up to the top deck. Parvez wandered off to explore the trawler. Despite the wind, Deen managed to light a cigarette. Maria melted into his arms to watch the sunrise. Deen was filled with tranquility. The smell of salt water reminded him of childhood.

There was a shuffle along the docks as fishermen began to arrive. Deen pondered the life of a fisherman, out on the raging river all day, at the mercy of the elements and the inconsistent whims of jhors. Jhors had many moods, all of them majestic and violent. They arrived without warning and could as easily decapitate a man or devastate a village. Heavy rains that blinded the world or electric storms that lit up the night. The lightening was sometimes a quick flash of black and white, other times it left a lingering purple haze. Deen wondered which one was on its way now. He pushed a strand of curls behind Maria's ear and sang softly, "*Love comes outta nowhere like a hurricane, and it feels like rain.*"

Parvez pulled off his shirt, preparing to jump off the stern of the trawler A neighbouring fisherman discouraged him. "No, bhaiya, don't swim. The water's unpredictable."

Deen stood up alarmed. "Hey kid, it's not safe!" he shouted out.

"Don't worry!" Parvez dived in. Expert dive, hands, nose, body, legs. No splash. Deen watched his friend disappear underwater. In an instant he resurfaced with a grin. "The water's warm."

"Bhaiya, get out!" Another fisherman shouted to Parvez. Several of them gathered by the banks.

Maria was disturbed. "Is he still drunk?" she asked.

Parvez circled the trawler. "I'm ok, bhaiya," he reassured Deen. "You two should join me! The water feels great."

Deen relaxed. He took Maria in his arms again, then heard Parvez scream. A desperate, choking child scream. Deen whipped around and caught the look of terror in Parvez's eyes, his arms flailing, just as he was sucked into a whirlpool.

Deen was stunned. Maria shrieked. The fishermen freaked out. Everyone scrambled to catch a glimpse of Parvez resurfacing. Deen pulled off his shirt to jump in after Parvez. Maria grabbed him by the waist. "You can't! You can't go in there!" she cried.

Two fishermen jumped onto the trawler to hold Deen down. "Let me go!" he screamed frantically.

The fishermen shouted at him, "The current is too strong!" Born and raised on the river, they knew the danger of swimming on the eve of a storm. Even the bravest among them would not risk it.

Several fishermen set out on small noukas to search for Parvez. Deen went numb. Maria sobbed. They spent an hour craning their necks on the deck of the trawler, then joined the fishermen on an unsteady nouka closer to the whirlpool. There was no sign of Parvez anywhere.

The wind subsided and the heat of the day returned. The promised storm never arrived. Deen drove Maria home and then, unable to get hold of AJ, returned to the ghaat with Rahul. They continued to search until noon, when Mintu chacha arrived with ten of his men. He found Deen there, red eyed, still drunk, and went into shock. He called the cops to arrest Deen, accusing him of kidnapping his son.

The cops found a red pill in Deen's pocket and agreed he must be guilty. Rahul was arrested too, but his father pulled some strings and had him released. To protect Maria from the ugly interrogation, Deen did not mention her in his statement. By evening, Parvez's friends heard the news and rushed to the white mansion to clear Deen's name. Parvez's devastated father needed someone to blame and his mind meandered into twisted conspiracy theories where Parvez's friends were agents too, in collusion with Deen.

* * *

Deen leaned against the lumpy green wall of his makeshift jail cell and felt like retching. He had let Parvez die. Self-loathing spread through his bones like poison. Cramps ripped through his stomach and legs. He remembered a time when they were kids. He had climbed the guava tree in Parvez's front yard. Parvez's eyes were full of awe as Deen rose higher and higher into the branches of green. When he finally came down with an unusually large guava, Parvez begged him to teach him how to climb. Though barely five years old, he was already more interested in the climb than the fruit.

He soon outdid Deen, scaling not only trees, but also buildings, walls and everything else possible. Parvez took his passions to the extreme. It was the same with soccer. No other player could match him. He ruled over the field, but in the kindest way, setting his friends up with goals. He was the best boy among them. Now he was gone. Deen was struck by the injustice of Fate. *God,* he thought, *why couldn't you take me instead?*

Maria arrived late in the afternoon, irate and crying. Parvez was still missing and a truck full of cops had arrested Nina, accusing her of collaborating with Deen in what the cops, instigated by Parvez's father, were beginning to suspect was a murder. Deen's car was traced back to Shagor who was subsequently arrested as an accomplice, but his father called a general in the army and had him and Nina released.

"Nina's a mess," Maria said, choking on sobs. "I feel horrible too. Parvez's dead, and funny enough, my father called me today. After so many months. He read about Parvez in the papers. He says it was a wake up call. He wants me to forgive him, but what of the hurts that never heal? The hurts that deconstruct your personality so completely that even after you finally pick yourself up off the ground and wipe away the blood, you're forever embittered, soul-dried, faith lost, all the important bastions shattered: loyalty, family, God, love..." Her expression darkened as she watched Deen lapse between shivers and profuse sweating.

"What's the matter with you?" she asked finally.

Deen felt sick to his stomach. He wanted to tell Maria everything, but he couldn't get the words off his lips.

"I'm late for class," Maria announced.

Deen watched her storm out, leaving him all alone once again.

Deen wondered what Nina was thinking. Did she know

how Parvez felt about her? Love is a precious gift. Treasure it when it shines on you. Did she wish she had given him another chance? *Just one more moon dance?*

Deen wondered about the purpose of life... to be a good human being? To love and be loved? To enjoy? To give? To worship? To believe in something greater than yourself that gives meaning to your finite time on earth? To make a connection, somehow, with someone or something, some union that lets you escape the unbearable prison of your own aloneness? Deen missed Maria.

Mintu chacha arrived an hour later to interrogate Deen. "Were there hard drinks at the party?" he asked.

Distraught and distracted, Deen murmured, "Yes."

"Were there drugs also?" he pursued.

"Ya chacha, there were a couple of joints passed around, just weed," Deen lied.

"So you kids do drugs often?" He probed for more information, trying to make sense of the past few hours.

"No chacha, just sometimes, to celebrate," Deen replied softly.

Parvez's father eyed Deen suspiciously then left the room.

Deen's muscles ached. The cell was hot. The sun was blistering. Even through the tiny window in his cell, Deen could make out how bright the day was outside. Daylight that Parvez would never see again.

Deen's mother arrived and woke him up, dark circles around her eyes. He tried to explain the situation. "We were at a party and Parvez was drunk so I took him for a drive to cool down and Ma, when we got to the ghaat he jumped in. Ma, there was nothing I could do."

"Oh my God," she sobbed. "I don't understand how you keep falling into these traps. I know I can't blame anyone but you, I just don't understand. Are you still doing drugs?" She knew all his symptoms. She could see how badly he was turquing.

"No," Deen lied.

"It breaks my heart to say this," she said, "but maybe it's best if you stay here for a few days, until the drugs are out of your system."

As she walked out, Deen saw how frail she had become.

Sergeant Akbar entered the room and slammed the door shut, startling Deen out of unconsciousness. He introduced himself, not recognizing Deen from their last encounter. "Minister Sahib has charged you with murder," he said, patting a wad of cash in his pocket. "We'll keep you here while the search continues."

The next day AJ and Shagor came with a pack of cigarettes. They told Deen about the search parties out on the river still. Deen wanted to cry. He missed Parvez. He despised his life. He asked the boys if they could bring him some sugar. Shagor said it was too risky, AJ said he would try. The boys left and Deen continued to wither away, tormented by mosquitoes, withdrawals and guilt.

Detective Khan entered the room. "Man is so alone," he said, more to himself than to Deen. Dazed Deen could barely keep his head up but he strained to listen to the detective. "By taking refuge in drugs, you're only isolating yourself further. You need to learn the art of loving." The detective sighed and stepped out, shutting the door behind him.

Mintu chacha arrived later that day. "You bastard!" he

shouted. "You killed my only son!" Sergeant Akbar held him back to prevent him from throwing punches, so instead he spat on Deen.

Deen lifted his head up with great effort and saw in Mintu chacha's eyes inconsolable grief.

Maria returned on the third day with a sandwich for Deen. He devoured it and then threw up. His body craved smack and refused to accept anything else. Maria offered him water, then hesitantly announced, "Amma received a marriage proposal for me. Some guy from London. He wants to marry a pretty graduate from NSU. That's what he told his mom. She's a member of Amma's charity club. They've been chatting. They think we'd be a good match, him and me."

Deen couldn't believe his ears. He was in jail, his body was a wreck, his life was disintegrating, Parvez was dead, and Maria wanted an arranged marriage? "What?" he muttered.

"I got drunk again last night," she confessed. Two guards watched with interest. "I can't stand it anymore! This life, what's it worth? Parvez's DEAD. You're in jail. I almost killed myself last night. This is not who I want to be. I need to get out of Bangladesh." She collapsed into sobs.

Deen's heart broke a little. He reached out to touch Maria's arm. He wanted to hold her, comfort her, but the guards were ready to pounce on him. Maria took Deen's hand and kissed it. A tear from her cheek wiped against his finger, warm and salty. She said good-bye and left.

Deen brooded over Maria's words. Would she seriously marry another man. She was lonely and depressed. Maybe it would be good for her. Why should she wait around for him? He was a waste of time. He couldn't save anybody. Not even Parvez.

Parvez had filled the world with light. Now he was nothing

more than a hole in Deen's heart. A collection of memories and regrets. A loss of love. Deen wished he had spent more time with him, the last few days, to help him come out of the trench he had dug himself into. Deen felt disappointed with himself, he had been too wrapped up in his own problems, selfishly stranded in his own drugged out world. His addiction had become everything, the very purpose of his life. It had taken over like malignant tumors and irreparable rips in friendship.

His friend was dead. Nothing he could do would bring him back. Deen wished he could be a better man. He remembered a prayer his father had taught him. *God grant me the serenity to accept the things I cannot change, the courage to change the things I can, and the wisdom to know the difference.* Suddenly he was weeping, unbearably lonely, God-forsaken.

In the morning, Deen's mother arrived and paid the cops to release her son. Not a word was exchanged as they drove home. She fumbled with her keys at the front door, then looked at Deen in distress. "There was no burial for Parvez because the body was never found. They had a milad for him, but his parents are still hoping he is alive."

Deen nodded silently.

"Maybe you should stay in your room today and reflect on how you want to live your life."

Deen nodded again.

"That could have been you." She placed her warm hand on his cheek. "Deen, don't give in to the drugs. Live, Deen, live."

Deen felt heavy with his mother's sadness. He wanted to thank her and tell her how much he loved her, but he couldn't find the words. Pain tore through his body. He wondered where AJ was. He locked himself into his room to wade out the withdrawals.

✦ TWENTY ✦

AJ lit a cigarette and examined his front door. The lock was broken. He had gone to the thana with some whiskey, but Deen had already left. He drank half the bottle himself to placate his cramps. He needed to chase. He needed money. He had to collect the diamonds from 31A. He had to find Raj's gun. He owed Quader bhai cash. In the midst of it all, someone had broken into his flat.

He wondered if it had been Raj Gopal's men or Quader bhai's men. Or perhaps it was Ronnie, unable to pay off his debt, coming to steal from the man he owed money to. Classic junky style. AJ blew out a smoke ring and stepped in.

A bulky man with a snaking scar on his bald head stepped out from inside and shut the door behind AJ. AJ could tell by the man's posture that he was an off-duty cop. A fatter, shorter man sidled up next to AJ and pushed him onto the couch. Hasan stepped out from the bedroom, reeking of cologne. "AJ, my friend," he said coolly. *Boom!* He punched AJ in the face.

AJ felt the skin under his nose break and he started to bleed. He was shocked and disoriented. "Why the fuck did you do that?"

"Where are the diamonds?" demanded Hasan.

"Chill out, Hasan, let's talk? I've got them. They're not on me right now, but I've got them," AJ lied. Instinctively he took note of the situation: he was outnumbered, but he had the key so they could not kill him.

Whack! Hasan slapped him, a violent blow to the side of his head that knocked him off the couch. "I want them right NOW."

The world blurred around AJ. He felt himself being lifted up by the shoulders and propped on the couch. Nothing made sense. Why would Raj have sent his goons to rough him up? The Don had too much to lose, there was no justification for this attack.

"What, AJ?" Hasan jeered. "Who is going to help you now? Your minister friends? Want to call the cops? Come on, show me your capacity. Guess what, little prick, I am the Government and the Mafia and the Cops!" He revved his fist and pounded AJ in the ear.

AJ's head exploded with pain. He felt his face swell up. His nose was bleeding. A numbing realization dawned on him. This had nothing to do with Raj Gopal. It was Hasan's personal vendetta. It was an ego war, no rationality guiding the process.

The bald cop left the apartment. Had he stepped out so that the others could finish off AJ? A cop could get into deep shit if he witnessed murder and did nothing. Had he gone for reinforcements? Or torture tools? AJ searched for an escape. "Hasan," he tried to reason, "Does Raj know you're here?"

Hasan slapped him. "I don't want to hear a word from you."

"Does Raj know you're here?" AJ repeated, sensing the edge in Hasan's voice.

Hasan punched him in the stomach, sending him reeling to the ground.

"He doesn't know, does he? It seems like maybe, your ass is on the line now too, my friend," said AJ, slowly, choking on the blood in his mouth.

Hasan laughed. "You're a bastard. You really are a bastard, you know that? You don't give a fuck if you live or die, do you?" Hasan started kicking AJ in the stomach.

The fat man stubbed his cigarette out on AJ's arm.

AJ flinched, more disturbed by the scar than the burning of the flesh. *This is it then,* he thought. AJ knew the mafia all too well. They would never scar a man unless they were going to get rid of the body completely. Too incriminating. There was no hope, he would never be allowed to walk out alive. *So this is it.*

"Fuck you," said AJ, with renewed arrogance.

"I'll kill you, you bastard!" Hasan shouted.

"Do it then. Kill me," sneered AJ, blood dripping into his eyes.

Hasan pulled out a gun and shoved it into AJ's mouth.

"Fuck you." AJ lunged forward sending the gun deeper into his mouth. Hasan freaked out and backed up. AJ understood immediately, it was easy to make a threat, but it was damn hard to pull the trigger. Even Hasan, mafia-cop-minister Hasan, Raj's own right-hand man, shat his pants when it came to pulling the trigger without Raj's backing. AJ felt like a king reborn.

Hasan stuck the gun back in his pants and screamed in frustration, pounding AJ with his fists. The bald cop re-entered the apartment and pulled Hasan off, whispering something into his ear. Hasan nodded. "Don't try anything funny," he warned, his voice trembling with hatred. "If you do, we'll kill your pretty little whore. What was her name? Sexy Sundari. She's quite fine, I've seen her naked."

"Fuck you." AJ scowled.

The fat man blindfolded AJ with a gamcha and led him down the stairs to the back street. AJ heard a swoosh as a car door opened, and a thud as the bald cop got into the driver's seat. AJ realized this was his last opportunity to escape. He started throwing up. The fat man, repulsed by the vomit, loosened his grip for an instant. AJ kicked him in the groins and bolted, ripping off his blindfold as he ran out to the main road, the fat man huffing in hot pursuit.

Adrenaline gave AJ a rush, so despite his broken body, he jumped onto his motorbike just as the fat man caught up with him. He kicked the hand that reached for his leg and sent the man stumbling back. Bloody, turquing, retching and throbbing in pain, AJ sped off like a madman.

* * *

Sergeant Akbar made his way through the narrow alleys towards the last shack on the embankment. His tea boy followed like an eager puppy, clutching the tape recorder to his chest. The basti boys eyed the newcomers suspiciously, but Sergeant Akbar paid them no heed. He was off-duty, dressed as a regular civilian in his best kurta, the blue one his wife had given him on Eid. He had not come to arrest Falani, he would have brought his men along if that were the case. The arrest warrant would take some time to process, even with the evidence. He could not

wait that long to see her and a harmless game of cops and
dealers seemed like a good way to pass time on a lazy Friday
afternoon after his visit to the mosque.

Perhaps he would play the tape for her. She would probably
squirm as she heard Majid confess her dealings. She would
recognize his voice and realize the depth of the betrayal. Perhaps
she would ask where Majid was. He might tell her of the
khor's death. Perhaps she would prostrate herself on the ground
and beg for mercy. The thought aroused Sergeant Akbar and
he felt irritated. "What should we do Samad?" said Sergeant
Akbar. "Now that you are Police Inspector Samad?"

Samad beamed. "Catch a khor!"

* * *

Musa and his brother approached Falani's shack to harass her
for smack. Majid had been missing for a few days and Kala
was no longer a threat. Falani's clients had not been around
either, so they saw an opportunity. Falani was probably home,
they could hear her daughters playing inside.

They were preparing their scare tactics when Musa noticed
a disheveled tuft of grass. He kicked it with the heel of his
foot to dislodge the dirt. Something had been buried in the
ground, as if by Destiny herself. He unearthed the treasure
and smiled. It was his lucky day. "Hey Issa," he called, limping
to his brother. "Check this out!"

Issa peered into the bag. "No way!"

"Smack! Four hits worth!"

"A gift from God!"

"Why do you think Falani left it there?"

"Who cares?"

They leaned against the krishna chura tree and began to chase.

* * *

As Sergeant Akbar arrived at Falani's shack, with Samad trailing far behind, he heard laughter. He skirted the decrepit structure and stumbled upon two basti men chasing heroin. "Stop right now!" he commanded.

"Who the fuck are you?" replied Musa without moving.

"I said STOP!" The sergeant aimed his gun at Musa.

Musa, who had already had his toe shot once, was in no mood for another incident. He dropped the smack and put his arms up in the air. Issa lunged for Sergeant Akbar's fat belly and knocked him off balance.

The sergeant stood up and grabbed a fistful of Issa's hair and pounded his face in with the butt of his gun. *SMASH* onto the bridge of his nose. *SMASH* in the centre of his forehead. Issa screamed as he exploded in blood. Sergeant Akbar tried to muffle the scream with his hand.

Musa hurled himself at the sergeant who tried to kick back, but lost balance and fell again. The gun slipped out of his hand. Issa grabbed it and pulled the trigger, sending a bullet straight into the sergeant's stomach. Bull's eye.

Blood drenched the sergeant's shirt. He stared down at his body in disbelief. His grip on Issa's hair loosened as he slipped into a slouch. The brothers bolted.

As he stared at his spilling intestines, Sergeant Akbar felt bitter. His parents, though poor, had raised him to be a proud Muslim. In a nation where liberal values were corroding the social infrastructure, he had nobly dedicated himself to defending the Islamic way of life. He had prayed regularly and fasted during Ramadan. He had loved his wife. He had worked hard in the police force and he deserved the respect it had earned him. He had only accepted bribes to pay for Daisy's school.

Jihad! Sergeant Akbar felt blessed to have been given the chance to act as Allah's own soldier in the war against evil. He had tried to do his part to destroy the terrorists and drugaddicts in his neighbourhood. In his last moments he thought, at least he would be remembered as a martyr who had died trying.

Sergeant Akbar started convulsing and the sight of his blood-soaked body scared him. He thought of his daughter and his wife and Allah and drugaddicts. He felt hatred, extreme hatred, as he breathed out his last painful breaths and he wished Falani were there, holding his dying body in her warm arms.

* * *

Samad hid silently behind the krishna chura, long after the basti boys had disappeared and a group of children had gathered around the bloody body of the sergeant. Samad sat in a trance, clutching the tape recorder to his chest. He had recorded the entire scene. Ev-i-dence. It had taken real courage to sit there and watch the fight, though it was over in less than five minutes, ending with a bullet into the sergeant's stomach. Still, he had done it. He had resisted the temptation to run away. He had stayed to collect ev-i-dence. He had done it out of love not duty.

Samad, who would later deliver the tape to Chief Detective Khan, felt sad rather than angry, as he listened from behind the krishna chura tree to the dying moans of his beloved boss. The killers looked like regular guys, not cold blooded murderers. They were probably friends of Majid's. Majid who had been killed by the sergeant, whom they had killed in return. Soon they would be killed too, by the police force, and so it would continue. Under the scorching sun, the fine line between Right and Wrong seemed to blur and Samad felt his childhood melting. Samad, who finally had the chance to be a hero, felt that victory did not taste sweet at all, but rather like a stabbing pain in the heart.

* * *

Sundari gasped when she opened her door. AJ, bruised and bloody, fell at her feet. He crawled past her, to her bathroom where he began puking, heaving stringy strands of yellow liquid and chunks of cherry red blood.

"What happened?" Sundari asked in a shaky voice.

"They followed me," he replied. He tried to haul himself off the ground, but instead collapsed onto the floor and blacked out.

Sundari closed the bathroom door and rushed to her bedroom window. A black Mercedes Benz pulled into the driveway. She grabbed her cell phone and dialed Raj's emergency line.

"What's the matter, Sundari?" he asked, recognizing her voice.

"Your men are after AJ," she said. "They're trying to kill him."

"Are you sure?" asked Raj, absorbing her words.

"Yes!"

"Ok, I'll take care of it."

She heard him punch numbers into another phone and then demand, "Hasan, what's going on. . ." Raj's voice was muffled, but she could make out from the tone that he was giving orders. When he hung up and returned to her call, his voice was chilly. "Is AJ with you?" he asked.

"Yes." Sundari replied.

"Send him to me," said Raj.

"Raj," said Sundari with hesitation. "I love him."

"Send him to me."

From her window, Sundari watched the Benz drive away. She returned to her bathroom with a bottle of pain killers and an antiseptic balm. AJ had regained consciousness and was doubled over the tub, groaning. His face was puffy, his nose broken. She helped him wash the blood off. She changed his shirt and gave him a glass of water for the pain killers. He emptied the entire bottle of pills onto his tongue then swallowed them at one go.

"I'm turqing," said AJ, finally.

Sundari narrowed her eyes. "You're destroying yourself."

"That bastard Hasan is destroying me," he argued.

"Weren't you frightened?" she asked, gently dabbing the gash above his eye with the balm.

"I thought I was a dead man, but you know what, it was no big deal." AJ was surprised to find how little he cared for anything anymore. He felt numb. Somewhere along the way, he had lost the passion to live.

"Aren't you ever going to do something good for yourself?" Sundari inquired.

"Don't nag," said AJ. "I need to chase. I'm in too much pain."

"I just saved your life, AJ, and for what? So you can go kill yourself with heroin?"

"Shut up," AJ snapped, the pain devouring his mind. He stepped out of the bathroom and into the bedroom and stopped in his tracks. His heart froze. He was scared for the first time that day. Slouched in Sundari's armchair, sat Raj Gopal, waiting for him.

"What happened?" Raj asked coolly.

AJ's first instinct was to lie. He mumbled an apology, then an excuse about the delay in the delivery. He tried to justify his actions by beating around the bush.

Raj stared at him, expressionless.

"I have a drug problem," AJ blurted out. It was the first time in his life he had admitted to his problem. He said it without conviction, a believable excuse to get him off the hook, but as he said it, it struck a chord, he realized it was true. The confession poured out of him cathartically as if he were vomiting up rotten food. "I was smacked out at my dealer's basti and I lost your gun. Maybe someone stole it. I would have told Hasan, but I pissed him off somehow. Your diamonds are safe, still in the bank. I have the key. I can bring the pouch to you this afternoon if you want. I'm really sorry."

"All right," said Raj at last. "You get help for your drug problem. That stuff will snuff you out quicker than any gangster in Dhaka city. Why don't you take it easy? Drink malt whiskey, smoke cigars. Enjoy your life. Heroin is dirty."

AJ nodded.

"Hasan won't be on your case again," he continued. "But you have to forgive him. He acted out of line. I want you to understand that what happened between you and him, it'll remain between us. Nobody has to know."

AJ nodded.

"If you need anyone to look at your bruises, let me know. My friend is one of the finest doctors in Dhaka. Ok?"

AJ nodded.

Raj was not being nice, he was just keeping his records clean. A trifling case filed at the police station could get costly. AJ was not worth such risks. The gun was small business. Even the diamonds were small compared to the trouble Hasan could have gotten him into. In their line of business, one could not afford to lose his cool.

"What's the name of your dealer?" Raj asked.

"Musa."

"Ok. Don't worry about the gun. The diamonds are in the locker still? Why don't you bring them to me this afternoon?"

AJ nodded.

"All right, AJ. I'll see you later. Take care." Raj stood up to shake AJ's hand then resumed his slouch on the armchair.

AJ said bye to Sundari and walked out.

Sundari watched from her window as he drove off. Her eyes filled with indignant tears and something inside her died. She pulled the front strand of her wet hair behind a diamond-studded hair clip and noticed a storm approaching in the sky.

✦ TWENTY ONE ✦

Falani's hair was still wet from her bath. She was preparing to oil it when the cops barged in, knocking over her can of coconut oil. She did not put up any resistance, but the eerie resolve in her eyes left them feeling emasculated and foolish.

As a cop pulled her arms behind her back to cuff her, Falani was surprised to find her thoughts drawn to Deen. He was a lost soul, misunderstood by most. He seldom looked up, but when he did, you'd see rare compassion in his sunken brown eyes. He had warned her of what she would face if she were caught. She should have given him the gun, but what did it matter now?

A lecherous cop grinned as he led Falani away.

Detective Khan shuffled uneasily. The five cops under his command made themselves comfortable, poking through Falani's belongings, eating her paan, waiting to avenge the murder of Sergeant Akbar. The idea of an ambush filled them with unambiguous excitement, much to the detective's dismay.

The detective shuddered to think of what they would do to the khors once they had them back at the station. How could he ask them to exonerate murder and forgive, break the circle of violence with love. They wouldn't accept the science of addiction or the desperation of poverty as explanations. *Justice?* He wondered about the rights and wrongs of society and the nature of life itself, at once so precious and so brutal.

* * *

Ominous clouds gathered in the sky and the day felt like evening. Deen stood shaking outside his building, resisting the temptation to chase. His withdrawals were worse than ever before, but he was determined to stay clean. He heard the wings of frantic birds trying to escape the violent wind.

His mother had claimed he had not tried hard enough. Perhaps she was right. He dwelt in denial. It was the only way he could accept his life, with all the mistakes he had made, all the people he had hurt. Parvez's death had shattered his foundations and Deen could no longer accept who he had become.

Fate? Deen pondered. Kismet? Kiss met. Where your kisses met the fate you had fixed for yourself. Where your life confronted the choices you made. Precious choices. Deen wished he had chosen more wisely. He had taken a wrong turn somewhere and now he was lost, unable to find his way back to inner peace.

At that fleeting moment between emptiness and despair, a butterfly landed on his knee. Dainty yellow wings. He could crush it if he wanted to. Deen lit a cigarette and blew a stream of smoke at the butterfly. Yellow wings fluttered in confusion. For a split second, the centre of the universe was located on his knee, all the joys and sorrows ever experienced, engulfed in thick smoke, enveloped in the density of hopelessness.

It reminded him of Falani. She had found happiness. It came from the joy of giving unconditional love. It came from her unwavering devotion to her daughters. They were her connection to something greater. Her saving grace. Deen wondered if she was all right. An uncomfortable nagging lodged itself in his gut, more distracting than the cramps even. He needed to check up on her.

His wallet was gone, probably yanked out of his pocket by the cops. He still had his cell phone though, he could barter that for a ride. Curly hair in disarray, sweat pouring down his back, Deen hailed down a scooter. Wind whipped against his face as the scooter hurtled down Airport Road. The scooter walla refused to accept the cell phone as payment and complained that he had been cheated.

Deen stumbled through the basti with a dying cigarette in his lips. Shaking. Shivering. Sweating. A group of snotty-nosed kids watched him with interest. He cursed them silently for witnessing his withdrawals. Withdrawals were a private affair. Not to be seen by children who did not know yet what it felt like to be empty.

Suddenly a shadow fell on the earth and darkness surrounded him. The jhor had come. Thunder erupted and rain poured down from the sky. Tin roofs clattered with madness. Women scrambled to clear the clothes lines. Children ran around in confused delight.

Deen thought of the bony boy with the deflated football and the 100 watt smile. *Resilience.* He had nothing and yet he was happy. Deen couldn't remember the last time he was happy. He felt like retching.

There were no shoes outside Falani's shack. Deen dropped

his sandals on the bricks lining the doorway and entered his sanctuary. For the first time ever, he had not come for smack.

He called out for Falani. No reply. He stepped inside. A can of coconut oil had fallen off its perch and spilt on the floor. The oil looked like a pool of blood. The room smelt of coconut. Where was everyone? Wasn't it unusually quiet?

Dooo dooo dooo dooo. Deen's ringer wailed. He reached for his phone and stepped around the cane partition to peek into Falani's bedroom, then let out a gasp.

Five fully armed cops open fired.

* * *

The sound of pistols shooting, man falling, phone ringing, created a strange harmony that would haunt the cops for years to come.

* * *

AJ was practically collapsing by the time they reached the basti. Shagor lit a cigarette and followed him as he stumbled through the maze of shacks. Suddenly a shadow fell on the earth and darkness surrounded them. Thunder erupted and rain poured down. The boys were drenched, but not dissuaded.

AJ tried calling Deen one last time. "It's ringing... no answer."

The air filled with the noise of distant gun shots.

"Cops?" whispered Shagor.

"Sounds like it's coming from Falani's place," said AJ. "A raid?"

"Let's get out of here!" said Shagor.

The boys returned to their car and drove off to score elsewhere.

* * *

Maria shoved a lipstick into her purse and stumbled around her room in search of her car keys. She tilted a bottle of whiskey to her lips and cursed as she realized she had finished it. There hadn't been much to begin with. Less than half. She pulled out of her driveway, knocking over a potted rosebush next to the gate. The pot shattered, red rose petals spilt on dirt.

Airport Road was the only road she knew that led out of Dhaka, out and away to somewhere else. Maybe out to the banyan tree in Kaligonj. She headed in that direction, tormented by skull bashing self-loathing. She wanted to drive away from her thoughts, away from her life. She yearned for freedom.

Life was not panning out as she had planned and she could not adjust to her reality. There was only one good thing in her life, one ounce of happiness. Deen was out of jail. She had gone to visit him there that morning, but he had already left. He hadn't called her since, not even to let her know that he was out. He could be cruel at times, indifferent to her needs. She wanted to hate him, but in the depths of her heart she knew no one had ever loved her like he had. When he loved her, it changed her world.

She realized she was sobbing hysterically though she didn't know why or when she had started. Blinded by her tears, she parked at the side of the highway. Her cell phone had no reception, so she stepped out to find a better spot.

Traffic was unusually light. Two cows were grazing in the ditch beside the highway, under the watchful eyes of a gaunt shepherd boy. The trees behind the ditch partially hid the tracks, but she could make out the blues and yellows of a train passing by.

Maria felt dizzy as Deen's phone rang. No answer. Maybe he was ignoring her intentionally. She didn't have to put up with him anymore. She was free to find a better man, wasn't that what she wanted? Someone stable, available, attentive. She felt a lump in her throat. Sour love. Stalemate.

She stared up at the dark clouds and wondered where he was. She wanted him to pick up the phone so she could curse him out. Or cry maybe. She needed to hear his voice, he'd make her feel better. He always did. Where was he now? In a fit of rage, she threw her phone into the sky and watched it shatter as it hit the ground. Life was too precious to waste away clinging to impossible dreams.

Suddenly a tire exploded and a blue truck full of pineapples swerved madly out of control. The truck hurtled off the road and crashed into the side of Maria's parked car. The grazing cows jumped up with a start and bolted. The shepherd boy scrambled to grab their leads.

Maria gasped in disbelief. She craned her neck to see if the truck driver had survived. Shards of glass, metal and smashed pineapples were strewn across the street. The truck had demolished the side of her car. She shuddered to think what would have happened had she been in it.

A shadow fell on the earth and darkness surrounded her. Thunder erupted and rain poured down, marking finally the first kal boishakhi storm of the year. The rain blurred out the world around her. Maria pulled off her rubberband, raven locks tumbled down to her waist. She threw her head back, threw her arms out to the side, and stared at the sky. The water felt cool on her face and she was grateful to be alive.

* * *

At that fleeting moment between emptiness and despair, a butterfly landed on Deen's knee. Dainty yellow wings. Infinitely fragile. A tiny miracle of life. It alighted and Deen was left in awe. The world was full of magic.

The afternoon was windy. The dark day, alive and vibrant. The colours of the garden were intense, a tropical burst of greens. The spring air smelt of bailey buds. Birds were singing love songs to the Divine.

Deen returned to his apartment and noticed the welcome mat at the door. Welcome, with flowers, home sweet home, welcome. He noticed the photo of his parents standing in front of the stage and felt warm with love. Life was sweet, really. Why had he let the little things bring him down?

He noticed two missed calls on his phone. Must be AJ on the way to Falani's for smack. No, he would not give in this time. Deen grabbed a pail from his bathroom to prepare for the heaving. He would survive this detox. He would quit. He would find a counsellor tomorrow. His stomach cringed, the withdrawals felt like bullets ripping through his muscles. The smell of coconut oil saturated the air.

Deen felt betrayed by the frailty of his body as he collapsed onto his bed, convulsing and dreaming: a vision of AJ, bloody and bruised, and Shagor parking his car outside the basti. "I'll try calling Deen," AJ remarked. They hurried through the alleys, past snotty-nosed kids. Thunder erupted and rain began to pour.

They arrived at Falani's shack and dropped their slippers at the doorway. Shagor called out for Falani. No reply. They stepped inside. The front room was deserted. A can of coconut oil had fallen off its perch, oil on the floor like a pool of blood, air heavy with the smell of coconut oil.

"Where is everybody?" said Shagor.

"Where's Falani? I'm in need," said AJ in a panic.

They stepped around the cane partition into Falani's bedroom and let out a gasp.

Five fully armed cops open fired.

Deen's head filled with the sound of gunshots, men falling to the ground and a phone ringing.

Dooo dooo dooo dooo. Deen reached for his phone feebly.

"Deen, can you hear me, where are you?" said Maria desperately.

Deen struggled to subdue the cramps conquering his body. He could see Maria in his mind's eye. She looked immaculate.

"I'm home," he managed to mumble.

"I'm coming to get you. I'll be there in ten minutes," said Maria.

Deen heard gun shots and thunder in the distance. *Dooo dooo dooo dooo.* The ringer wailed.

"It's me, I'm downstairs," said Maria on the phone. Deen crawled out of bed and staggered to the gates. There was Maria, smelling of whiskey, her shirt soaked in tears, her hair tangled, her eyes wild. Deen stepped into the car and suddenly his cramps were gone, he felt fine, strong and healthy and fine.

Maria pushed in a CD, pumped up the volume and drove

towards Tongi. Deen rolled down the window to let the wind in. He felt invigorated. A smile spread over his face and settled into contentment. He was happy to be there with Maria, happy for their connection, happy for all that was left to share. He had so much love to give and he felt joy. Exquisite joy.

Then things started happening all at once, a blue truck headed straight at them, Maria screamed, his mother wept, Parvez shouted, they crashed into a ditch, broken glass, blood everywhere. The world around him began to dissolve. He heard his phone ring. He heard thunder erupt. He heard the sound of gunshots in the distance. He heard his own body fall. The sounds blended together and he felt like he was drowning.

Huddled on the floor of Falani's shack, Deen felt the warmth of frothy blood and stale vomit in his mouth.

* * *

The cops walked over Deen's bloody remains in silent discomfort. They were disappointed that their ample supply of bullets had brought down only one useless body and not a gang of murderers. They had hoped for a fantastic blood bath. In their secret hearts they were also worried. The boy they had gunned down, nice jeans, expensive cell phone, was probably not a basti boy at all.

"Tell the men at the thana to release Falani," Detective Khan ordered. The second in command grumbled, but the detective silenced him. "We've killed one man. That's one death too many. It's best we don't disturb the balance any further." There was no scope to argue with the authority in his voice so the cop complied, calling the thana to order Falani's release.

"Let's go," said Detective Khan. He had not expected the

men to open fire like maniacs. High-strung and afraid, ill-trained and hungry for vengeance, teeming with misguided anger. He did not blame them, but the blitz of bullets had startled him and he did not want to face the riot that was sure to erupt soon.

"Let's go," echoed his second in command. "I'm tired of breathing in this coconut oil air."

***

Futility, thought Deen. He began to pray. *O God, let the warm breath of Spring drive away the negativity in my heart. Let the new year be fresh. Come new year, come, come.*

As if in answer to Deen's prayers, a warm cyclonic wind ripped off the roof of Falani's shack, thrusting it into the dark sky. Dust and rubble lashed at him. The openness of the world surrounded him as the downpour of rain collapsed into the shack. Dense, heavy rain drenched his body. Sheets of water cascaded down, washing away the blood and vomit and coconut oil around him. Deen remembered a Robindro Shongit his mother used to sing during storms and the sweet melancholy of her voice. The grief caught up to him and he felt like he was choking.

On such a night you can tell her, heavy dark rainfall, dark dense rainfall, on such a night you can open your heart, the sound of thunder, the rain drops falling, the sunless dense darkness, on such a night, no one can hear your words anymore, all directions are empty, emptiness everywhere, on such a night, when two people come face to face, heart to heart, heavy with deep sadness, each has his own, the rains continue to pour and it seems there is no one else in the world, society and family all seem like lies, all the noise and celebrations of life seem pointless, on such a night, with soul searching eyes that are ready to drink in her sorrows, ready to feel the pain you see in her eyes, share in the pain, share what's in her heart and yours, feeling her heart with your own, everything else has disappeared into the darkness, who would be hurt by this compassion? If only you could lessen the heaviness of your heart, alone in the corner of your room, if you said a few words to her, what would it matter to anyone? The wind sweeps by with the dread of someone awaiting a lover who will never return, lightening erupts, those words which in this lifetime stayed within the confines of your heart, those words which you could never utter, those words can be spoken on a night like this, today you could say it all, in this sort of heavy downpour.

Deen felt himself floating up, like a diamond in the sky, high above the world, looking down on himself, on his ravaged body. After the visions and revisions of how things might have been, in the last few moments of his life, Deen was overwhelmed by a sense of deep, irrevocable regret. He felt sad, not frightened, not trying to make sense of his fall or the bullets that had torn through his body, but rather, desperate to open up into tears, he felt the uncontrollable urge to sob, but could not. He thought of his mother's hand on his cheek. He thought of Maria's manicured nails and vulnerable smile. He thought of Falani's indomitable spirit. He thought of the summer his father had taught him to swim and the salty water he had swallowed, the aftertaste still lingered in his mouth, and the school of yellow fish swimming in the tranquility of his childhood. He thought of green cat eyes, fierce and reprimanding. He thought of the endless heroin he had consumed, the endless heroin that had consumed him, and the past six years that were now just a dark blur of meaninglessness. He thought of his addiction, not with anger, but disappointment, starting to realize how much he really loved the people he had hurt the most. He felt a devastating loss that knocked his breath out and he was nostalgic for his wasted life. He thought of the butterfly on his knee and he wished for a second chance. *Let me live, God, let me live!* He had forsaken God for too long. He remembered Kala, with his bandaged stubs, hopeless and forlorn. An unfamiliar tenderness for life spread over him, so overpowering that it hurt, swelling within him like an unbearable burden, and then he felt his heart burst.

Acknowledgements

I am deeply grateful to all the people who inspired me and believed in me. Lubna khala, Rezina khala, Firdous khala, Tarico, Preeti, Urvashi, Sahana, Ornob, Doctor Yusuf Merchant, Boshi, Buno, Keyur, Pavan, Naureen, Sarah, Jaferi, Zulquar, Sheehan, Sabah, Kelly, Biko, Mash, Rubai, Liz, Shamer, Tamazer, Writers Block Bangladesh: Abeer, Mahmud, Sam, Saad, Muna apu, Sal, Aaref, Sadaf, Farah, Ashu, Monica, Shujon bhaiya; Deepa phupu, Maggie, Deepak, Alizeh, Baba, Almer and Shazly. Thank you!